The Last Hanging of Ángel Martinez

The Last Hanging of
ÁNGEL MARTINEZ

Kate Niles

University of New Mexico Press | Albuquerque

ISBN 978-0-8263-6704-4 (paper)
ISBN 978-0-8263-6705-1 (ePub)

Library of Congress Control Number: 2024942697

Founded in 1889, the University of New Mexico sits on the traditional home-
lands of the Pueblo of Sandia. The original peoples of New Mexico—Pueblo,
Navajo, and Apache—since time immemorial have deep connections to the
land and have made significant contributions to the broader community
statewide. We honor the land itself and those who remain stewards of this land
throughout the generations and also acknowledge our committed relationship
to Indigenous peoples. We gratefully recognize our history.

Cover illustration by Felicia Cedillos
Designed by Felicia Cedillos
Composed in Adobe Jenson Pro

For New Mexico, where I learned how to find love again

Every love story is a ghost story.

—DAVID FOSTER WALLACE

Acknowledgments

My career as a writer would be far more limited if it were not for Joan Sch-weighardt, who recommended I submit this book to UNM Press. She has seen all three of my full-length manuscripts to fruition in one way or another and holds a very special place in my heart. I also thank Lynn and Lynda Miller for their crucial support in seeing this book to print, as well as Elise McHugh at UNM Press proper. I love the feminine empowerment behind all these alignments, and the ease at which this has all come together.

Those familiar with New Mexico Probation will surely know that I plastered Colorado's version of said state entity onto the operations depicted here. There are some crucial differences, but I am grateful for my years spent as a Probation Officer for the 6th Judicial District in Durango, Colorado, and the guidance of Tom Harms and Charles Schwabe in particular.

Nina DeCreeft Ward is my godmother and the muse for Nina Montgomery as far as her art is concerned. Please check out her website at www. ninadecreeftward.com. Her presence in my childhood made a great deal of difference in that she gave me permission to be creative and to live a creative life.

To my therapy clients throughout the years, and to my probationers—you are such muses in and of yourselves and I am grateful for the pain you have shared with me. Writing is my way of metabolizing all of it.

Finally, Jonathan Niles—I owe you so much. Thank you for co-creating a stable container for all the trauma I have lived through and processed in various ways. Our home is a wedding basket, a weaving of it all.

The Last Hanging of Ángel Martinez

Prologue

Taos, 2014

Carmelina

She wakes up from a bad dream. The dog is dead again. Every night the dog dies. It is getting to the point where she doesn't like to go to sleep.

"Mamma! Mamma!"

And Mamma comes, as Mamma always does. She sits with her and rocks her, smooths her hair. "Is it the same dream?" her Mamma with the long brown-blonde hair asks her.

Carmelina sniffs away tears. "Yes. Where did he go?"

One day she had a dog, a little Jack Russell terrier she named Barney after her favorite show. Then the next day there was no Barney. Mamma said Barney must have run away. They put signs up all over the place. Mamma said she called the animal shelter, the place she said where sometimes stray pets end up. But no Barney. And Mamma always looked weird when she talked about Barney missing. A week in and she said maybe they had to think about Barney being gone.

Now, though, it has been a month. Now, "Mamma, want some juice."

"Juice isn't good after you've brushed your teeth."

She pouts, her black-brown-auburn hair a mess from attempted sleep. She crosses her arms with resoluteness. "Juice, Mamma."

Her mother sighs. Smiles at her. "Okay, little one. Just once."

Carmelina smiles and moves back down under the covers. Just the thought of getting some juice makes her happy, relaxes her. She begins to drift off. Somewhere in there, in the back of her head where dreams reside, where what is real and what is not collide, it's as if a strong wind shakes the house. A kind of urgent shuffling, like when branches slap a window. A squawking noise, like a chicken. Her eyes fly open. Low voices. A thud.

Silence.

"Mamma?" she murmurs, burrowing further into the covers. Nothing. Her body is a coil. "Mamma?"

She does the opposite now, springing open from the coil, the covers flailing off. "Mamma!"

In the kitchen her mother is face down on the floor. Something dark pools under her neck.

"Mamma! Mamma! Mamma!" She shakes her. A kind of low moan escapes, then a gurgle that makes the girl want to throw up though she could not tell you why. Then nothing. A deep, nothing nothing. A cold silence even the newborn understand.

Now the child is sobbing. Not Barney, now Mamma! She's four. She knows. She lies down on the body. On Mamma's back, where the last of her warmth keeps Carmelina warm.

That's how they'll find her, when they come. Asleep on her mother's dead back.

Chapter 1

I AM COMMUNICATING WITH the dead this evening, as the flies die on the sticky strips I've laid for them over the kitchen sink and Ernest Borgnine, the dog, the big lugubrious Great Dane, sniffs under my feet for scraps. This is what a person does in New Mexico—communicates with the dead. You'll see it all over, though not in the way the tourists think. It's not all Indian dances from the past or squash blossom necklaces sold on the plaza for three times what you'd pay in winter. No, New Mexico is the kind of place where if you know someone or if you were actually a friend of the family, you'd get the necklace for free. A friend of mine's dad, who's ninety-two, makes and sells the stuff, an old white Mormon who got into the business when Harvey Houses were still the rage. My friend has scads of turquoise, silver, tourmaline, coral, an obsidian bracelet.

In this neck of the woods, if you live here long enough, it doesn't take much to understand what you're looking at is the colors of the earth resurrected and polished into something else. The ancient geologies, veins of uplift and volcanic weeping, fissures of some violent melting and freezing. The Dallas socialite usually doesn't get that part, because she doesn't know someone who goes to the old mines, or traces one-thousand-year-old trade routes, or puts out shrines along with the prayers. Even the old Mormon went with some of his wholesalers a couple of times to do that. He had no trouble with the whole concept; he knows there's a way you pray here just by tracking the winter migration of sandhill cranes or watching the urgent feet of flamenco dancers cry their sorrow into your heart. This is a land-scape of *descansos*, crosses by the side of the road, prayer sticks stuck in the cracks of basalt escarpments, sage smoke rising up in the same plaza where church bells ring. Jesus is not over the altar at Taos Pueblo—the Corn Mother is. She's been resurrected too.

I have a casita in Arroyo Seco, a little village north of Taos in the first miles to the ski valley up NM 150. We just call it Seco. Here it is still high desert and I'm surrounded by sage and piñon and juniper. Back when I did archeology, piñon and juniper were never referred to as "piñon and juniper" but simply as p-j. As in, I am surrounded by p-j, or "I found it in the p-j." Hector Griegos mumbles by my house each evening, pulling a red wagon like it was a burro. He's one hundred fifty years old, says his great-great granddaughter Helena, who also says she's nine but I'm not sure I believe her. Helena brings me fresh tortillas and eggs once a week from her mama, who I got off probation early a long time ago, since I knew her domestic violence case was largely her ex's fault and not hers. Helena is the last of four from that match by ten years.

DV is like p-j; no one says "domestic violence" in my office. We all say DV. As in, "Are you recommending DV treatment for him?" or "How many DV cases do you have on your docket?" DV guys are, sadly, cookie cutter most of the time—toddlers in size twelve shoes, Poor-Me tricksters with attachment issues. The control freak in them has to do with a baby needing a mama, needing an Anything. And when Anything doesn't meet their baby needs—well. *Bam.* Out comes the fist or the shotgun or what-ever. Therapists have the luxury of understanding that those boys are really two years old; that the only difference is a two-year-old can't load a gun or tower over a woman.

DV guys tend to find DV gals—*mujeres locas* who are also needy and put up with fight, fuck, and fight cycles because when it's fuck time it's headier than hell, it's ecstasy, it's datura and red roses and the darkest rich-est chocolate out there. Then it all goes to shit pretty quick.

I try, honestly, not to know any of this about Seco folk. Of course, that's fairly impossible, seeing as Taos County only has thirty-three thousand people in it. But I aim my caseload for points south and west—for Taos proper, Ranchos de Taos, for the hippie Earthships out on the mesa in El Prado, and the trailers set back on the last of their occupants' ancestral land grants. Helena's mom slipped by this "no neighbors" rule of mine—I put it down to my being new at the job then—but Loretta, who also goes by Mama, has morphed into a kind of a friend and definitely the best neighbor you could find. Helena is now at my door this morning with her mama's basket of eggs, some tortillas, and something else—*carne adovada*. I let her in, fumbling the latch as my hands are otherwise engaged in brushing out my long mat of salt and pepper hair, inherited from an Irish father and an Italianate mother.

"Mama made me carne?" I ask.

"Yeah, she said she had extra."

"How's she doing?"

Helena wrinkles her nose. "Grumpy. She says she wants you to stop by later."

I can just see Loretta scowling with arms folded over her stout frame. She's small boned, plump, brown, and short. She cooks like a pro. "Okay . . . so why did you bring these over and not her?"

"She's feeding Hector." Helena rolls her eyes. "He's like a baby. No teeth. Takes forever."

I smile at her, that brown-eyed, black-haired imp. Helena will grow up and run away to join the cast of *Saturday Night Live*; I'm sure of it. She holds her hand up. "High five me."

"High five." Our hands slap and she's out the door.

A silence always follows. I live in a lot of silence here. Sometimes I sit out on the back patio and just listen. Crickets, a faraway car, the shout of a kid down the street in summer. Now, March, it's cold and still and sharp. You smell more than hear. Cedar fires, cold river birch. Then the sky falls into soot and the stars loom. I can miss old lovers then, or I can just be awestruck into grace. Either way my heart's pierced, raw, open, and often as not I'm crying a little bit. I've always been bitten by desert skies, though as I've aged it's harder because William's not with me anymore and hasn't been for five years. Damn damn damn this death business. Who the hell dies of a heart attack at forty-seven? Lots of people, I'm told. Well, right.

I crack eggs and make a breakfast burrito with the carne. After—it's Saturday—I decide to go to Helena and Mama's, down the winding street, the dirt rutted and unstiffening in the morning sun. March means windy and sharply cold in the morning. I sneeze at least five times because juniper pollen is raging; that incongruity between 25-degree mornings and spring pollen defines northern New Mexico this time of year. By 11:00 a.m. it will be 65 degrees and the idea of frost will linger only in far north shade. I hate juniper pollen. It turns me into a red-eyed, sniveling bandit. I'm kicking myself for not having taken an antihistamine, on the verge of a pleasant bout of self-pity as I sneeze a sixth time, when a shriek hits my ears. I stop. Mama's house. Then a moan, and the sound of something dropping. "Mama! Mama!" Helena is begging, and I stop sneezing and start running.

Mama is on the kitchen floor, an old linoleum pattern flowering out beneath her. Helena's holding her up by the shoulders and looking up at me with big saucer eyes. A cell phone has skidded halfway toward me, and Hector slumbers, unperturbed, on the couch in the living room, a slight shift and the smack of his lips unsupported by teeth the sole disturbance of his atmosphere.

Mama moans and I take over for Helena. Her eyelids flutter and she starts to focus. "Mama?" I ask. "Loretta?"

"Ay, Nina, it's you. Nina. Should be Niña. Do they tell you that?"

I smile. "No, and I'm older than you, I bet. So don't Niña me."

She reaches up, touches my hair a bit, at the end of my braid. Like my hairdresser (God bless his muscled soul), she finds my silver beautiful, not faded to some odd off-blonde color, and still shadowed by plenty of near-black. But she goes away from me again, quickly. "Ángel . . ." she says. "They'll arrest him for sure now. Ángel . . ."

I scowl. "Why? What happened? What about Ángel?"

Her hand comes down off my hair and flops in resignation in her lap. I'm still holding her shoulders up in a kind of squat. I shift and lower us both to the floor. She begins to cry. "Liza's dead."

"What?" Liza is Ángel's estranged wife. Ángel is Mama's nephew. Mama tried to raise him on and off when his own mother—Mama's sister—was on a bender, in jail, off with another guy, or otherwise deemed unfit for mothering by her family or, often, the county child welfare office.

"They found her—oh, Nina, they found her stabbed to death on the kitchen floor."

Helena emits a cry from over by Hector and just as I realize I'd totally forgotten about her presence, she bolts out to who knows where, to some comfort zone of her own where wife-beater nephews do not exist, and their victim partners live forever free from harm.

Ángel Martinez fits in that category of wayward sons Mama no doubt was trying her best to circumvent in her intermittent mothering of him. He is currently a probationer of mine. The discovery file on him reads like the bedside journals of the Marquis de Sade. He stands out in his cruelty. One charge had him twisting Liza's knee till the cartilage snapped. Another, and another, and another, had him kidnapping, manipulating, and/or using their now four-year-old daughter, Carmelina, against her. Liza mostly dropped charges. This could exasperate me until I see how frightening he can be; until I remember that seventy-five percent of all DV-related murders happen when the woman tries to leave; until I run across—again, as I perused through his file recently—the incident where he hung the dog in the globe willow in the front yard. Mostly probation work is a litany of human stupidity begotten in a stewpot of poverty. Every now and then, though, it chews the stomach up. Ángel's file is on my desk because of the dog and two black eyes on Liza. He's been on my desk twice before. This time I am recommending prison, both because previous attempts at control haven't worked and because my fear is that he is easily capable of homicide. He is out on bond, of course, and his defense attorney is doing his job trying to get everything pled down to the usual misdemeanor. It galls me how a state can decide property damage above five hundred bucks is a felony, but that beating the shit out of your significant other and choking her to near-death is a misdemeanor.

Just maybe, though, I was hoping Ángel had too many marks against him this time. And though I didn't tell Mama that I knew all about him, as we sat there on the floor with her shoulders in my hands, what I really thought was—well, good. Maybe he's nailed for sure now, what with Liza's death. Mama'd done her best to love him, but by the time she first got him he was seven and feral as an alley cat. She'd have him for three months, then not see him for six months, a year maybe. Then she'd have him another three, and so on. Each time it was like being handed a hotter and hotter branding iron, a fiercer dust storm, a sheath of vacant rage and misdirection. Finally, she threw up her hands and told the state no. They'd have to find some other placement for him. For Loretta, where family is all, this must have been a knife in the heart.

She looks up at me. "Nina, *por favor*. Can you find out more about Liza for me? From Larry? Your cop *amigos*?"

I sigh. She sits up and I release her shoulders. "Sure, Mama," I said drily. My heart sits heavy and shriveled. Of course. This is not an uncommon request. I do what I can within the confines of the law and my own ethical guidelines. Probation officers know all the dirt, what scuttles like trash along the bases of low adobe walls; what squats, lethal and unseen, in the backyard junk piles of dilapidated singlewides. We know which prominent attorney has four DWIs. Who beats their kids, who has a problem with bouncing checks. I work hard to shift my vision once I leave work. I do a mental smudge with smoldering sage; I go on runs; I take showers; most of all I do my art. But then my friends and neighbors have a crisis and come to me, and my job spills into my other life.

I make to leave. "I'll be in touch," I say, and go quietly out the front door.

The phone rings in my office as I stash Ángel's file back in my stack. It's now Monday, and I've hid from Mama and Helena all Sunday. Ernest Borgnine the Great Dane did not mind, though he failed to understand why we went for our walk up canyon in the cold and still somewhat icy mountains instead of in the more pleasantly warm (at least by 3:00 p.m.) and certainly more familiar neighborhood. I gave him an extra doggie biscuit upon returning home as recompense.

The phone keeps buzzing.

I pick up. "'Lo," I say, attempting to neaten my desk. I have a couple of Bauman prints and Ansel Adams's iconic *Moonrise Over Hernandez, NM* hanging on my walls, and I've added a huge bunch of Carmen Miranda paper flowers in a vase on my back shelf, but it still feels like a boring place.

"Mom."

"Hey! Jackson! Where are you?" Jackson hates my day job because I've been threatened a couple of times and now that William's gone, he thinks I should take his pension and "just do art."

"Coming into Santa Fe. I'll be home soon." His voice sounds tired and though he's twenty-six and doing okay the old mother worry creeps in.

"How was your trip? You're out a day early."

"It was okay."

"Jack? Are you okay?"

"Mom, I'm fine. Just tired. We hiked twelve miles today. I'll pick up tamales for dinner. From Mr. Santa Fe Tamale Man you like so much."

"Tomas's Fine New Mexican Cuisine, thank you very much."

"Yeah, him."

"Thanks, sweetie." I let out air. We hang up but I've got my lips rolled into a tight ball. *Mijo*, my only child, my grace, my light . . . my boy. Christ.

I stand up to go home, putting stray things away. You can't win, I think, and then consider that idea both inane and clichéd. Life is not a "win" thing. He'd had everything, Jackson. In some ways, he had too much in that way only children do—too much attention, too much pressure, too much parental pride. We were like bees to him, or wasps—annoyances, possibly toxic, always capable of sting. You give yourself trauma in order to grow if none already challenges you, he once said—at fifteen. There it was, that Old Soul business, that uncanny wisdom, unmoored until his brain could catch up to it.

But he is here now, back from two weeks in the mountains to the south, where March truly speaks of warmer weather. Before that he was in the Peace Corps, in Indonesia. He doesn't know what's next for him, but I don't care. I have my boy home for a night or three, and he is bringing tamales, and his face is such a perfect mesh of me and his dad. So I will get to bask in the echo of what is dead but never gone for me; I will get to relish in the thick eyebrows and quiet temperament that were William's—William who left us both five years ago, on a solid sunny morning so ordinary in New Mexico you hardly knew what to do with the shock creeping in. You looked for portents in the grass, the lone upset crow, the whirl of carrion birds high above the house, the sudden isolated rustle of sage. But there really had been nothing. Nothing but the distant wail of a siren, the result of a call I must have made, before clattering my phone to the floor just as Mama had done Saturday, and starting feebly, shaking, moaning a little, to do CPR until the wail closed in and a small army of EMTs took over.

Needless to say, there'd been no point.

I swallow and find a tear leaking out one side of my face. The desk is neater than it was ten minutes ago and I'm blowing my nose when Larry Baca walks in.

"'Sup, homegirl. You're looking mighty sorrowful. The four o'clock hour doesn't suit you, it seems."

I gawk at him. Larry is classic northern Rio Grande Valley born and bred, wears cop boot-cut polyester pants in the universal beige of all sheriff's departments, and has a handsome moustache as well as a history degree from UNM. He usually sounds kind of, well, *male*, and straight to the point, but today if his speech could act it would bounce around like Tigger. "What language was that?" I ask. "Larry Baca mushing together the Crips with Scarlett O'Hara and Shakespeare?"

He laughs. "Something like that, yeah. I am a linguistic Samurai." He fakes a karate chop and leans over with a fresh tissue, proof he saw me crying. I blush. "Just trying to get you to laugh, sister."

I take the tissue and manage a smile. "Well, you definitely knocked me back to the present. What are you doing here?" Larry works for the sheriff's office as a detective.

"To give you more possibly bad news about Liza."

I frown. As per Loretta's request, I'd left a message for him about it first thing this morning. "Okay . . . so what is it?"

"It's not Ángel."

"Huh?" I look at him dumbly for a moment. "What do you mean?"

"I mean Liza wasn't killed by Ángel. At least not so far. He was in Santa Fe at the estimated time of death. He's beside himself, wailing and carrying on. Or at least that's the rumor."

I make a face. "DV guys are always wailing and beside themselves when the object of their brutality leaves their orbit."

"Man, you really don't like this guy."

"His discovery file makes my stomach do back flips."

Larry lets out a low grunt. "I know he's no charmer. But he's got a tight alibi."

"'No charmer'? Larry, he's a sadist." I sometimes think law enforcement sees so much their eyes glaze over and their hearts get leathery and prehistoric. And I like Larry. He's on the Sexual Assault Services Organization board. His wife runs the victim advocacy program for the DA.

"I'll have to read the file sometime," he says drily.

"Yeah, you will." A March wind sprays a clot of dust against my only window. My view is of dun-colored buildings leaching out to a dun-colored mesa, which at some point out there is ripped in two by the Rio Grande Gorge. "What's his alibi?"

"He's a *santero*. He was at an art opening for his work on Canyon Road at the time of Liza's death."

"What? He's a what?"

"A sant—"

"I know what that is."

I can hear Larry grinning. "Doesn't fit with your sadist image, does it? You should see his Christs. Man, I've never seen such sorrowful faces, such tears of blood."

"And to think you come from a culture that makes a fetish of such things. Great. I suppose he's a millionaire if he's showing on Canyon Road."

Larry makes a face at me. "That was for the bloody culture reference. And not yet for Mr. Millionaire. This is his big breakthrough."

Fuck me, I think. I let out a sigh. My little ceramic sculpture gallery, the one in bustling downtown Arroyo Seco and shared cooperatively with three other artists, seems a pale failure. "So, fine. I'll just assume he has no new charges pending and write up my recommendations as per his currents."

"That where he hung the dog?"

"Among other things. Liza had two black eyes and three cracked ribs." Something occurs to me. "If he didn't kill her, who did?"

Larry shrugs. "Beats me. She didn't think much of herself, Nina. Could've been any number of lowlifes she let in too close."

And that's the sad thing, isn't it? That's the thing you're left with when all the perps are in jail and the women's bruises have faded. It's a ringing silence, the bleak portrait, the banal repetitiveness of people who hate themselves inviting other people who hate themselves into their lives, just so they can prove they were right about their unworthiness, all along.

I stop by my gallery after work. My studio is out back, a shed with a space heater, a block of clay. I shouldn't say I'm a failure. I don't do pots and bowls and coffee mugs. I do heads of animals, hooves, glazed pelvises, human skulls, abstracted a bit, warped as clay allows for warp, fired delicately. Half my pieces used to blow up in the kiln, though now I have mastered that craft so that I lose far fewer. Still, the ones that survive I've managed to shape and hold and burn into a sacred creation. An alchemist's art, ceramics, as is anything that requires burning to form—a mirror, then, to the journey of the human heart.

I do sell, now. I sell in part because, ironically, I've kept myself "exclusive" to Seco. I've done this because I need to work thirty hours a week at probation, both for the mortgage money and for the pension. In truth, I am also scared to completely quit. William's death benefits, stashed in mutual funds, beckon like a new love interest. *Try me*, they whisper. *You could go international.* And then *clunk*, the Voice of Reason, that hyperparental annoyance—*yeah, right.* You're hot one year, a bust the next. Besides, *mija*, you love the job too much. And it's true, my best artwork comes often as stark release, as counterpoint, as refuge, from my intense human work. Too much art time and I feel like an introverted narcissist. Too much probation and I feel defeated by the human race, burnt out, in need of a spa retreat. *Hohzo*, as the Navajo say—balance. They're right; it's the key to everything.

I pat my latest antelope head—one of a series—and blow a speck of dust from the base. Antelope Head #3 is spoken for. I was sort of hoping to sell the whole series to some rich movie star, but no go. Still, I've sold two of the six in less than a month. Rumor has it our resident billionaire is interested in #4. The ex-secretary of defense, who has a ranch near here, took #3.

I am trying not to hold my nose. *Think of it*, Luis, my flamenco dancer friend says, *as payback.*

How so? I ask him.

Mujer, you paid his salary for four ghastly years. Now he pays some back.

I have to smile at this, at Luis. Worse, I feel a flush of heat. He is in Spain now, leading workshops for beautiful young dancers. He'll be back in a month to begin choreographing the summer season in Santa Fe. The last time I saw him—and I've seen him exactly twice when he was not onstage—I caught the hungry look of a wolf on him, and I felt the brief touch of his hand as he flicked a stray hair out of my eye.

That split-second intimacy. A rekindling of a fire I thought died with William. Disturbingly, it seems to take on real flames with each e-mail he sends me. I snort at myself. I'm fifty-two. Really? I flip off the light and go home to my big silly dog and my thoughtful son with the packet of steaming tamales.

Chapter 2

LIZA MONAGHAN'S FUNERAL IS a small, somber affair at a Catholic church in Bayfield, Colorado. It is Friday and has been almost a week since they found her body and still no leads. This is looking like a cold case, rapidly, which makes us all want to blame Ángel that much more. I go because Mama has asked me to, for her. She feels intense guilt for Liza's death, as if the sporadic months she kept Ángel from ages seven through fifteen should have prevented his rage. She doesn't listen to Larry Baca, who's her second cousin by some convoluted reckoning only large families understand, nor does she believe in alibis. She certainly doesn't believe in Ángel's art, and her eyes widened when I told her about that.

"Santero," she spat. "Lucifer's artist, maybe. *Nada de Dios.*"

"Lucifer was close to God at one time," I said, hiding a smile and slicing my eyes sideways toward her. I am trying to lighten her up.

She flapped her arms at me. "Not funny!" And she dissolved into a pool of tears.

"I'm sorry, Mama." I put my arm around her. "I'm sorry. I'm just trying to get you to see it's not your fault."

She blew her nose. "I wouldn't be surprised if he couldn't fly out of his body and come kill her. Devil boy. *Brujo.*" She spat again. Loretta spitting out Spanish for "witch" was something to see. Her short pear-body shook along with her head of dark curls.

Now, at the funeral, I'm relieved to see Ángel has stayed away. He's got an arrogant idiocy to him, a blundering pride, that might compel him to make an appearance. No, he's mourning elsewhere. Or at least I sincerely hope he is.

Liza's parents are thin, pinched-looking white people. Her mother's face has the red bloat of someone who cannot stop crying. Her eyes look as if bees got to them, and she wipes her nose frequently. Her father is more stoic, staring straight ahead, vacantly, at the altar behind the casket. I feel he's gone, somewhat permanently, to some other locale, where he will function mechanically and without emotion until he himself dies. It's plain to me his heart has not survived his daughter's death.

I mill around a little aimlessly after the service, thinking I ought to do something Loretta would like me to do. In truth this would entail falling on my knees, dressed head to toe in black, wailing and asking for penance. Mama's guilt at Ángel's failures hits me like a wave, how deeply she would beg and beg Liza's parents to forgive her. I shake my head. I have no business here.

It's a four-hour drive back to Taos and getting on in the afternoon. I drove up to Colorado yesterday and treated myself to a spa night at the Pagosa Hot Springs. Rumor has it the owners use the business to launder drug money from South America, but when I'm soaking, postmassage, in 104-degree heat in a pool next to the San Juan River, I don't really care. Now, the church hall echoes with murmured voices. I head to the coffee urn where a man with a goatee stares sorrowfully at Liza's parents as they endure condolences.

"Poor kid," he mutters.

"Yeah, she didn't have it easy," I say, overhearing him. He turns to look at me and I stick out my hand. "Nina Montgomery. I knew her in Taos." Needless to say, I don't tell him I am the PO for her shithead boyfriend.

He takes my hand. "Dave Schaefer. Principal at the high school here."

"You knew her in high school?"

"Yeah. Her poor parents had no idea how to deal with her. They adopted her when she was five. Really messed up birth family."

I blink. "Liza was adopted?"

"Yeah. Classic RAD kid."

"Come again?"

"Reactive Attachment Disorder. Her birth parents were meth users, partiers. Lots of sex abuse . . . made Liza a perp too."

I cringe. I hate hearing yet another story like this. "When she was a toddler?"

He shrugs, as if the world is a hopeless place. "Yeah. Who knows."

"Crap," I mutter.

"She might as well have had a 'V' for Victim on her forehead by the time she got to junior high. Kids used her all the time and she thought it was normal."

"How so?"

He looks at me like, *Lady, you don't want to know*, at which point I ever so slightly blow my cover. "I'm a probation officer, Mr. Schaefer. I've probably heard it all."

"Your Liza's PO?"

I shrug and let him think what he will.

"Well, then, she'd trade—er—blow jobs for pot and talk about it like it was the most normal thing in the world. We think at one point she was muling for dealers."

"Crap," I say again. "Here in Bayfield?" Which, as I drove into town, seemed unencumbered by ethnic diversity and was proud to boast about its football team on a sign next to the "Welcome to Bayfield" one.

Dave Schaefer chuckled. "Surely, you're not that naïve, Ms. Montgomery. But you're right that Bayfield doesn't really want to *look* at stuff like that. Who does?"

"How'd her parents handle all that?"

He gazes at them again and shakes his head. "No tools, those two. They meant well, but they had no tools for handling it. I didn't tell them half of what went on. Liza finally did a spell in a treatment center in Colorado Springs, but it made it worse, I think. She came back, dropped out, and ran soon after."

I let out a sigh. "I'm sorry, Mr. Schaefer." He strikes me as one of those True Principals, for whom losing even one kid in his charge is a personal pain.

"Was she muling in Taos?" he asks.

I lurch into my coffee. "What?"

"That's the rumor here. Drug deal gone south."

I'm staring at him. He looks baffled.

"You know, why she died."

I shake out of it. "Sorry. Maybe, I mean, that's an intriguing idea."

He barely holds back a smile. "But that's not what the good cops of Taos County are thinking."

"Well—no. They don't know what to think."

He pours me more coffee and fishes out a business card. "None of us did either." He swallows. "She was pretty and smart and filled with a thousand demons."

Silence steals in while I take the coffee and his card.

"It sucks, doesn't it?" I finally say.

And we part on that note, as the sun goes low and beams long shadows, and the March snow lurking on the north sides of so many ponderosas seems to seep its coldness up into my boots. Back to Taos, I think, where the juniper pollen will sear my eyes and the snow, such as it is, stays high on the peaks to the east.

On Saturday I go visit my friend Margot, who lives in an Earthship on the sage plain west of town. Margot dresses the same way she did in college—Birkenstocks, batik tops, flowing skirts from India. It has always irked Margot that our generation missed the sixties. We became friends in part because our first presidential election involved Ronald Reagan actually winning, and people in our dorm—*eighteen years old, for chrissake*—voting for him. She, like me, lived off the fumes leftover from Kent State, the SDS, radical feminism. We thought we were progressive, only to find frat boys ascendant. I haven't really gotten over this.

Margot owns a gallery on the plaza and does okay by it. This is what truly cemented our friendship, as late adolescent idealism can carry you only so far. She curls her nose at my probationary tendencies, and I bite my lip when I find myself wishing she'd ditch the Birkenstocks for good, with their ugly footbeds, even uglier leather straps, and Germanic failure for anyone to wear sandals with any grace. It's an in-joke throughout the Southwest that you can spot a German tourist a mile away by the pairing of ghastly summer sandals with even ghastlier black or argyle socks. The Germans come in droves, too, because they were all weaned on Karl May—their equivalent of Louis L'Amour—and have nothing like a red sandstone cliff in their country. Paired with wool socks in winter, Margot's Birkenstocks reach their apotheosis, and my aesthetic sensibilities wince each time.

Yet Margot loves art. She isn't an artist per se—her creation is her home and the gallery—but we shared classes in art theory and history back in college. I love making art but hate the marketing; she is most creative at the latter. Margot, born a fortunate daughter of a Dutch shipping magnate and an heiress to a snack company pile, foundered in depression until she figured out a way to take the family genes and subvert them into the brilliant selling of artists she loved. She also used her trust fund to start a nonprofit in town, for environmental stewardship and alternative energy development. What a great way to flip the bird to the old man, I said to her once, and she just laughed. "The old man, as you put it, has more resources than God at his fingertips and makes sure all his lobbyists are cozy in bed with the right senators. I am but a pimple on his arse."

"But he loves you, O Pimple."

She sighed, squatting in front of a tomato plant and plucking off ripe fruit. "I know. He'd just be happy if I got married."

The Pimple comment was ten years ago. Margot did not get married; instead she built an Earthship. The more elaborate of these structures look like Barcelona's Gaudi and a hobbit had architectural matings using old tires, bottles, and mud. For Margot, this betrothal has kept her occupied ever since, though now as she's down to daily maintenance and small improvements, she's been suspiciously lively about "community meetings" and a guy named "Richard." I don't ask anymore. She'll tell me if it gets important. I'm visiting today just to say hi, and because she wants to do a ceramic show with some of my stuff in it.

"I fired some raku horses this morning. And I have some new mountain sheep," I tell her.

"I like the raku, that red quality. The horses aren't too RC Gorman, are they?"

"I don't think so." I blink. *Are* they too cowboy? Too Romantic Western schlock? You have to be careful with horse art. I pour more tea from the pot she's made and help myself to a ginger snap. I'd felt so in love with my horses this morning, but a lot of times I have learned that this can be a red flag, a signal for Not-Ready-For-Prime-Time art.

"You're unsure about the horses."

I make a face. Margot can read me very well. "Come look at them when you're in town next," I say. "I think I've got what I want. But you are right—horses can be . . . cliché."

She nods. "Every week I have some Western art yahoo in my gallery, wanting me to hang paintings of cowboys on horses, backlit by a dying sun, the dust poofing at their feet." She sighs, waving a long, ringed hand as if shooing away flies. "I tell them, look around. Do I look like a cowboy gallery to you?"

I laugh. "Yeah. But I have oodles of gray squirrels, jackrabbits, and cottontails I sell for twenty bucks a piece. They fly off the shelves. Cute stuff."

"Bring some of those too. Little hooks. Like bait."

I slump. "There's going to be a reception, isn't there?"

"Oh yes, sister. Wear your finery."

"I hate schmoozing."

"I know." She reaches over and puts her hand over mine. "But they love you all the same."

I am unaccountably melted by her gesture of affection. I could tear up if I wanted to. I put on a rueful smile instead, though I'm fairly certain Margot is not fooled. "Thank you."

"Any time, *chica*. Now," she says, getting up, "I made a vat of green chile stew for my silent auction the other night and have too much leftover. Please take some home." I wait while she ladles a substantial quantity into an old cottage cheese tub. "I'll stop by the studio and see what you've got."

I take the tub. "If I'm not there just go around back. The key's hidden you-know-where."

She nods. "How's Jack?"

"Good. It's nice to have him home. He brought up tamales the other night and is figuring out what's next." My heart goes a bit leaden, unexpectedly. That this still happens annoys me. I step toward her front door and am reluctant to face the relentless sun outside. Trees are a rarity on the plain, and the wind can scour.

"See?" Margot says, reading my face. "That's why I never had kids."

"Why?" I look back at her. Am I that obvious in my moods?

"'Cause they grow up! Imperfectly! And nobody gets over it."

"True," I say. "That's true."

Outside I glare back at the sun as it glares at me off my windshield. I put the tub of stew on the passenger seat next to me. In the truck bed are sacks of clay. The sides have whitewash stains. I don't think, at that moment, that I am ever elegant, and I am sick of the damn sun. I'd like to go to Portland for a week, until my tennis shoes start to grow mildew. But then I look up and see the purple hulk of Taos Mountain and catch a whiff of sage coming in my window.

My heart relents into a clutch of unparalleled attachment.

Damn this place, I think. *I cain't never leave.*

A new child plays with Helena in Mama's yard. Children in New Mexico cavort on dirt in front of sloping pink-beige walls. This one looks younger than Helena, a big toddler, and sorrowful. Ernest Borgnine lies next to her, tongue lollygagging, the child's hand on his shoulders. A tiny alarm courses its way, capillary-like, through my body. Ernest knows immediately who needs comfort, who is sick, who might even be dying. He is a natural, an ideal therapy dog, though the *Taoseño* painter who lives up the road says he's a shaman and we'd better respect that.

I slow the pickup, roll the passenger window down.

"Ernie! You want a ride home?"

Borgnine's ears perk up and he stands by way of a yawn and what I suppose is an upward facing dog, where he seems to pull into the sun, his front paws aligned and his head titled back. The little girl next to him is dwarfed, even as she scrambles to her feet. She slaps the dust off her backside and stares at me.

"I'm Nina," I say. "Ernest's dog mom." I gesture at my beast, who by now is at the door, wanting in. Helena comes over and obliges him, opening the door while I wince in anticipation of my enormous hound completing his graceless leap into the front seat.

"Who's your friend?" I ask Helena.

Helena makes a face. "Not my *friend*," she says.

"Oh?"

"Mama says I should think of her as a *sister*."

"Why?"

"'Cause she sort of is. She'd be—lemme see—some kind of cousin. Aunt Lolo's son's kid."

"Aunt Lolo . . ."

"You know, that nasty Ángel's kid."

The little girl listens to this hollow-eyed and without defense of herself or her dad. I stare at her. Of course. Where else would she go? And how else would Mama feel she could redeem herself?

"What's your name?" I ask her, craning past Helena, who hangs in my window petting Ernest's head. I can barely see the top of her dark hair. "Helena, move," I say. Helena scowls but steps back.

"Carmelina," she mumbles.

"Well then," I smile, in that fake but sometimes effective and definitely well-meaning way adults who are trying to rectify the world do, "come over tomorrow, you two. At one. We'll make cookies and you can feed raw dough to Ernest. He'll love you forever."

A glimmer of something like hope flits across Carmelina's face, a breeze rumpling ever so slightly the glassy surface of a lake. Then it's gone. But Helena looks excited. "Ooh! Okay," she says.

"Not too much dough, Helena, to the dog," I say.

"I know I know. But you never eat very many cookies so we'll get a *ton*." She takes Carmelina by the shoulder and starts steering her for dinner inside. "C'mon, we gotta go. See you tomorrow, *tía* Nina."

Tía Nina. My honorary aunt-dom. Tía Nina. In my driveway, Jack's Jeep. Mama Nina now. Let's hope he's kept the place clean. Inside, I find him asleep on the couch. I gaze at him unremittingly, tears and pride swelling all at once. I could never gaze at him like this when he's awake. He would say, "Mo-om," just like he did in junior high, and blush with embarrassment, even at twenty-six. In sleep, too, I can see traces of the boy he once was, the vulnerability in his slack jaw, the way he balls his hands up under his chin. He has done that since birth. Mijo. I take Margot's stew to the kitchen, and rattle a pot just a hair too loud, to make him stir for dinner in this rare, fine time I have him home.

Chapter 3

ON MONDAY LARRY BACA and I carpool to Santa Fe for Drug Lab Awareness Training. I've taken this course before, as every five years the state thinks it's a good idea that its probation officers be up on what drug labs look like these days, in case they run into one on a home visit. They make us do other trainings repeatedly too; some of these are asinine, but I've learned with drug behavior that things shift wildly depending on black markets, real markets, new laws, and who's trafficking what. Larry's on the Northern New Mexico Drug Task Force and he coteaches the class. Yolanda Rodriguez, a new PO, is also taking it from our office, but she wanted to drive separately so she could have dinner with relatives afterward.

Larry's friendly today, in a short-sleeve, button-down blue Oxford and chinos, looking like a better paid detective than a beat cop. He really is the former, but he finds his pay isn't that much better (this is New Mexico, after all), and a lot of the time at home he wins more respect with the uniform. Look office-like in Taos and we think you're selling real estate. Wear a tie and we think you are a pharmaceutical salesman from Phoenix or Dallas. He still has his gun at his waist, though, which ought to tell people.

"Seen Ángel yet?" he asks me.

"He's supposed to have a hearing tomorrow."

"They'll continue it, won't they?"

I nod. I look over at Larry. "What time do we get done today?"

"Three, four. Somewhere in there."

I get a glint in my eye. "Want to go look at santero art on Canyon Road afterward?"

He looks over at me. "Check out the alibi?"

I nod. "Who interviewed who about where he was the night Liza was killed? I mean, you farmed that part out to Santa Fe, right?"

Larry colors a little. "I had three deaths that week. A nasty car crash too. So me and Ted and Alicia were pretty busy."

"I know. I wasn't suggesting you were incompetent, Larry," I tease, though Larry can be such a perfectionist about his job it borders at times on annoying. "I know you guys do stuff for them too."

"It seemed good. They interviewed half a dozen people at the gallery. He definitely had a show that night." Larry lifts up the console between our two seats and fishes around with his fingers till he hits a curve in the road and tells me to look. "I think I have a brochure in there."

We're at Pilar, down through the Gorge. The first part out of Taos down to Santa Fe is beautiful, stark, winding. Depending on the season the river happily roars or rumbles or trickles over basalt rocks that can turn places in the canyon into ovens come summer. The little towns—Pilar, Embudo, Velarde—are startling pockets of agricultural beauty. Water glistens in the *acequias*. It's starting to green, and glory of all, now that we are farther along in March, the fruit trees bloom.

I find the brochure. Ángel Martinez's name sits in big letters over an eye-catching close-up of one of his Christ *bultos*, or carved statuettes—lots of red, anguished blue—on a black background. On the bottom are the dates of the exhibit. Inside, I find that he's Mariposa Gallery's chosen "Young Artist of the Year," a series they apparently sponsor. Smaller photos of complete triptychs accompany this information. We're supposed to call for pricing.

"I'll bet," I mutter. My jealousy has returned. How come *I* was never "Young Artist of the Year"? How come they don't have "Middle-Aged Artist of the Year" awards? Hell, you need more huevos to keep going now when your thumb's arthritic, youthful abandon has left you, and you wake up every morning in some pool of grief, than you do when you're twenty-one and an idiot.

Larry's looking at me in between checking the road. "You look like you're about to cry."

"Fuck him," I choke. "He's such a shit. Even if he didn't murder Liza, he would twist her knee till the cartilage snapped. He'd kidnap their daughter, then drive by the house, taunting Liza. He fucking hung the dog."

"And he gets an art prize you wish you had."

I turn to the window because the water works are right there and I'm wishing it was Margot next to me and not Larry. My decision to marry, have a family; my discovery ten years ago that when I quit a day job, a frontline kick-your-butt social work job, my art languished; my ridiculously complex brain and personality that can't just sit there and do nothing but churn out sculpture for the masses like some genius with autism—it all floods back.

Ángel's a simpleton with a wracked heart and a good eye. At least that's what I want to believe. I sigh heavily. I turn to Larry. "I mean, what if they're all heroin dealers who *agreed* to back his alibi? What if Liza's been dead even an hour longer than the coroner's giving it right now?"

"It's okay to hate his guts, Nina. And you might have a point about heroin dealers."

"What do you mean?"

Larry's turn to get a glint in his eye. "Mexican tar's big right now, ever since the state clamped down on OxyContin prescriptions. The task force has been working with the feds in Taos on a ring for a while now."

"Great."

"Rumor has it that it gets funneled—or maybe laundered—through some high and mighty places."

"Hmm. You know, when I went to the funeral for Liza last week her high school principal told me she was a born victim. She'd been adopted out of a hellhole at age five. Sexually abused, forced to perp herself, lots of drugs and alcohol. He said she had Reactive Attachment problems. At any rate, giving a blow job for pot was normal for her. And he said the school thought she'd been used for muling pot around."

Larry's turn for pique. He's chewing the inside of his cheek; I can tell. He's got a grown daughter who teeters in and out of meth use. He and his wife Clara are raising her two girls.

"Shitty world," he says.

"Yeah." We're down at Ohkay Owinge now, or what the Spanish named San Juan Pueblo. Española next—the heroin capital of the Southwest. It's not even 8:00 a.m. yet, and we're both furious with grief.

Drug Lab Awareness boils down to this: Here is what a grow house looks like for pot. They take up an enormous amount of electricity and turn into hazmat sites because of the mold that starts growing and the five thousand electric plugs overheating the system. Then: Here is a meth lab. I've seen those before, though given the movement around legalizing marijuana and the clampdown on Sudafed and other allergy drugs used in meth production, grow houses are currently more abundant and meth labs less so. Here is Mexican tar, a gooey, bubble-like caramel in a spoon up there on the power point, getting cooked for the needle. This leads into Naloxone, a new drug that when administered reverses, suddenly, the low heartrate of a near overdose. Law enforcement and EMTs use it now to revive a potential heroin OD on the streets. Here we get to see short YouTube videos of Deepest Albuquerque and stereotypical addict-types groaning under freeway bridges as their partners are near death and the cops come in to revive them. I've had a couple probationers saved by this, whether they like it or not. We then cover Fentanyl, what the patches look like, how much stronger it is than Oxycodone, what kind of market is blowing up for this. It's enough to make a person leave in disgust.

Larry talks about a bill he is sponsoring to strengthen state child neglect laws, as he sees what overwhelming pot use looks like. The idea that a person "can't get addicted" to pot is one I have to fight to debunk in my probationers on a near-daily basis. If meth leads to kids being exposed to porn, sexual abuse, and beatings, pot addiction leads to unchanged diapers for weeks at a time, three-year-olds trying to find crackers or anything to eat in the pantry, an extreme parental inertia. Larry is not a fan of legalization, barely a fan of any kind of medical use, though he has known some people whose judicious use of pot has kept them off opioids, and for that he has some respect. I can tell at times it's hard for him to talk about drugs, given his daughter's on-again, off-again struggle with meth. But that's also why he is on the task force.

His Santa Fe partner—Tom Garcia from the Santa Fe police—talks about gangs and who's into what. West Side Locos, Sureños, the prison gangs, Mexican Mafia. In a different training—Gang Awareness—we'll have to endure pictures of beheadings and so forth; I still have imprinted on my brain from the last Gang Awareness training an MS-13 victim, with no hands, feet, or head, left in a galvanized steel tub, like the kind you use to water horses. It is disturbing to find out that MS-13, a notorious Salvadoran gang that (of course) started in US prisons and then got deported back to the old country as its members were released and sent packing, has begun to put down roots in New Mexico. But today it is just gangs and drugs: who moves what, what niches are occupied, what is shifting in the market.

We finish on high-end stuff, the difference between poor people's drug use and the wealthy. Most of the Santa Fe wealthy seem to tend toward the prescription opioids, and not heroin per se, though it seems there is a possible pulse toward heroin being chichi, like coffee these days. I roll my eyes. By four o'clock I've had enough, my mouth ashy with human detritus, my body wanting a shower. I wait for Larry to pack up his computer and notes, and we head out the door.

Mariposa Gallery is de rigueur Canyon Road: sloping adobe wall abutting the street, wooden Spanish-style gate, a lilac bush guarding its entrance, just leafing out and squeezed between wall and road. Inside, a courtyard with fountain; more lilacs; Russian sage; Talavera pots not quite capable yet of being planted with annuals, since they could freeze still; a cherry tree flowering. Flagstone walkway, gravel between the bushes, a tiny grass area tucked in one corner with a bench. The gallery itself is more sloping adobe, cozy inside, a kiva fireplace in the corner of the main room. Larry and I smirk at each other upon entrance and slow up. A buzz of people mills about. We were not expecting this—it looks not only as if we have stumbled into a reception, but that it is Ángel's, a second honoring for his Young Artists award, perhaps. Larry suddenly screams Cop! in his chinos, close haircut, and Oxford, even though he's left his gun in the car. I feel as if I scream Frumpy Probation Officer! though at times like these I'm glad I've got my long braid of salt and pepper hair and my co-op made earrings (silver and lapis today). At least I look like I vote Democratic, and someone might even suspect I harbor artistic ambitions.

I'm more well-known than I thought, it appears.

"Nina Montgomery!" A tall woman in a red clingy maxi-dress approaches. She's raven-haired, a well-trimmed sixty, a single, blindingly polished silver cuff at her wrist. I think it looks like a bow guard, but I would never say that to her.

I have to smile. "Gert." Gertrudis Kahn. Married to the one and only Reza Kahn, owner of the big gallery at the mouth of Canyon Road, the one you see driving Paseo de Peralta as you pull out of government buildings and head easterly. Gert and Reza are the height of what I'd call local color. Reza has an Asperger's love of objects—art, artifacts, suspiciously procured pots, Clovis points, Spanish treasure chests, ghostly mantillas of black lace, colonial coffins, governors' canes. Gert is the human side, a consummate marketer and, to her credit, makes it her business to know every artist worth what she considers salt in the state. A little thrill goes through me. *You rate!* says a voice.

"Listen," she says, sotto voce and handing me unasked-for wine, "rumor has it Jade Kirchner wants your entire antelope series."

I nearly spill the wine. Jade Kirchner is Taos's biggest movie star part-time resident. Larry grins and I tilt my head ever so slightly for him to go make rounds. *Look for needles in the men's urinal. Eavesdrop on Ángel. Pay attention to gang colors.* My look says I'll be along as soon as my brief bask of fame has faded.

He's laughing at me and leaves. Gert is oblivious to him.

"Really?" I say to Gert, feigning recovery.

"Yes. We were at a reception for John Billings and Jade saw your antelope head that he bought and she kept circling it the whole night."

Billings is my billionaire purchaser. I'm fighting two emotions—elation and *goddammit it really is all about who you know. It's all luck.* Shit. I feel as if I'm at the artistic equivalent of Davos, but then my long-dead father's voice whispers not to look a gift horse in the mouth and I muster a glossy, welcoming smile for Gert.

"Well, I'd have to make new antelopes to replace the ones I sold."

"You could. Or just hold the remaining three until I talk to her."

I squint my eyes a bit. "And your commission on this, Gert, would be . . . ?"

She laughs. She has a great, belting, Spanish queen laugh. "None. Because, *cariña*, once she buys the world opens up for you and *then* I represent you. Consider it PR."

"Ah." Now my smile is genuine. "Well, all right, then. I'll hold ten days, but that's it." I learned long ago that applying a deadline could help pressure a pending sale.

"Good. Now . . ." she says, putting a hand on my arm and turning my attention to the room. People mill about with wine. Cheese platters shine on a couple of waiters' arms. Candles wink in the niches. On an old Spanish table Ángel's wooden carvings—triptychs, solo figures, a wailing Christ who looks like an intriguing New Mexican transfiguration of Muench's *The Scream*—greet me. "You must be here to support a fellow Taoseño."

"Something like that," I mumble.

She pats my arm. "Good to see you. I need to circulate. You know," she sniffs, and I know then that she knows it's all a game, "I have to *rub elbows*. If I don't do it, it won't happen." For a flicker I feel for her, married as she is to a man who tracks objects over people. Her red-bedecked back blends into a loose sea of other well-appointed souls, and I turn my attention elsewhere.

Ángel Martinez has his dress shirt securely buttoned at his wrists. My first thought is that he's hiding all his jail tattoos. He clutches a beer bottle in such a way as to shield his West Side gang marker—tatted in the webbing between thumb and forefinger—though with this crowd they'd probably think it a mark of Santa Fe authenticity. He looks dazed, as if he can't believe his good luck, but he's also turning on his psychopath *cholo* charm. He looks *muy guapo* in a snarky kind of way—black hair slicked back, silver tips polished to a high sheen on his black cowboy boots. He is too skinny, and a white guy who seems vaguely familiar lurks right behind him. I circumnavigate, hoping he doesn't spot my braid, combing the room for any sign of his lowlife friends, or—with Larry's notions in mind about wealthier drug purveyors—for opiated wanderers. I don't see much, just the buzz of tipsiness.

I catch a whiff of conversation between two women looking at the *Scream* Christ figure. "I nearly bought that one last week when he first opened," one says. She dresses like Margot, in a batik dress.

"It's beautiful. A little unnerving, though," says the other. She has a simple little black dress on.

"Yeah." Margot Wannabe shoots a look toward him. "I don't think he's had the easiest life." And off we go, into the Tortured Artist conversation.

I move away, cringing at the cliché, and find myself being stared at by a Hispanic man with a scar dragging down the right side of his face. I stop dead. In this probation business, every now and then you feel what Jerry and Roni in the office call the Lizard Soul, a truly psychopathic cold piece of meat. His eyes are utterly blank. I've seen eyes like that before and I don't like them. They are eyes beyond help, beyond the usual criminal pleading or pretending. They are eyes that don't care. I have no idea why he is here.

I turn away and pretend to admire a *retablo*, the flat wooden tablets on which biblical scenes or people are painted. This one is of the Virgin Mary, who looks surrounded by a kind of harrowing halo of porcupine quills. Larry sidles up, much to my relief, coming out of the back hallway by the bathrooms. We make eye contact and come together near the door.

"Anything?" he asks.

I nod my head toward Scar Face. "Who the hell is that?"

He squints. "No idea. If I didn't know any better, I'd say he was deep into some lifelong shit."

"Yeah, me too. Did you find anything?"

"Open your purse," he says.

"What?" I look at him, startled, but do as he asks.

He drops a baggie with one neat syringe in it.

My eyes bug out. "Where'd you find that?"

"You'd be amazed what you find when you rustle the bathroom trash a little."

"Eww." I make a face. "I am so glad I don't have your job."

"*Muchacha*, that's not the half of it. Besides, it could just be insulin."

"I know. Still."

I survey the room one last time. Ángel's eyes graze mine and do a double take. "Shit," I mutter. Ángel's gone stiff. I give him a little smile. If I had a cowboy hat, I'd tip it. And then Larry and I are out the door, into the cold March night, making our escape.

Chapter 4

AT THE END OF March, our Great Old Broads soccer team has a mud match with the Grumpy Old Men soccer team. The sad thing is we just *think* we're old, because we're in our fifties and the first meaningful experiences with age have appeared: a dead spouse, shoulder surgery, warnings from the doctor about weight and diabetes. The West is full of active retirees, so the seventy-somethings who still ski Taos every year formed their own soccer team—*Truly* Great Broads and *Really* Grumpy Old Men. They play co-ed to make enough of them, and travel to Albuquerque and Santa Fe and Durango and Farmington to play others like them. We fifty-something women just stick to Questa and Angel Fire and Pilar, with a daring run to Española and the casino (if we feel like it) at Ohkay Owinge when we're done dispatching the Española Conquistadoras, as those uppity women down there like to call themselves.

The match today is less mud and more frozen grass and dirt, a scruffy field at the middle school. Taos has a FIFA 2 Eco Park soccer field made of synthetic grass, but we like our low-class operations as well as real grass and so shun it for the "authentic" rutted grass of the middle school. This idea of "authentic" is a kind of crude joke for those of us who live here—a way to snigger at all the romantic hype.

The idea of the March Madness Match is to make ourselves as miserable as possible for two hours, starting at 7:00 a.m. when it's likely to be 20 degrees, if that, so that by 9:30 we are ensconced at our reserved Great

Table behind the pastry case at Michael's downtown. It's a wonderful social gathering, a kind of ceremonial return from hibernation. We also catch a preview of ourselves for the upcoming season—who's likely to be out with knee problems, who's leaving for the summer and will need replacing. Finally, it's a great excuse at our age to eat like a pig and feel utterly justified.

I play defensive back, generally. I'm not a soccer player the way, say, Margot has been all her life. But I like how I get winded and I like getting a little physical to protect the goal. I don't look anything like the elaborate, balletic, true soccer players do, their long legs scissoring with a grace I didn't realize was so integral to the game until I caught a UNM match one year when they were good. Then I went Holy Cow and started getting much more interested. Margot was with me that day and just smirked. This morning as I tighten my cleats, Ernest looks at me forlornly because he knows soccer days mean no walk for him. I scratch his head. "You know, Ernest, if you could be a good dog and just sit on the sidelines like everyone else's spouses, you could come with me." He worms his nose into my lap and looks up with Doggy-Guilt-Trip Eyes. I bend down and rub his muzzle with mine. "But nooo . . . you'd lope onto the field and chase the ball." He looks at me, defiant. "Yes, you would, and you know it."

Jack stumbles into the dining room during my dog chat, coffee in hand, hair an updo of chaos. "Take Ernie for a walk," I plead.

Jack scratches Ernest's head, which noses its way to resting on the table-top. He laughs. "He can really pull the Poor-Me shit."

I smile. There's a small, small silence in which the depth of an absence makes its way into every pore of the adobe. Tears sprout before I am finished tying my laces. Jack's hand comes to my shoulder even though he can't see my face. I look up at him from my hunched over position.

"I miss him too, Ma," he says.

I forget the lace and we reach for each other. For the first time in a long while a good sob erupts from me as he holds me.

That's the other reason March just sucks. He died in March.

This year Margot has batiked lion tee shirts because by late March we will have determined whether it is going out lamb-style or lion-style. This year is lion-style: wild, flying snow that doesn't stick, wind, more wind, a freezing rain last week that flooded the streets and then slicked over into ice. The next day it rose to seventy and put on a fake lamb face before returning to its usual pollen fest of wind. We don our tee shirts, a lioness with her paw on a soccer ball, and meet the men. This year they appear to have cleaned out the sale rack of a hunting supply store and are all wearing camo.

"Good lord," says Margot before she moves up to center the offensive line. "Do they think they're Rambo?"

"Probably." I move to the right of the goal, my usual perch.

What the men have in strength we like to believe we have in agility. Margot is an obsessive yoga practitioner, as is Judith Keel. Marta Gomez is a tiny soccer wunderkind who was Albuquerque High's Player of the Year back in the day. She continued playing at New Mexico Highlands University until her career was ended in the usual way good Hispanic Catholic girls' careers were back then (and, to judge by my caseload, still are)— pregnancy. She married the man, had four boys, and coached them all into college scholarships. She currently sells turquoise jewelry and cowboy paraphernalia to tourists in her store on the plaza. Lisa Schlanger is an archeologist. She invented the name Great Table for the Michael's feast, after Chaco Canyon's Great Houses and Great Kivas. She hopes, however, that we don't follow into the apparent evils and downfalls of that ancestral bunch. Karen Hodges sells real estate. Maria Benavidez is a Native Taoseño who runs an environmental nonprofit designed to protect sacred land. Jenny Trujillo is a cop.

The men we face pretty much span the same spectrum. Larry's playing today; Ted Martinez, with Karen "the face of Taos real estate"; Mark Farrell the Hippie Potter. Taos Taos Taos we all shout collectively—old hippies and land grant Spaniards and Indians and cops and teachers and artists. None of us will ever be rich. A generation ago, our forebears more than likely detested each other, when the New Buffalo Commune was raging and *Easy Rider* was Hollywood's idea of documenting the whole phenomenon. But our sheer staying power in a place wracked by drought and violent storms and poverty has forged a kind of respect.

"Play ball!" says the ref, and we're off.

Today's forecast, I decide, while the action moves downfield toward the men's goal, is for frigid dry air. It hurts to fall on the grass, small icicles cracking under the body. The ball moves my way, a header coming from Margot. I capture it, move it toward Judith Keel, who is acrobatic when it comes to sliding a ball out from under a six-foot man. I punch it out as Larry runs into me and we fall to the hard ground, laughing. He blows into his hands.

"Wear gloves," I say.

"*Cállate*, Montgomery." He grins and gets up.

"Don't tell me to shut up," I growl.

Our game is interrupted by loud shouting against the wall of the middle school facing the field. Four or five boys, a couple of girls, two colors, a lot of black, chains, baggie pants, a blur of pomaded hair—and Larry's running, Larry and Jenny Trujillo, who works for Taos PD. We all quit playing and my stomach bottoms out. I want to scream at Larry to stop it, Larry who is already on his cell calling for backup, Larry who I can only imagine is heading straight into the barrel of a gun.

I know these kids. Or I know their type, and if I could get closer, I would be willing to bet one or two of them have been on my caseload at various times. Their clothes, their colors and postures, give them away. Shit. That does it—we will play on the FIFA field in the future, the one with no school close by, no contested turf. A kind of rooster warning springs up from one of them, a girl on the edge, pointing at Larry and Jenny. The boys, some of them already involved in grabbing jackets and hands back with fists or god knows what, freeze midfight. Margot, pulling up next to me, attempts a chuckle.

"Jesus. They look like some postmodern sculpture."

"Shut up," I growl. "Get down."

She looks at me funny, but crouches on the field as I do. We are thirty yards away, maybe, but I don't want a stray bullet hitting any of us. There is not much between us and them, no bleachers, no grandstand, nothing but a hip-high chain link fence demarcating the field from the track around it. Others, seeing us, follow suit, sending me—the sole law enforcement representative left on the premises—nervous looks. For some reason we all go quiet, as if, squatting like grouse in the middle of an open field, being quiet would make us less visible. I feel ridiculous and a maniacal urge to laugh metastasizes inside. I shake my head as if ridding of flies. *Cut the crap, Montgomery.*

Larry shouts, Jenny seems to pretend she has some weaponry behind her back, and they keep running right at them. "Sheriff!" He screams, again not wavering, in full charging bull mode. I peek out to my right and see his wife Clara gone white, clutching a thermos of hot tea. Her lips are moving and I know she is saying Hail Marys over and over.

But Larry and Jenny know what they are doing. They know, somehow, these are kids, at bottom they are kids. The frozen fight all of a sudden releases, and the kids spray in all directions.

Jenny shouts, "Those two!" And they sprint after two boys in particular. I didn't know Jenny could run that fast, but she closes quickly on one of them, while Larry corners the other, whose low-rider jeans have slowed him down. A battered Nissan Sentra, its windows tinted and its suspension dropped, spins out of the parking lot carrying half the crowd, while Larry does what I don't like seeing Larry do, and that is slam his kid into the middle-school wall and wrench his arm up behind him. I turn away. We all slowly stand up.

Karen lets out a huge sigh and Judith just gawps. "What was *that*?" She looks wildly at me.

"Gang warfare crap," I say.

I can't help it. I leave my team and jog toward the scene of the fight. By now two cop cars have shown up and Larry and Jenny are busy arresting their respective culprits, cuffed and shoved into a car apiece. I look down on the ground. Brass knuckles, a loose bullet. Someone had a gun. Whether it was loaded or not, who knew, but someone had a bullet in the pocket of a hoodie, or one of their jackets. I circle around, careful not to touch anything. Against the wall of the middle school, a vial. Prescription. I don't touch that either, but as I crouch down to peer at it, I can already tell it contains a cocktail of different pills.

The dirt is a hopeless smear of scuff marks. I see a mascara wand, a barrette—the girls' contributions. Also a razor blade. I let out a kind of half-snort. Perfect for cutting. For making mark after mark on arms, thighs, stomach. Beads of blood, their own crown of thorns to alleviate the other pains in their lives, the rapes and murders and addicted dads and conniving sisters and relentless poverty. It works, they say; it distracts off everything else; it shuts down pain by spilling endorphins into the system. Later, it will sting. Later, they will regret the scars. Some of them. Others will wear them as badges of pride. Others become addicted to the whole practice.

When I get back to the field, players and spectators alike are wrapped up in jackets, sipping hot drinks, wondering what to do. Larry and Jenny jog toward us, their job done, and find us gathered like refugees, looking a bit shocked and uncertain.

"Sorry," says Jenny. Larry goes to Clara and puts his arm around her.

I clear my throat. "Do we want to keep playing?"

The energy is collapsed, slightly angry, timid.

Judith, who'd been doing downward dogs and warrior poses to keep warm, seems to have recovered. "I say hell yes, comrades! I have been stretching for five minutes now, and I tell you, let's get those kids out of our system!"

You'd think she was Henry the Fifth at Agincourt. We stare at her, our turn to be frozen. Then Larry grins.

"Hell yes!"

The Law Enforcement Seal of Approval breaks the uncertainty. And we are back on the field, reeling out piled up cortisol and adrenaline into each other, into the running game, into something that goes on, furiously, for half an hour more, until the ref calls time and we move, sweating, off to our cars and to Michael's, for something warm and more comforting.

Chapter 5

ÁNGEL MARTINEZ INSTILLED SOME sympathy in me two years ago when I'd first met him, but by the time he walks into my office today to update his last PSI for his current crimes of hanging the family pet, felony assault on Liza, and attempted kidnapping, I am not inclined to be very nice.

"Hola, señora," he says in his best fake *maricón*.

I squint at him in mock horror. "What's with the gay Spaniard approach? Just 'cause you know I know you do art now? Does that make you gay?"

His usual vacant stare settles back onto his face and I sigh. Getting crap out of Ángel would be difficult now. "Look," I say, "can't you take a joke? What do you expect, coming in and talking like that?" I know he can't take a joke—most cons can't—but I am trying to appeal to his Tough Guy side.

He puts his hands, fisted together, on my desk. "*Mira*, Officer Montgomery, what do you need for this plea? Why I'm here, no?"

Cocky bastard. I swallow. "I want your version of what happened, for one." I always have to get this for a PSI, comparing what they say against the police report and describing both without bias. I don't want to hear his excuses and justifications, but that's the job. "Let's start with the dog," I say.

A shadow crosses his face, a brief ghost of pain. I suppress any impulse at speech because that will just snap him back to vacancy, but I'm surprised. I see him begin to adjust his face back to that hard nothingness anyway, so before he can shrug himself to insolence I murmur, "the dog . . ." as compassionately and softly as I can.

He actually covers his eyes with his hands, his head bowed.

"That bugs you, huh? The dog." I keep my voice low, soft.

He nods, head still in his hands. Then he looks up, eyes now far away. "I just got so mad."

"So you hung the—"

His eyes snap to me, blazing. "I did! After I kicked him! Damn bitch. Not the dog. Her. Damn bitch."

"Liza?"

At her name his eyes widen and he crashes back into his chair. Now he's actually crying, his anger useless against the fact of her death and his own crocodile pity. Out in the hall over Ángel's head I see Jerry Wright patrolling, sending a questioning look my way. Jerry is six foot four and two hundred seventy pounds, a former UNM linebacker who all of us call quietly over when one of our neighboring officemates seems to sense tension coming from our room. It's why we leave our doors open, unless it's a juvenile and parent, and even then sometimes we do. Roni, my neighbor in the little office to my left, must have picked up Ángel's remarks and dialed Jerry. I nod imperceptibly to Jerry that things are okay and hand Ángel a Kleenex.

"Ángel," I say, going for a totally different tack that I hope both throws him off and endears him to me for all eternity, "I like your art." This at least is true. As much as I begrudge his newfound Canyon Road infamy, Gert Kahn's offer on my own stuff softens me a bit.

He actually looks quasi-human for a second and smiles his skinny Spanish boy smile at me. It strikes me how gaunt he is, as if all the years of malnutrition as a child will never quite leave. Pencil jeans and cowboy boots wear well on him, of course, but they cover up a basic starvation. "Like yours too, señora," he says quietly.

My heart does this odd melting thing as my brain gets set on stun. "You've *looked* at my art?" I'm staring at him.

"The antelope are your best yet," he says.

I emit a strangled noise. *The antelope are my best yet?* How long has he been scoping my gallery? I refocus so I don't let him get the upper hand, but the human connection is everything, so I try to keep it. "Thank you," I say. My mouth has gone dry.

He nods into his hands again and I keep going. "So you admit to the death of the dog."

This time he nods vigorously. "I took a plea for all of it, señora. Whatever the cops say, sure."

No con ever does this. I can't figure him out. "You don't want to justify your actions? Like you have before?"

This time he really does shrug. "What for? She's dead. Liza's dead." And he sounds pitiful, genuinely devastated.

"So you didn't kill her?"

He looks horrified. "No! Ay, are you all thinking that? No!"

"Ángel," I say, gently as ever, "your track record sucks here. With her."

He blows out his nose like a furious horse, tears leaking out the sides of his coal eyes. "*Yo sé, bruja*," he spits.

I start laughing. I can't help myself. "Bruja? Did you just call me a witch?"

He lets out a buckling noise, half sobbing, half crackling with laughter himself. "Not such a good idea with my PO, eh? Who's writing my report, *¿que no?*"

"No," I say, "I mean yes, I'm writing your report. And no, not so hot on the bruja bit." I'm shocked that I want to reach out and pat his hand. "But I promise not to put that part in, okay?"

He relaxes and smiles a cocky-ass smile, which I think is about as sincere as he can get right now.

"I've had a tough life, officer," he says.

I sigh back into my seat. "Don't get all pity-pot on me, Martinez."

"Fine," he says. We're back to our usual roles. "But I loved her, Montgomery. *Quiero que se conozçala.*" I want you to know that.

"Yeah, and she was a 'damn bitch.'" I'm not falling for this.

He looks back into his hands, then up with his vacant stare. "*¿Andale? ¿Por favor?* I've got a buyer coming in at five."

"Fuck me," I say, at a bar half a mile down the road, Larry and Jerry and Roni Hawman and some other office people with me for happy hour. "That was exhausting."

"'I've got a buyer coming in at five,'" Roni's snorting into her beer. "Did he really say that?"

I nod miserably. Larry hands me a pink cocktail.

"What's this?"

"A strawberry daiquiri. I know tequila makes you sick, so no margaritas for you."

Larry knows me too well. This little gem of information was revealed at a training in Santa Fe, three years ago, when everyone else was gulping down salt-rimmed drinks and I was nursing a gin and tonic.

I drink it slowly. Larry sits next to me and hunkers in close so the others don't hear. The place is loud anyway with happy hour banter.

"So now you really don't think he did it?" he asks.

I chew my lip before answering. "No, Larry. He might know something about it, about why, though."

"Drug connections?"

"Maybe."

"You want to read the coroner's report?"

"Not really, why?"

"Maybe you'll catch something I've missed."

I smile in a small, sad way at him. "Okay, Larry. If you think it will help."

He smiles. "That's my girl."

"Why's it important?"

"It's a murder, Nina. We get what—? Two a year here? And most are self-explanatory."

I slurp my daiquiri while looking at him blandly. "You're putting in for chief of police, aren't you?"

He pretends to be offended. "That has nothing to do with it."

"Bullshit, Baca," I smirk. "It has everything to do with it."

"Okay, okay," he says. "Sure. But Liza . . ." He trails off and like the insensitive cad I can be I flash too late on his daughter's own history with drugs.

I put my hand on his wrist. "I'm sorry, Larry. I know you must see Eva in Liza."

He nods but looks up and away as if swallowing a river cobble, his jaw set. I leave my hand on his wrist and squeeze. He puts his other hand on mine to acknowledge this, and then we break apart, gently, into the sea of conversation around us. Roni is regaling Jerry and Rich and Laura with her attempts at sheep-dog training. She has a border collie she spends all her free time with. Someone at the bar laughs like a rooster. A mariachi band tests the microphone, and I know we'll all soon drown, ever gratefully, into Mexico's version of polka, and our own sorry drinks. I finish my daiquiri and head home.

It's March 31st and I find my walk strewn with blood red rose petals, just enough for me to puzzle whether a bumbling floral delivery boy has made a terrible mistake or whether I have an unknown admirer. Or perhaps Jack does! I smile at this, but on my doorstep, blocking the way, is a bottle of Spanish red—imported label, everything in Spanish—and my stomach does a flip-flop. I pick up the bottle and slowly open the door.

My house smells like a gourmet Latin kitchen. There is a sweetness—nutmeg? chocolate? squash, pulverized, and mixed with cinnamon?—along with a red chile smell. Ernest Borgnine's rear end sticks out from behind the half counter separating my kitchen from the entry way. He's lying down and his tail is wagging.

"Ja-ack?" I call out, not believing he would possibly cook a meal like this but at a loss for any other answer.

"Ah, señora!" a voice calls, and from my pantry at the far end of the kitchen emerges—my God—Luis.

I just stare at him with my mouth open. His grin widens.

"I—uh—Luis!" Ernest sits up and gazes fondly at me, as if I were somehow responsible for bringing home this fine-smelling creature.

Luis comes forward with his hands extended and takes mine in his. "Nina, I hope you don't mind . . ."

"How—I thought—how did you get in the house? How—?" I look

down at Ernest, who usually distrusts strange people on his turf. "How did you woo *him*?"

Luis laughs. "I came by today and met your son."

"Jack! Where's Jack?"

He chuckles again. "He's out, down in Santa Fe with a friend."

I can barely absorb this. We're *alone*. I'm alone in my house with a beautiful flamenco dancer who can cook and who apparently wants to impress me in a romantic way.

Luis squeezes my hands gently and lets go. "Is it all right? All this?" He gestures toward the kitchen. "Jack told me to *please* do so."

I relax a little and give a wry smile. "Oh he did, did he?"

"*Se adore su mama,*" Luis says, "*puedo a verle.*" He adores his mother. I can see that.

His voice is soft and gentle and masculine. I am melting inside in an embarrassing way, and stumble to a dining chair. Luis pours me a glass of the red wine and Ernest nuzzles my knees, howling. He always knows when I am thrown for a loop.

I look up at Luis and give him a feeble smile. "I never expected this kindness . . ." My voice is hoarse. "Yours or Jack's."

Luis pulls up a chair and puts a hand on Ernest's flank. He stops howling and licks Luis's hand. Luis is close and smells of the sweet-savory dinner he has been making. "Jack said," Luis swallows, "that five years is long enough and he's sure his father would think you needed some fun."

I must look like a human fly; my eyes feel so big. I start to cry again. All the loneliness, self-imposed after the grief settled out, and I was left, simply, with an ashy taste in my mouth, and the ordinary, lonesome, demands of my art overwhelm me. I wasn't aware I had been this lonely. I wasn't aware my heart had become a walnut, but one now cracked. Embarrassed, I blow my nose.

"Luis, you are—too beautiful! You dance with beautiful women! You are the most graceful man I've ever met, and I will tell you in no uncertain terms that women pretty much drool when you come onstage. I know I did."

He lets out a laugh. "Flamenco is supposed to make you drool! Or cry, or moan into your sangria."

Close up, I see the laugh lines, the fact that he's gray at the temples, the little wobble under his fine jaw that tells of age. In the right light he could even look tired, haggard. "So it's all an act? In real life you take out the trash and have a fat wife and seven kids?"

"If I had a fat wife, I would not be here." He takes my hand into his palm, then looks up at me. "I'm a widower, you see," he says. He traces my lifeline slowly with his finger and I'm suddenly on fire. "So I understand your position."

I clamp down on his finger to stop it. To go from crashing release with its realization of devastating abeyance to hot and horny is too much. I'm almost dizzy. I pick up his clamped hand and kiss it quickly. "Luis," I say, looking at him without tears and more lightness, "Jesus."

He laughs. "Okay, then?"

"Okay."

We smile shyly at each other for another minute and then he gets up. "I've made *mole*, with *calabacitas* and spices. *¿Bueno?*"

"*Muy bueno.* Can I help?"

"Ah, no . . ." he says. He tops off my wine. "Your job, *mujer que linda*, is simply to sit there and drink."

So I am in a dreamy daze when Larry plops a large manila envelope on my desk late the next morning. I ordinarily do not do a lot of full-strength coffee, but I have this morning. Luis did manage to leave around one, but my body and head were in such altered states it took me another hour to go to sleep. We came close to rounding third base and it has been a very long time since I have been in that kind of territory. I'm staring stupidly at my computer screen looking up the criminal record for another PSI when Larry comes in. I stare, bovine-like, at the envelope.

"What's that," I manage.

"Up late doing art?" He smirks. I squint at him.

"Why are you smirking?"

"I take my delights where I can find them, Montgomery. You look like road kill this morning. *Ahora*, help me with this *miedra*," he says, gesturing at the file he has just called shit.

I smirk back. I want to tell him never to run straight into a pool of armed gang kids again, but I can't help smiling. "*La Miedra de Taos.*" I brighten momentarily. "Let's name the Sheriff's Department that."

He laughs. "Better yet, that'll be our affiliated, nonprofit art gallery."

I snort. "We'll feature Ángel Martinez!"

"Art from the jail."

"My horse heads."

"Dang," whistled Larry. "The tourists won't know what hit 'em."

I'm on a roll. "It's a perfect match for my upscale housing concept."

"What's that?"

"*Villa Pendejo.*" Asshole Village.

Larry's turn to snort. I spread my arms out to mimic the idea of wide-open space. "Lotsa land. Gated ranchettes."

Larry gazes fondly at me. "Awesome."

I pick up the manila file. "Liza's stuff?" I am immediately sobered.

He nods. "Gotta run. Tell me what you think."

Chapter 6

I FINISH THE ONEROUS task of writing up the lengthy insipid criminal history of one Tony Roybal. I don't mind it when there are some fun charges on there, like bank robbery, or attempted murder (usually pled down to manslaughter), or even a good old-fashioned distribution charge of some import. But Roybal is like thousands of other unrepentant, lifelong alcoholics: five DWIs, a zillion license suspensions and revocations, four misdemeanor assault charges, three Disturbing the Peace write-ups. Finally—finally—Mr. Roybal is facing prison for a more serious assault and driving under a revoked license, having at last triggered into the state's felony statute for being such a repetitive road hazard. This job, I swear, makes me want to outlaw alcohol. And don't even get me started on prescription meds.

By the time I'm done it's lunchtime. I close my door, eat a premade burrito using Mama's tortillas and carne, and manage to snooze twenty minutes. I have two clients early in the afternoon and then some time to read Liza's file. For that I close the door too.

Liza was born Elizabeth Destiny Jackson in 1991. *Destiny.* That right there nails you as white-honkey trailer-trash in this neck of the woods. How many hapless Destinys have sat across from me, their lives derailed by poor choices and sexual abuse and mothers infested with meth? But Elizabeth is a beautiful name, timeless, powerful. Like Queen Elizabeth. And I always liked Liza as a nickname—it got the long version off its high horse and into a blues bar or honky tonk; it suggested a girl with personality. So I had better hopes for this girl than what happened to her.

At age four, after a year of lengthy and sordid investigation, Colorado Child Protective Services took her and her baby brother into custody. Liza got lucky fairly quickly—six months later she was adopted by the Monaghans. The Monaghans had tried three times to have a kid of their own; Patricia Monaghan had miscarried all three. So they took on Liza, attending pre-adoption classes but not following through, post-adoption, with recommended family therapy. When Liza predictably acted out—masturbating in front of the introverted Ralph Monaghan, humping a classmate at school, biting and attacking when they tried to set boundaries—they took her to treatment but never entered it themselves. The therapist recommended they learn skills, and they half-heartedly attempted the suggestions on worksheets handed to them when they picked Liza up. But they did not participate. This seems to have been a recurring theme; summations of therapeutic notes for much of Liza's early childhood read like this.

Then Liza seemed to improve. Freud's latent phase seems appropriate to me here; I'm perpetually impressed at Freud's powers of observation, despite his sexualized interpretations. She does well in school, has friends, seems to stabilize—until puberty. Then all hell breaks loose.

I think back to Patricia's and Ralph's faces at the funeral. I look at their photos in the file. Patricia has a stern face that reminds me of an overworked pioneer woman scowling as she hangs up the laundry in a stiff breeze. Too much work and too much strait-jacketing religion make them rigid and old before their time. Being her daughter would give me the willies—if you were less than perfect, or even decided that you liked, say, hip-hop, I didn't see how Patricia Monaghan had any room for that. Ralph was softer, kinder, but largely silent. Married to Patricia I imagined meant being a bit bullied. My guess was that Patricia's emotional ups and downs ran the show. How difficult to be needy there.

The file also has Liza's criminal history—mostly minor drug possession charges, a couple of stupid late-teenage false reports to an officer when the dipshit boyfriend she'd been driving with (twice this was Ángel) was pulled over. A note of her daughter's birth, when she was nineteen. A couple of DV charges against her, though most, of course, had been against Ángel. A prostitution charge.

That makes me sit up. Most of the time the drugs-for-sex trade is an implied part of a life like Liza's; women admit this to me six months into their probation, when they've cleaned up enough and been forced to curtail their acquaintance with the worst of their men. The debasement—the truth of their humiliation—begins to hit them and they fall apart in my office. Most of them have been raped as kids. Most of them understand early on the equation between sex and food, clothing, shelter. But very few of them are ever brought up on formal prostitution counts. Maybe in Albuquerque, in the Breaking Bad motels along Central, but not around here. Not in southern Colorado, either.

The charge had been dismissed. Two years ago. Down near Española, south of here. Española, with its quagmires of heroin.

I put down the file, breathe deep. I have a little sage bundle I keep strictly for altering my state of mind when I find my head closing in. I sniff it. Something about that charge bugs me. As if prostitution was a red herring. Who prostitutes these days? The mafia? Gangs? Who? Or was she that desperate for food or drugs that she'd do anything? Or was it a sick fantasy of Ángel's? Christ, who knew?

I stick my nose into the sage again, then look to see what's left in the envelope. I know there are photos of the crime, waiting for me. And a small, faux-leather journal. I take this out, palm it. This is probably the best thing I've got—her relationships, her woes, a ticket to her thinking. But I also feel as if it's a tender and private thing. Who am I to read her most intimate thoughts? I put it aside. I'll work my way toward believing it's in Liza's best interest for me to read it. For now—it's 4:45 and I want out of here—I brave the crime scene photos.

Blood everywhere. A great big pool under her inert body. Close-ups of her slashed throat. Not stabbed to death, as Loretta said, but slit. Her hair's a tangle. She'd had her pajamas on. No sign of rape. Her facial expression is a masterpiece of horror, so alabaster it could've been carved from the purest stone. I clench. She hadn't expected to die. The toxicology's not back yet but it did not appear she'd been out of her head with booze or pot or anything else. No sign of drug use in the house. Her daughter asleep in the back bedroom, but she woke up—and, shit. *Found asleep on top of her mother.* I put down the photos, cover my eyes. *Who does this?* Leaves this mess for a four-year-old to find? Mommy Mommy Mommy—*stop.*

I get up. Put the photos away. Lock up the file. I want the journal but I'll get it later. Read it somewhere secure. The kitchen had been neat. Liza'd been working four months as an aide at Head Start. She got by on food stamps and her small income. She was taking parenting classes. I shake my head. Fucking Ángel. She was getting her life together, and *you couldn't stand it, could you?*

But maybe that wasn't it at all. Maybe it was something else entirely.

I get into the studio the next day and furiously knead clay. I managed sleep last night with some uber-melatonin supplement I get from a naturopath and my previous exhaustion from my time with Luis. But today I am all fury. I take Ernest on a fast run, shower, go to the studio. By ten it's promising to be almost warm, so I'm outside, firing the kiln for a little heat, burning a fire, too, in the outdoor pit we have out back. I have a thermos of hot tea. I bang the clay, roll it, sweat over it. I have no idea what I'm making, but whatever it is, it needs to be made.

I start shaping and soon I have flared nostrils, a spiked back, tiny T-Rex hands. I've got some monster, some amalgam of Guernica and dragons and dinosaurs. I draw out string-bean legs. I keep shaping, pulling the clay into what turns out to be cowboy boots. Now it's T-Rex with Slim Pickens legs. I laugh a little. Fine. If that's what it is, fine. I move up to the neck area, which is not yet differentiated from the barrel chest. I scoop it out a little, find myself fashioning a bolo tie, raised out from the rest of the clay. I can paint it later, glaze it a gaudy blue. I want the stone outlandish, with the glittery tastelessness of a certain kind of Southwest nouveau riche. I roll out skinny mica-flecked black clay for the ties themselves, and I can fire them to make a burnt, corrupt look. But I roll them first against a tight basket, to make them look braided. I could tip them with silver but I'm feeling that's too pat; the ends especially will show the graying, the burn marks, the black marred by sienna, rust, the colors of fire. I like the glitter effect of the mica; after firing with my burn marks it'll still shine through the smudges, looking like a drag queen after a bad night. I want this whole piece to reek of corruption.

By twelve-thirty I'm starving, a bit spent, and no longer enraged. I have done the equivalent of Luis dancing a fevered flamenco set piece. As ever, I'm taken by the power of art to transform. My half-finished monster is human, is animal, but most of all it is the disgust at Liza's death and her daughter's pain, starting to turn into ordered expression. My monster is T-Rex with Ángel's skinny-jean legs; it is all that is beautiful about the Southwest, stretched and made gauche and feral. I slump onto my stool with my piece in my hands. I stare at it a few minutes, determining if I am truly done for the day. God knows if it will survive the kiln.

Ernest snorts in his Great Dane sleep, lying as he does in the sun. By now it's lovely out.

"Come, dog," I say.

He sits up.

"Time for lunch."

He exhibits an impressive downward dog Margot would squeal at, and licks my hand.

"You old fool . . . I love you too." I scratch his ears, and we walk back together to my little manse, the world almost kind again.

Two days later I take Liza's diary and Ernest to my favorite dog-friendly bed and breakfast in Tesuque, just north of Santa Fe. I come here when I need quick refuge; the owners love Ernest and will take him out on wood-chopping expeditions or trail rides if I need time to plot some art, draw, write in my journal, or go to the spa down the road. Ernest and horses get along fine, though his first encounter with one was comical. He slinked behind my legs, trembling. The horse tried to nuzzle him as if he were her long-lost colt, confused by his size and gentle nature. Eventually I coaxed him out and since then he's learned that horses are generally more skittish than he is and not worth the bother of terror.

This was where I holed up after William's funeral. Death brings a lot of initial hubbub—financial arrangements, funeral arrangements, condolences to answer. Mama took good care of me and Jack, living in my guest room and cooking nonstop for two weeks. His reception consisted of her posole, enchiladas, and horchatas. She made flan, tortillas, and the largest vat of pinto beans I'd ever seen. Each table had a sachet of six biscochitos in the center, which our nieces and nephews devoured. There was Mexican coffee using canella, Mexican cinnamon; Hector sat in the corner and strummed incoherent riffs on an old guitar, all to himself. Sopapillas were torn apart and slathered in honey. There was enough beer to swill a biker bar. William would've been quite happy.

But after that, when the flowers had wilted and the last thank-you note had been written, a crass silence descended, quickly, like a flash snowstorm rolling in black and lethal over the great sage plain. My house felt hollow and as though its walls must be made of metal, not adobe, so if you hit it, it would gong and echo. I could not sleep in our bed. I would smell his shirts and weep, relentlessly, for hours. I had a lot of leave built up from work and my boss insisted I take some of it. He was right—any sign of human stupidity, tragedy, or despair sent me over the edge. It all seemed hopeless. Jack went back to school because that seemed the best way to distract off his dad's death. Then Margot left, in my door jamb one day, reservations for La Chamisa B and B, of Tesuque, New Mexico. I caught her on her cell.

"What is this?"

"Shut up and go. They're friends of mine. They know the deal. My treat."

"Margot, it's a week's worth of a hundred-fifty-dollar nights!"

"Plus a deluxe spa package."

"Margot!"

"Plus dinner at Bishop's Lodge one night."

"Margot!"

"Shut up and go. Talk to me when you get home."

"I love you," I said, weeping.

"I love you too."

So I went and found a toehold into peace, because if nothing else Margot's gesture had begun to teach me that true love comes in many forms, and is much, much bigger than even the marriage I had so recently and utterly lost.

Liza's little journal is half-filled and begun two months before her death. This makes me wonder if there are other journals, if she had a stack of them in her bedroom, going back to junior high. This one had been on the kitchen counter when she was murdered, a pen beside it, as if she was settling in to write, or had written, just before her killer showed up. I go to the last week of entries. Yes, March 9th through 11th. Some short sentences—*cooked Carmelina dinner. Bath. Sweet girl. Asks about Daddy. Where'd Daddy go? Is he coming back? Can't tell if she's terrified of him or in love with him or both. Fuck it probably both. You remember. Liza dumbass you remember. Sure Dad I'll give you a fucking blow job cuz I love you and if I don't—Shit the abyss—have to fight—have to fight either crying my ass off or breaking glass times like this.*

She's the age I was when—when. Well anyway that skinny vato better not come anywhere near. Last of my heart went cold when he hung the dog. Jesus.

Why don't I know what love is? How it works? Trying to raise a little girl with love and I don't even know. Man sometimes I want back on the dope. That's what does it. That I fucking can't love. Pot, meth, coke, please. Too much. But I can't. Not for her. Maybe that's all I get to wring out of love—staying off shit for her. Maybe that's all I get. FUCK I'm crying. Can't stop. His cholo West Side gangbanger friends come around, purring in that vato way vatos purr, holding out little white baggies in their creased brown hands . . . the ones he owes shit to. Hey Liza, stash this for me, Chiquita, por favor. Just till Wednesday. If I said no? He'd break my face.

I put it down, my first thought that of her school records, which revealed an A student, a writer, a lover of history. My chest caves in, to some small deep point in the middle of my sternum. Headlines of kidnapped Nigerian schoolgirls float by; Pakistani women's faces ruined by acid for daring to want an education; the countless bright women I see in my work whose lives have been derailed; my own complicity, a remnant of self-excoriation that results in crumbling in the face of selling my art so that I might live by it and it alone. Every woman feels at times they are not far from them, those beaten girls. I don't know if I have learned I can't live by art and art alone because I live in a time and place where to get by cheaply is no longer possible, or if I don't want to fail so some part of me refuses to try. But I've come down to Tesuque and Santa Fe partly to see Gert at her gallery, to see if this hoary promise of movie-star sales can come true. I spend a lot of time lowering my expectations in anticipation. I spend a lot of time bucking up my self-worth while trying not to get overly excited. Words of Margot float in, from her Vipassana training—be aware of outcome but not attached to it. O Great Buddha, so easily said, so hard to do. The thousand little cuts women make to themselves so that they will not infuriate some internal patriarch who fucking hates their guts.

I wish, fervently, for just a moment, that Liza was alive and could tell me about her life.

I wipe my eyes. I've got a fire going in the little kiva fireplace and Ernest snores in front of it, exhausted from an earlier run with me and then a lope with the resident horses. So Ángel was into drugs, and he was into them through West Side. West Side Locos. WSL. XIII, X3, 13. Numbers chiseled onto the soft cheeks of teen boys via tattoo ink. Some with tears at eye corners—how many you kill? How much of your soul have you lost? Gangs confuse me. One-on-one, in my work, their members are just dumb, lost, tormented fifteen-year-old boys. But it's amazing how much damage they can do. These dumb lost boys will kill. Easily. Their cruelty is legend and appalling. West Side is locally in battle with Barrio Small Town, a homegrown south Taos County organization. The Westsiders are mostly local, too, but with Santa Fe roots and real outside connections that worry the crap out of Larry and his Northern New Mexico Drug Task Force guys. Nobody likes the idea that little Johnny Rivera or Armando Gonzales or Gabe Candelaria has some head-chopping drug lord at his back. I'd seen photos of gunshot kids, slit throats—*stop*.

Slit throats.

It takes a little expertise to do this cleanly.

Liza. No ragged slice, that. No DV passion leaving something fumbling and jagged and messy. *Little White Baggies.* No. Hers was methodical, cold. I punch Larry's number, leave a message.

Ángel's gang ties need looking at more closely.

Chapter 7

IN THE MORNING I feel oddly happy about Liza's journal. I thought I'd feel vaguely ashamed for peering into a murdered woman's life, but instead I'm pleased at the strength of her voice. Liza was a rock in her own house in a way, or at least learning to be one. I'm on a run the next morning with Ernest when my phone rings, interrupting Green Day ("Don't wanna be an American idiot"). Damn, I think, but I see it's Larry and slow up.

"'Sup, homegirl. Where are you?" he squawks via Verizon into my ear.

"T-suck." I am forever perverting proper names. "My refuge in times of need."

"You're needy?"

"Liza's journal. I wanted to give it appropriate space."

"Plus you want to visit Gert Kahn and bat around princely sums for your antelope." Larry is in a bantering mood today, it seems.

"Maybe." Gert had texted me two days ago, said her movie gal was going to buy, and I needed to meet with her. It kind of sealed the deal about coming down here.

"A-a-and I hear something about a hot flamenco dancer," Larry adds, going coy on me.

"Jesus H. Christ. What do you do? Mainline Loretta's gossip hour? Download my Neighborhood Watch security cams?"

"Oooh, good idea."

"Larry," I growl.

"Okay, okay. Anyway, what's Liza's diary got that interests you?"

"Am I the only one who's read it?"

"Only girl."

"What's that supposed to mean?"

Larry sighs. "It means I think jaded male cops can't get past the whining about shitty relationships and wanting to go back on the dope. They just see another hapless victim girl. That's about all we ever arrest on the female end of things. Though she did mention the vatos . . ." His voice trails off as if some new light is beginning to dawn.

"Well, fine." The light is not dawning fast enough in my opinion. My ears are getting a little hot, my voice testy. "I'd have thought y'all were a little better trained than that. But yeah, she mentions Ángel's gang affiliation, and makes reference to past requests on his part that she hold drugs for him till he's ready to move them."

"He's a Westsider, right?"

"Yeah. West Side."

"They mostly move coke."

"I know. And in Drug Lab Awareness Training you revealed that they are apparently strengthening in outside drug ties. You know, people who routinely decapitate. Slit throats. Execute with a bullet to the brain without batting an eye."

"Ri-ight." I think light *is* dawning on Larry.

I plow ahead. "Liza's throat was slit. Expertly. Clean sweep. Larry, you don't do that in a fit of DV rage. You'd stab her instead . . . or make some shitty ragged cuts. There'd be yelling, screaming. Carmelina would have woken up right away. Report says, in a brief interview they did with her, that she heard something and tried to go back to sleep first."

"He could have snuck up on her, premeditated."

"He could've," I say, flatly.

Larry sighs. He knows I don't believe that story.

"Even if he was 'trained' to slit throats," I go on, "which I doubt, he's too dorky somehow—I don't think he'd do that do her. He wouldn't kill her that way. He'd do it in a drunken rage, or accidentally, one fist too far into her head."

"Okay, you got a point." He sighs. "I ran this whole thing by Garcia in Santa Fe, and he snagged on the slit throat too. They just had one like that. The premeditated thing doesn't really fit with his impulsive MO, I have to say."

"Not at all. I think we've—*I've*—been blinded by that DV history. I think it's time to focus on his gang ties." Something occurs to me. "Did you ever get that syringe analyzed? The one you found in Santa Fe?"

"Yeah. That was interesting."

"How so."

"China White."

"Huh?"

"Heroin," Larry says, "but not Mexican tar, which is overwhelmingly what you get around here. China White's more East Coast. Brought in originally from Vietnam in the sixties. Nowadays it can just mean really pure, or Fentanyl. But this was the Oriental stuff, poppies from Afghanistan."

"So maybe some New York art fart was using that night?"

"Apparently. Or maybe there's some high-end Santa Fe shit I don't know about yet."

"But offhand that's not West Side stuff."

"No."

"Hmmm. . . ."

There's a silence, just my feet crunching on gravel as I approach the B and B. Ernest has loped ahead to the lawn.

"Okay, Nina, I'll look into the gang stuff."

"Thanks, Larry."

There's a pause. Then he says, "Just don't have too much fun with Flamenco Man, okay?"

I scowl at my phone. "What? Why? What business is it of yours?" This is not the Larry I know. He's acting either like a protective older brother or a jealous boy.

"None," says Larry, too quickly. He's going for lighthearted, but it sounds as if he has marbles in his mouth.

"Are you *jealous*? Larry? Larry?" But he's hung up.

Bastard. I shake my head and round up Ernest, who's got his head in a bush, rustling, it seems, for some rodentia invisible to the human eye.

Gert ushers me into a cramped side office at the back of the Kahn gallery.

I was expecting opulence—space, high ceilings, vigas with etched flowers painted in turquoise. The vigas are there, but they are plain, dusty, and hold up a low ceiling. The walls slope, thick and adobe. A kiva fireplace, cold and ashy and smelling faintly of old cedar, sits in one corner. Gert's desk is huge and antique and takes up half the room, squatting at the back opposite the door. Invoices, artist PR, gallery openings, reviews, all manner of paperwork pile high on top of it. A tea stand with a red metal tea set, circa 1955, sits under a deeply recessed window, and what light there is emits primarily from two Tiffany-style lamps (probably the real thing) set in the corners. The window itself can only muster up an opaque filminess, its pane too recessed and old to do much else. High-backed Spanish chairs, two of them, face her desk. These are adorned with turquoise-colored leather seat cushions and it's not until I'm about to sit in one that I see the other is occupied by a slim woman with brown wavy hair and a wide smile.

"Nina, meet Jade Kirchner. Jade, Nina."

Jade stands up and offers her hand. I'm sure I look like a horse accosted by an out-of-nowhere thunderstorm, eyes wide and nostrils flaring. I somehow manage to take her hand.

"Nice to meet you," I say. Then I turn to Gert, who's almost smirking. "You could've warned me!"

Gert grins and even her grin is elegant. "And ruin this moment? No, my friend. Please," she gestures with a bejeweled hand, "sit down, both of you." She turns to Jade. "I've only met Nina a few times. But she possesses a face wholly incapable of dishonesty and it's such a pleasure to tease her as a result."

I'm scowling and both Jade and Gert laugh. Gert's point is proven. I sigh.

Jade looks over at me. "I would kill to have a braid like yours," she says.

My hand flies to my hair. It's thick, almost black, shot through with gray. A braid is my best method of control, though if I wanted to, I could whip it up into some high formal do worthy of a Spanish grand dame. But it doesn't come with olive skin or sepia eyes; my skin is light and my eyes are, in the right light, an unearthly deep blue that Margot likens to the elves' eyes in the *Lord of the Rings* movies. Margot is smitten with *The Lord of the Rings* trilogy. I could care less except for the Ents. I fully believe in the aliveness of trees, and it does me in to watch the scene of their destruction.

"Thank you," I say to Jade. "I'd kill to be a successful movie star." My hand flies to my mouth. Sometimes my sarcasm is completely inappropriate. I was trying to be funny but instead I sound flip. And when Jade—the beauty!—had done the most graceful move by complimenting *me*.

Jade just blinks back at me like a placid mule, with a hint of a smile. "No, you wouldn't."

We stare at each other and then I can't help smiling after I think about it for a minute. "Yeah, you're probably right." I crane my neck out the poor window. "Do we have paparazzi outside?"

"No," says Jade. "But I wore shades, put my hair up, and—as you will note—am wearing the sweatpants I painted my barn with."

I look at her lower half. "Nice. An artist always appreciates messed-up clothes."

Jade grins. "*People Magazine* doesn't think movie stars wear pants like this. So they're not on the lookout."

"But what about *Us*! The Fashion Police! My God!"

"'They're just like us!'"

"Fifty-seven percent like Jade in this dress!"

Pretty soon both of us are snorting and start regaling each other with more gossip magazine parodies.

Gert has to pull us back to the subject at hand. "Ms. Kirchner would like to buy your remaining antelope." Her tone carries an exasperated dignity and I get a flash that Gert's demeanor is a familial defense against having been pogromed out of Russia, or having only one aunt survive Dachau, or discovering that some Nazi pig had all your family's long-lost art stashed in some house in Switzerland. I decide I love Gert a little right then.

I cock my head. "Do you want me to make three more to make up for the ones I sold?"

"No," says Jade. "That's okay."

"She's trying to stay away from any replicas. Especially ones similar to the piece owned by, ah, our ex-secretary."

I squint at Jade. "You don't like our ex-secretary of defense?"

She blushes, as most people do who aren't familiar with the political breezes of new company. "It's not that I don't *like*—"

"Oh, horseshit," Gert says, and even this sounds classy out of her. "Never fear, Ms. Kirchner. You are among friends here."

Jade looks down at her hands. "I get invited to his parties, that's all."

"See?" I perk up. "Another reason being a successful movie star must suck. Forced appearances with Republican warmongers."

"The Taos Elite. That's me."

"Ooh la la!"

For some reason I'm having a gas with this woman. All three of us are quite capable of some sort of dignity—well maybe more Jade and Gert than me—but Jade and I have devolved to a lower life form.

Gert throws up her hands. "I was going to offer you coffee from Ohori's and fine pastries from our little bakery down the way, but I think you all are beneath that today."

Jade sniggers. I look at my shoes as if they hold the secret to the Ark of the Covenant.

"Nina," Gert says, in a nearly parental voice that says *shape up, chica,* "I am here to represent you. I want to represent you. From now on."

I really owe this woman due respect and a vague whiff of cringing insight floats through me that my infantile behavior has to do with my own discomfort with finally, *finally,* having some real artistic success. I raise my eyes and meet her gaze. "Thank you, Gert. I appreciate that more than I can say. What are your terms?"

"That's better," she says, and I rightfully blush.

Gert, ever the businesswoman, gets down to it and saves me any opening salvos. We haggle over her terms, and the selling price for the antelope. Jade and I shake hands and express genuine delight at having met one another. I give her a business card—an art one, not a probation one. "Come by the gallery sometime."

"Can I watch you work?" she asks. She's almost shy.

I love, I suppose, most of all, discovering Jade's humanity. I love her interest, her appreciation, her unexpected timidity. By all reckoning the world is her oyster. But to her it's not. To her—like the rest of us—the new territories must be navigated, tenderly and with great courage, despite (and maybe all the more because of) the success. I smile. "Of course. I'd be honored."

She shoots me a wistful look and is out the door.

I am high as a kite when I step into the small dinner theater at the Santa Fe Lodge. It's early evening and sound checks are in full swing. Luis comes over after ten minutes of directing and dancing, kissing me serenely.

"I just sold three antelope to Jade Kirchner!" I spout.

"This must be very good."

"You don't know who Jade Kirchner is, do you?"

He laughs—and this is the thing about Luis that makes me think we actually might work at some level. Despite vast cultural differences, he can laugh at it all. That and I find his refusal to take American pop culture seriously very refreshing. "Not really," he says.

"Big movie star!" I extend my arms out as far as they'll go to demonstrate how big.

"Can you get her to come to our opening night?" Like any good artist, he knows this would be good publicity.

I become coy. "May-be . . ."

He holds his handsome face in a checked smile. "What do I have to do?"

God, flirting! I haven't done it for years! "Nothing," I say, almost blushing. "Just dance as beautifully as ever."

He grins and goes back to his dancers and musicians. The rehearsal's on a music piece now for the most part with one lone female dancer moving slowly about as catcalls ("*Allez!*") and hand claps—those tortured stylized flamenco hand claps—accompany her. Luis is right. Flamenco is meant to rip your heart out and leave it dripping on the floor.

A movement catches my eye to the right and through a side door a man with a damp rag enters the room. It's fairly dim lighting, but I watch him come closer as he wipes down tables and lines up chairs in prep for tonight's performance. He comes near me, and I see he's covered in tattoos, sleeves on both arms. He pauses to work on a stuck bit of old food on the little table next to me and I catch the three dots in the webbing of his hand, and WSLXIII on his wrist.

"West Side," I mutter. He stops scrubbing.

"Half of Santa Fe is," he says, covering his surprise rather adroitly. His accent's fairly thick but I can't tell if it's authentic or cholo'd for effect. He's getting a beer belly, but his upper body is beefy. He probably doubles as a bouncer here.

I take a calculated risk. "Do you know Ángel Martinez?"

He goes stock still. "No," he lies. Then he squints at me. "Who's asking?"

I fish out a state business card. "His PO. Why?"

He takes my card and moves very obviously to the next table further away from me. "No reason."

"Who's Ángel to you?" I press.

"No one. Really." He looks almost frightened.

"I'm sorry to bother you," I say, and turn back to watch Luis and his crew.

A few minutes pass and then a glass of ice water appears in front of me. I look up in surprise.

"I don't mean no disrespect, señora," says Beefy Sleeves.

I smile at him. "None taken."

"Ángel's not one to be scared of."

I'm puzzled. "Then who is?"

He sets the chair next to me straight and begins to move on. "Chuy." He draws a line down the side of his face with his finger.

"What's this?" I ask. Something about it jars me.

"*Cicatriz*," he says. I get the feeling he is using Spanish not because he usually does but because he wants a layer between him and me, the nosy gringa.

I trace my own face, rummage my brain for my Spanish. I sit up. "Scar."

He just stares at me, a deer ready to bolt.

Now my mind is going. "What about drugs," I ask, thinking of syringes and slit throats. But as soon as I say it, I feel I have gone too far. He's fled to the door to the kitchen and I'm standing up. I run to catch him. "Wait! Who's Chuy?"

But he's slipped the room, into a vast kitchen full of various males producing vats of tonight's food. I slink back to my table. I'm not that up for creating a scene in a kitchen, and I'm aware he's given me more information than he probably should have. I don't want to blow any cover for him. I spy my ice water. Nice gesture, I think. Very sweet, very nice. He's probably gunned down five guys, but he knows how to treat a lady right. I lift my glass to Luis, consider what to say to Larry given this information, and settle in to watch the show.

At intermission I follow directions upstairs to the ladies' room, down a wide hallway with Oriental carpeting that seems somewhat deserted. After that, I go outside for fresh air. I am used to mooning the stars at home, where the night sky is less impeded by electric light, but I still like the cool air on skin, the way it shifts me out of whatever mood I'm in. Besides, I want lip balm and I left it in the car.

My back's to the driver's side door when something enormous claps itself onto the back of my neck, picks me up and flips me over against the side of the car. The only image I have in my brain at first—which suddenly feels as slow as molasses—is of a giant sea creature burping up out of the Cretaceous underground, long dormant, and plastering itself all over me. I'm okay with this till it dawns on my neurons that this creature seems to want to kill me. Then, immediately, I cannot breathe.

Another hand holds my neck in a total lock, and I am aware of hot, beery breath on my face. Even beard stubble. This makes me want to throw up. I try turning my head away and dimly try to ready my knee for a crotch shot but then I realize with horror he is plastered over me there too and I am now frantically worried he has a hard-on. I can feel all of me paralyzing. *Fuck this, fuck.* But he has a thick flannel jacket on and I feel nothing that distinct, just an enormous body.

I do my best to try to breathe deeply and slowly, to keep some small part of myself out of freeze. I am not doing a good job. He leers. Even the urge to vomit is locked in, halfway up my esophagus. It is as if I am acknowledging this from outside my body. He's huge, and as I try jerking my head again, he says, in a snaky loud whisper, in the lilt of Hispanic

English that usually I so love, "Stay the fuck away, señora." Then he drops me, rag doll, onto the pavement. I hit my hip hard, and my head bangs against the door. Someone cries out, though it does not feel like me. Swimming, I paddle up, my eyes paddle up. In the halo of a far-away parking lot light I see not only the gigantic hulk, but another figure, leaner, familiar, walking away backward, eyes on me. The eyes flicker. I feel he is smirking, and one side of his face seems creased in a shadow the other side does not possess. I have been face-to-face with evil before, but it has been a long time. *Don't move. Don't move till they've gone. Let them think you're down.*

I start shaking. I let out a loud burp and my throat unlocks. I am shaking so hard I can't steady my hands. I sit there on the ground next to my car, a few people here and there off in the lot, me in the shadows. The giant octopus and his wiry piranha friend are now disappeared. Do I need to call for help? That sobers me a notch. *No, not yet. Not yet.* I rise off my hip, wincing, and move to sit with my back against the car. I feel in my coat for my cell, but I am still shaking so hard it is difficult to get it out of my pocket. On the third attempt, I manage it. The only person I know in Santa Fe right now who is not on stage is Jack. I stall. He'll hate this. His worst nightmare, come true. Mom the probation officer, truly assaulted this time. And besides, he's couch surfing. What's he to do? Put me up at the El Rey?

Larry's voice comes in. *Call the fucking cops, Nina.* I slump. He's right.

I dial dispatch because I don't want ambulances and to waste 911 resources, but the lady on the other end thinks I am nuts and says someone will be there right away. "Are you hurt?" she asks. I have to say yes, and then I hate myself for thinking I am just a burden and no one should waste resources on me. Christ. I thought that girl had grown up a long time ago.

Then I call Jack. "Mom?" he says, in a voice that says he already knows something, the way kids and parents just know.

I collapse. I start crying heavily. "Jack, Jack . . ."

"Where are you?"

I get out where. I know he'll come, and I know, after the cops are done and we've either gone or not gone to the ER to check things out, he'll be furious and worried, all at once.

I close my eyes against the car, my head throbbing. A long, distant wail of a siren starts in from some other part of town. I don't remember them coming.

Chapter 8

I WAKE UP AT dawn on a strange couch in a messy living room, a thick blanket over me. I have no idea where I am and I move to sit up, startled at my disorientation. A searing pain goes through my right hip and my head immediately throbs. It all comes back, and a flash of the beery octopus is so intense I whimper. I slump back down to the couch, sniveling automatically, hating the helplessness. I am abnormally groggy. *Where the fuck am I?*

I gaze out at the view from under the blanket. A flat screen TV on the wall. A coffee table piled at one end with magazines and lightly strewn with small plates and a coffee cup over the rest of it. A nice-looking chair by the window full of clothes, a blow-up photo of some kind of dancer. I squint. Flamenco. The top magazine is in Spanish and appears to be a dance magazine. Under that is a *Santa Fe Reporter*. I breathe a little easier. I think I must be at Luis's.

I take a light sip of water from a glass I now see before me. My stomach seems okay with it though earlier I seem to recall some nausea. I dimly remember a hospital, perhaps a morphine shot. Fuck. Where's Jack?

I take another sip and look around for my coat. I see a heap on the chair by the door. Is that it? I squint again. The idea of walking over there to retrieve it makes me slump in despair all over again. Something rustles behind me and I jump.

"Nina," says Luis softly, trying to smile but looking very tired and concerned. He is wearing pajama bottoms straight from Walmart and a white tee shirt. My lips feel dry and cracked. I want to talk but I feel incapable.

He comes over and sits at the end of the couch, putting a light hand on my feet under the blanket. He swallows. "I am so sorry."

"It's not your fault," I croak. I take another sip, testing my left arm as a prop to half-sit up with. I can only lie on my left side. I look at him. "I hope—I hope you got to finish your show." It occurs to me that he only had an hour to go after intermission and that between being hit and taken off in an ambulance it would have been about that long until someone knew to contact him anyway.

He nods. "At the end, I saw you weren't there and a cop was waiting for me."

"Where'd they take me? St. Vincent's?"

"Yes. Jack met me there. They gave you a morphine shot."

I am startled and feel my hip. "Nothing broken?"

"No. Just a concussion and a pretty bruise on your hip bone. That will take a while to feel better." He smiles wanly. "I remember that from falling on stage once and bruising my own hip."

It is hard to imagine him falling, being less than graceful, and for that reason I admire the messy house, the cheap pj's. He seems to catch me looking around. "I am sorry for the mess. I wanted to make it beautiful for you the first time you saw it."

A lump bigger than I imagined possible rises up in my throat. "You did?" I squeak.

"Yes, Nina." His hands clasp my feet more warmly and he gazes at me with such tenderness I start crying all over again. Here it is . . . I've wrecked our second real date; and here it is . . . this man not caring about that.

"You are very sweet, Luis," I snivel. This feels inordinately dumb and inadequate, but I try for a meaningful tone. My head is really throbbing now. "Do you have some Ibuprofen? My head just sucks."

He smiles. "You can have a Lortab if you want. The doctor left you some."

I shake my head. Like many of us who work with opioid addict after opioid addict, we recoil at them. I'd rather smoke a colossal doobie. "Let me try the Ibuprofen first."

"Of course." He gets up and says on the way to the bathroom cabinet, "Jack will be here at eight."

I crumble for the thousandth time. "He will be so angry," I whisper.

Luis stops in his quest for drugs and shakes his head. "Nina, he's twenty-six. Do you remember twenty-six?"

In my foggy head the first memories of William float by, how dumb I was, how much I tried to sabotage it all because I had a terrible con man alcoholic father and when any man got too close they turned into him. I must have been twenty-four because by twenty-six I was pregnant with Jack. I am startled now that I would have thought I could rear a child given my mental state. God, the idiocy.

"Ye-es," I say, as that all runs through my fuzzy brain.

"He will forgive you. Mostly he has to forgive himself, work with the anger." He starts twisting his wrists and doing the agonized hand movements of flamenco.

"What are you doing?"

He looks at me. "When I first start teaching flamenco, they have to learn it's all about working with anger. These little ballerina princesses—" He shakes his head. "You have to have experienced pain to do flamenco. Be older."

Now I am squinting at him from over the couch back, best I can on my elbow. "So who are you, then? My dance therapist?"

He laughs. "Apparently I am Jack's."

And I allow a little laugh too, just enough so my head doesn't hurt.

By the time my son comes, I have managed dry toast, and to comb my hair. I don't bother with other clothes. I seem to be wearing men's sweatpants and a tee shirt. Jack just comes over and holds me lightly, tears leaking out. He looks as if he hasn't slept. Like my assailant, he's wearing flannel—the uniform of hipsters and gangsters alike these days—and I hate that. I try to reset my mind, to stay present, to say, *This is your son.* I smell the flannel, and miracle of miracles, this works. It smells like faint bacon and coffee. It smells like Jack. My body slumps into his.

"I worry about you," he blurts out. "You all alone up there in Seco. You without Dad. We were always such a small family."

This truth—that there were just three of us, and it always felt precarious, especially against the loud and sprawling Catholic families surrounding us—settles over us like a cloak. Now we are just two. Now Jack is one person away from total orphanage.

"Oh, Jack." I clutch his shirt. I don't know what to say. I feel guilty for not giving him seven brothers and sisters. I want to tell him to get married as soon as possible to start his own family, but even in my addled state I know that won't go over well.

Luis goes to the kitchen tactfully, saying nothing, and the smell of brewing coffee reaches me. I had worried, an hour ago, that it would make my stomach churn, so I ate the dry toast with just a hair of butter and more water. But now it smells fabulous and all of a sudden I am ravenous.

"Good lord," I say. "I want *huevos*."

Jack makes eye contact with someone behind us—presumably Luis—and then his tears turn into hysterical laughter. "Shit, Luis," he brays through a few tears and some spit, "she's okay. When my mom wants huevos rancheros, she's better."

Luis comes over with coffee, clearing plates and neatening the magazines. "Huevos it is," he says softly, and we give ourselves over to the making and eating of food.

I still have to eat slowly, and I only manage half of it, but it helps. I'm about to talk about how to get me home when there is a knock at the door. I look at Luis.

"The police. They said they would come by in the morning to interview you."

I somewhat aggressively slide some beans onto my fork. "Of course," I mumble. My head starts to rumble again, as if the merest stress will piss it off.

I recognize Tom Garcia from Drug Lab Awareness. He comes in with a female partner named Lucinda Watkins, a name I appreciate. I feel she must have another life as a country western singer.

Jack and Luis state that they are going to Trader Joe's for some necessary items and leave me with Santa Fe's Finest. I understand but everything makes me pissy anyway.

"Tom," I say. I assume he's just the officer on duty, but then I wonder about the drug thing.

"Ms. Montgomery," he says. "Can you tell us what happened?"

So I tell him about the Octopus and the Piranha, the attack itself. Then I stop. I remember the waiter, me asking about Ángel. The waiter must have said something to somebody. I must have come too close for comfort for someone.

"You ever met Chuy Martinez?" Tom asks.

"No," I say. "But I think I might have seen him. At Ángel's art reception."

"His son is an artist?" Lucinda asks.

"I know. Startling, isn't it? He's a santero. Bultos and retablos, mainly. His religious figures generally look as if their hair is on fire. He seems to live in Dante's Ninth Circle of Hell in terms of his muse."

Lucinda smiles. "Nice description."

"You seem to appreciate this."

Tom rolls his eyes. "Her husband wins awards every Spanish Market. Mostly paintings."

She swats him. They remind me of Larry and me. "Larry!" I say, blurting out my thoughts. But they don't appear baffled. God, he'll hate me.

"Yeah, he's pissed off at the moment," Tom says.

"He knows?"

"Of course he knows. Jack called him; I called him."

I sigh back into my couch. "Fuck," I say.

Lucinda brings me a glass of water, more Ibuprofen. "It's okay. Your stomach can handle two more."

I am grateful for the feminine touch. I swallow them and gingerly move my position. "Chuy has a scar, I think."

"Yes."

"The waiter said that. 'Cicatriz.' He said that and I remembered a man who didn't fit with the rest of the crowd at the reception, who had a scar."

"Yes."

"The waiter guy seemed very afraid of him."

"As well he should be."

And Tom gives me Chuy's sordid history, his prison time and gang ties and general life of psychopathy. "We'll interview the waiter. Anything else you asked him besides if he knew Ángel?"

I realize now how stupid I was. "I asked him about drugs." I say this slowly. Larry will be even more pissed. I made my own shit pile and then stepped in it.

"Why'd you do that?" asks Lucinda.

"Because we found a syringe at Ángel's art opening. Larry did. In the bathroom. I think you knew that," I say to Tom. What I don't say is that I so deeply wanted Liza's death understood that I lost sight of good detective work. I smelled a whiff of true crime and saw a WSL tat and just started asking questions. Christ, what a dumbass.

Tom nods. "What about the guy who attacked you? Any ideas?"

I shake my head gently so as not to infuriate it. "No. He was huge. It was dark. I couldn't see any tats or anything. Hispanic."

Something stops me a bit, and I must look puzzled because Tom asks, "What?"

"His voice. You know, I think it was more, uh, not local. He only said one sentence. But you know . . ." My mind feels like a slug in fog.

"Not Santa Fe classic?"

"No. Not Rio Grande. I don't know how to say this. It's subtle."

Lucinda and Tom exchange glances. "That doesn't sound like West Side," she says.

"No. Also most of our local boys aren't tall. They can be bulky, but usually they aren't six-foot-four. Or whatever he was."

Lucinda puts a hand on my arm. "Thank you, Nina. I know this is tiring."

I swallow. I try to not snivel again. "I'm sorry. I was dumb. It's just— well, Ángel's ex was murdered in Taos County and we all thought it was DV—Ángel's a shit, long history . . . Anyway, I don't think it is. I want to convince Larry and everyone else it isn't. I just—I just want her life—" I break off. *I want her life to have mattered.*

Tom is still, respectful. Lucinda's nodding. "I know," she says softly. "I know just what you mean."

By Monday I can walk without looking completely crippled. I show up to work dearly wanting both to avoid Larry and to debrief everything with him. My boss said to work only a half day the whole week, concussion advice from the ER doc in Santa Fe, whose notes I handed him.

I spent Saturday on Luis's couch with brief fits of walking; we laid off much kissing, as if wanting only to heal this time for something later. In the afternoon we went to Ten Thousand Waves Japanese Spa, where he treated me to a private tub and a detoxifying massage. It did wonders. Even the little expensive Japanese plates we ordered at the restaurant next door seemed full of health and rejuvenating qualities. Nothing like pure sea kelp to make the cells tingle, the brain start working. On Sunday I managed to get in my car and handle a gas pedal home, though by Sunday evening the "two days after an injury is the worst" rule had set in, and I took lots of Ibuprofen and rubbed my hip with a ton of arnica in order to sleep.

I am out of luck in the Larry Avoidance category. I am not ten minutes in my office, organizing the criminal file of one Fred Galvin for a PSI, when he walks in.

"I'm not going to talk to you if you are mad at me," I say. Boundaries first, talk later.

He sighs. "I'm not mad anymore, Nina. I just care about you, that's all."

I soften. "I know. I'm sorry for being so stupid."

"I got Chuy's file from Tom."

"And—?"

"He never mentions a kid in his PSIs or elsewhere."

"Ángel doesn't mention him, either," I say. I think back to my PSI and the Family History section. "Said he didn't know his bio dad's name. Two brief stepdads.' They were Troy Griffin and Manny Baca." I grin, and risk teasing him. "Any relation?"

Larry makes a face. "Really, muchacha. You are so untrainable."

I laugh even though it hurts my head. "I know, I know." If Ángel Martinez is sort of a Hispanic version of Bob Jones, Manny Baca is a New Mexican Joe Smith. There are probably three Manny Bacas in the state legislature alone. The one I conjure up in this moment wears polyester boot-cut leisure suits and has a prominent love of pinkie rings. His bolo tie is an ostentatious hunk of veined turquoise, his district West Albuquerque. He's been elected so many times I'm fairly certain he's got a mini-machine full of nepotism, greased palms, and twisted arms assuring his success.

Larry chews one end of his half-moon reading glasses. "Talk to Loretta."

"Huh?" I ask, still basking in the reflected light of Manny Baca's pinkie rings. I'm wondering how I might make a New Mexico State Legislature Caricature Series out of ceramics.

"Talk to Loretta. Her sister's his mother. I betcha she knows who dad is."

"Or something." Now I'm peeved at myself again. Why have I overlooked Loretta? Or Carmelina, for that matter? What might that reveal?

"Good point," I say.

"Oh, and Nina?"

"Yeah?"

"Nice job with the antelope."

I blink, disconcerted to have completely forgotten about my big sale. But then I smile, and he smiles back. I know he is not mad at me for sure now. My biggest fan, Larry.

I go directly to Loretta's after work, deliberately famished because a person doesn't get out of Loretta's house without having eaten. Loretta's definition of a snack is most people's idea of a meal. Loretta herself, however, stays the same modest pear-shaped size she always is, which is a mystery to me. I'd be obese if I cooked as much as she does.

Cooking is her art form, though, her anti-anxiety remedy. Today when I come in, Helena and Carmelina are watching *Dora the Explorer* and Hector is asleep on the couch. His wagon's next to him, and in it is a little yap dog who barks at me and then desists into a growl as I move along. As long as I don't come close to its master it holds its tongue and leaves Hector to slumber on.

"Mama," I say, handing her a bottle of red wine Luis left the other night, "Who's Hector's dog?"

She kisses my cheek as she takes the wine. "Ay, who knows? He calls her Bettina. Bettina! We think she's a cross between a Maltese and a Chihuahua."

"Unusual for a stray."

"I know." Most strays around here are working-dog mutts—heeler crosses, Border Collies, Aussie Shepherds—or rejects from the pit bull / guard dog camp. The latter give me the willies and are favorites among gangs, MMA fanatics, oil-field workers, and heavy-metal biker types.

Bettina has her own pink blanket and pink collar. Where Hector gets this stuff is beyond me. She appears well fed and is not scratching for fleas. Mama reads my thoughts as she puts a glass of the red and some corn chips in front of me. "We took her to the vet last week. So she's clean."

I smile at her. "Can I help with anything?"

"Nada." She pushes me back in the chair. "I'm making chile rellenos stuffed with lamb instead of queso. Better for me." She pats her hips. "Borderline diabetes. *La doctora* has been lecturing me."

I nod and sip my wine. Carmelina laughs at something on the TV, and I see Helena looking exasperated. Babysitting a four-year-old is not her cup of tea.

"How's Liza's girl?" I ask.

Mama sighs. "Okay. She has nightmares. She asks for her mama. Sometimes for her dad."

"There's a restraining order against her seeing her dad," I say, making sure Loretta's heart doesn't go into its periodic soft places ("More like codependent," Larry growls inside my head) and lets Ángel see her.

"I know, I know. Ay," she tut-tuts and shakes her head. "So sad. It's all so sad."

"I'm just worried he'd kidnap her."

Mama puts down water glasses, mats, silverware. Her brow stitches. "Do you think he really would, now? With him up on felonies?"

I look over at her. "You think he knows better?"

She shrugs. "Mira, his girl's dead. His art's going places. And like I said, he's up on more serious charges than ever, no?"

"Yeah."

"So why dig his grave for good?"

Because he's Ángel, I want to say. An impulsive idiot. But I don't. He's her kin.

"Mama . . ."

"Yes?"

"Who was his daddy?"

She looks sharply up, but not at me. *Dora the Explorer* has suddenly gone silent and the two girls appear to be staring at us. I do a quick assessment and decide Carmelina can't possibly have a clue about the significance of my question, and I'm not sure they've heard it anyway. My next surmise—in all hope—is that *Dora* ended via pure coincidence to my asking it. But Helena's locked on her mama and Mama's locked on Helena, and no one's breathing except Hector, who snores gently in his corner on the couch, with Bettina curled up in her wagon beside him.

"*Madre de Dios,*" Mama mutters under her breath. "I'll talk to you later." Meantime she claps her hands once, Helena unlocks, and the spell is broken. Mama orders her daughter to pull the rellenos from the oven.

Helena glowers at me as she puts the rellenos down on the trivet in front of me. "Who were you talking about?" she hisses.

I shake my head. "Not your business, Missy."

She pouts. She's used to being thought of as beyond her years because she's precocious. That, and I can tell she sometimes feels infantilized by Carmelina.

Carmelina sits on a phone book placed onto her chair. She's busy with a plastic spoon and fork, her plate a Winnie the Pooh relic from Helena's toddlerhood. Mama gives her tortillas, some beans, a little lamb meat from the rellenos and says, "Be neat."

"Juice?" asks Carmelina.

Mama shakes her head. "I don't have any, *lo siento.*"

Carmelina stares at her. Spanish seems utterly foreign. "Juice?"

"We ran out yesterday," says Helena, exasperated. "You have milk. Here." She thrusts the sippy cup at Carmelina.

But Carmelina is looking from adult to adult to older child in some form of desperation. "Juice!" she screams.

"Oh, God," Helena says.

Carmelina's face collapses as her wailing escalates. "Mommy Mommy Mommy! I want juice! Mommy get juice!" I swoop her up into my arms before I know what I'm doing. I hold her even though every ounce of her is squirming to get away, shushing into her ear over and over again. "Mommy—juice!" And I'm flashing back to the crime scene photos, past the pooled blood and the dead woman to the kitchen floor, to a corner of it under the counter, to a spilled sippy cup lying crookedly right there, its contents leaked out as terribly as Liza's blood.

I must be white as a sheet because Mama and Helena are staring at me. But I don't care. I know what it's like to have someone go on you with no warning. As Carmelina shrieks for her mommy, for the juice that never came, I see in one fell swoop how her daughter will think for an eternity that it was her fault Liza died like that—if only she hadn't asked for juice! And then we collide together into that terrible, shared, keening pain. I feel my own tears running rampant down my face, dropping onto her dark hair. I've got her and she's no longer squirming but seems to have surrendered into me, as if some innate animal wisdom let her know that here was a creature who absolutely understood her loss.

I find myself rocking the both of us back and forth. I'm sobbing; she's sobbing. Then comes an ebbing of it, and, finally, an abatement. I'm aware of an appalling silence. No one moves. The two of us glaze out at the world from strands of unkempt hair and blurry eyes and runny noses. We're met by Helena's shocked face and Loretta's grimace. Then Mama picks up her fork and scoops up a mouthful of beans. The sound—the sole sound of a fork against a plate—sets the world to ticking again. I let out a heavy sigh. I position Carmelina on my lap, let her feed by hand from my plate. It goes like this, quiet, no word uttered, the snuffling of feeding creatures the only noise, till, miraculously, all of us are full and she and I have taken up residence on the other end of Hector's couch.

She will not let go of me and has fallen sound asleep on my chest.

Loretta puts a blanket over both of us. "Stay, Nina," she implores. "She hasn't slept like this since I got her."

I nod and shift to get more comfortable. Mama somehow moves Hector to his bed in the spare room, and I have the whole couch now.

Sometime later I hear toenails clacking on the tiles and I open one eye. Ernest licks my hand. Mama has seen fit to get him. I can't help but smile and feel oddly as taken care of as Carmelina does, in her baby girl repose.

Chapter 9

THURSDAY MORNING AFTER MY attempt at a run I find a note tucked under the wiper blade on the driver's side of my truck. I unfold it and turn away from the blinding morning sun to read it.

Ángel's father was a man named Jesús Alarcon Martinez. Went by *Chuy.

I stare at it. It's Mama's writing. I follow down to the little asterisk at the bottom: **P.S. Lolo used to bring Chuy around when she was seventeen and with him. Gangbanger. Scared me to death.*

Then: *P.P.S. I have to go to Pilar a mi tía's so that's why I left the note instead of finding you. In the house are some biscochitos for you and your man!* And a wicked smiley face followed by . . . *Te quiero, vaya con Dios—Loretta* that makes me smile in return.

I go back in the house long enough to find the cookies, which are in a plastic container and sitting next to the drainboard. Once I've showered and eaten breakfast, I tuck them under my arm. The work crowd will appreciate their showing up next to the coffee pot.

Lolo. Ángel's mama. Short for Dolores. Dolores and Loretta, the Garcia sisters of Arroyo Seco. Lolo died of an overdose three years ago. They found her in a desiccated South Valley trailer in Albuquerque. Ángel would've been nineteen, Carmelina, one. Mama said no one knew where Ángel was by that time, except maybe hiding out in southern Colorado with Liza. DV incidents, DUIs show him up there about then, when I get interstate information from Colorado. So I have an idea where he was, but for now I don't share this with Mama. His rap sheet would crush her.

I drive to work, lost. Assuming Chuy was more or less Lolo's age, that put him around forty-five or forty-six by now. Loretta was the older sister, the Responsible One, the Parent in a family where dad drank and mom let him. Lolo was the one with attitude, Dad's princess until she hit puberty. She didn't listen to anyone then and carried all the entitlement of a Princess Child whose older sister inadvertently enabled her petulance by her own role as Perpetual Saint. The entitlement piece I keep to myself, but the rest I get directly from Loretta. I held her hand through most of Lolo's funeral. Loretta considers the rot of her sister and her eventual death as her biggest failure. No matter how many times I tell her Lolo was not her responsibility, Mama doesn't hear me. It finally occurs to me that if she drops that role, with all its guilt and entanglement, she won't have a clue who she really is.

I have to go to court for three clients, which takes the morning. Two I'm arguing have done well and deserve early termination from probation; the other I'm arguing for revocation after three hot UAs. But he no-shows and earns himself a bench warrant as a result. My clients are strung out in a lengthy docket full of petty thieves, check frauds, assaults, and possession charges. Roni and I sit together and play Words with Friends surreptitiously on our silenced phones, back and forth, one ear to the proceedings. Judge Lawrence's courtroom has two large photographs of New Mexican landscapes—one of the famed Rio Grande Gorge in long evening light; the other of Taos Pueblo in what looks to me like favorable morning sun. I find this a relief from the drabness of other courtrooms, and something to counterbalance the people in chains and orange jumpsuits sitting behind the railing in the jury box. The dreary business of repeat offenders, neck tattoos, missing teeth, poor decisions, abusive childhoods, and, most of all, no way out of family ties and poverty to show them a different path. Some make it, yeah. Others, no way.

I start grazing the pile of cons for an enormous one, for the Octopus. But they are all New Mexico scrawny or stocky; if they are white, they are stringy and pallid, done in. There is, in typical representation for these parts, one black man. One fellow towers above the others in the back, but he's strawberry blonde and pocked with meth marks. When he answers the judge, he sounds vaguely southern. Not my guy.

Larry beckons to me out in the corridor afterward. "José Hernandez ring any bells?"

I look at him. "You have got to be kidding." There must be thirty thousand José Hernandezes in New Mexico alone.

He chuckles and hands me a booking photo. "That him?"

"Who?" I look at it. It's just a head shot, but he seems large.

"The guy who attacked you."

"I don't know." Already my skin is crawling. Already I want to shove it in his face and run out of the hallway. My hip starts throbbing, my head spinning.

Larry's watching me closely. "Is it me just mentioning him or something about this pic that's making you want to punch me?"

I set my jaw. I hate this. I have been here a time or two before. Acute trauma shit. If I don't want lasting PTSD, I better go do a little shrink session.

He gently returns the picture to his folder.

"Who is he?" I ask.

"An MS-13 creep."

"MS-13?" Now I am doubly startled. My predominant image of MS-13 doings is the headless, handless, and footless man in the cattle tub in Gang Awareness training. My stomach plummets. "How'd you—how'd you come up with this guy?"

"Tom has this nifty software that will sort people by things like height, weight. Unlike me, he spends time getting grant money for stuff like that. Also, he did a little asking around and heard some rumor about Chuy and a large guy, scary. This is who he found for now."

I pucker my mouth. I'm afraid if I open it I'll start to cry. I look helplessly at him.

"It's okay, Nina," he says. "And it's okay you didn't get an ID. Why would you?"

I swallow. "Thanks," I squeak.

He looks back at me as he walks away. "Clara says come to dinner tonight."

"Is that mandatory? Is that a Mandatory Clara Request?" Ever since William died she has occasionally made these.

"Yes, muchacha," he says, his voice tired, and then he is gone.

I doze in my office at lunch after heating up two leftover lamb rellenos I took home from Mama's. Then I start pulling up records. I am officially off the clock and my boss is in Santa Fe so he will never know I am disobeying concussion protocol. I have Tom's file but it seems cursory, as if he did a quick search of convictions and got his prison records, some arrests. Mostly what Larry has from Tom is Tom's long memory, his sense of Chuy as a pretty disturbed Bad Boy from day one. I want to see if Taos County might contribute something. I wish electronic records went back twenty-three years, to when Ángel was born, since it seems our boy Chuy was at least in Taos County at that time, wooing Lolo and loitering. Lolo didn't have Ángel till twenty-two—qué milagro—so it seems she and Chuy were an item of some sort for quite a while. I look up Chuy Martinez, Jesús Martinez, Jesús Alarcon, Chuy Alarcon, and hyphenated versions of the two. Chuy is a pretty common nickname for Jesús. I target Taos and Santa Fe counties, since both Tom and my buddy, Mr. Beefy Sleeves, at the Lodge seemed familiar with Chuy. And I look, possibly, for later Santa Fe records and earlier Taos ones.

This hunting records biz is a triple drag in New Mexico where (a) Hispanic mother and father's last names are both on the birth certificate, and so, therefore, (b) criminally minded sorts will often use the mother's name (in this case Alarcon) to evade capture, instead of the more standard paternal surname. Add the usual evasiveness of gang mores, in which being a snitch is considered incredibly poor form and a death sentence, and you usually get difficult PSI interviews and multiple police records for the same person.

Ángel was born in 1991. So Lolo was born in 1969 or so. I start winnowing Jesúses and Chuys down to those born between 1960 and 1971, in part because if he'd been too much older than Lolo, I think Mama would have said something.

Two possibilities become apparent. Given that I think of Chuy as a gangster extraordinaire, the rap sheets I do find are spare, stupid. Reckless driving, DV, minor possession. But one Chuy—and I sit up at this—had an attempted murder charge that got dropped to conspiracy. This was in '95. It looks as though he went to prison for five years for that one. This Chuy is in our very own jurisdiction and, oh look!, he was on probation too, in 2004, for assault, which means we should have the file. I get up, find the keys to the old jail cell that now houses our old files, and mosey down the hall. It's thick, that file. Most of it will be of little use. Drug treatment reports, anger management completions, revocations. But I am hoping there is a good PSI. I'm hoping it says he had a son, age thirteen, in 2004, named Ángel.

I get a cup of tea and the remaining biscochito, go right to the PSI, to "Background." The writer was spare. Jesús "Chuy" Alarcon Martinez was born in Santa Fe in 1972 and was the oldest son of Chuy Sr. (I knew it) and a woman named Leila Candelaría y Alarcon. Leila had four kids by three different dads, and Chuy Jr.'s dad dropped out of his life a lot of the time. But then—the cryptic sentence—"He would show up randomly and take him for weeks at a time." Chuy Jr. at this time said he was pretty sure he had one of his own progeny, a son, but he wasn't totally certain.

I was willing to bet that Chuy Jr. knew he had a son and "randomly" took him for weeks at a time, too, in fine family tradition. I think he lied a lot in the PSI about his family, including whether he knew for sure he had a son. This was a common theme in the tribalism of poor New Mexican families, though sometimes the patriarchal pride took over and, in that case, they bragged about sons. It's interesting that did not happen here, suggesting to me that Chuy Jr. wanted to protect Ángel from something fairly serious. Mama might never know about that end of Lolo's life. But other than that, not much else can be gleaned from the PSI.

It's after two now. Talking to Mama might be more fruitful anyway (maybe she knew Ángel's dad was in his life somehow?). Also, Larry is up on the coke angle given the WSL connections and the reference to white powder in Liza's journal. He and Tom Garcia have been delving into this and Tom apparently roughed up my bouncer at the Santa Fe Lodge. I groan when I hear that. I am already timid about going back to the Lodge to see Luis dance. How do I avoid Beefy Sleeves altogether? And what was Ángel doing with said coke . . . or setting up Liza for—I may never know now. But increasingly I feel he left her pegged at her house, planting a haul she either had no idea about or was forced to harbor. And when she couldn't or wouldn't produce it—well. One murder at 10:00 p.m., one sippy cup spilled into one kitchen corner, one little girl who fell back asleep on her mother's back after finding her prone on the kitchen floor.

That night after dinner at Larry and Clara's, I tackle Liza again. Jack is still in Santa Fe, with some word that he has an interview with the graduate architecture program at UNM in the morning. I say nothing other than a generic "that's great," and ask if he plans on coming up for the weekend. I have learned over the years that to mother him after a certain age is a fatal mistake. Even to say, "Oh that's wonderful, dear!" like my grandmother used to do, and then want to ask thirty questions about it, is an exercise in watching his fight-or-flight response magnify and squirm. High hopes are the harbinger of maternal criticism when offspring look as if they are finally getting their act together, but then the next minute they're "finding their own way" and it looks to said mother like a disaster in the making. Better to keep expectation at bay, offer kind and friendly support, and simply wait in the wings if anything really falls apart. Besides, tonight all he cared about was that *I* was doing okay.

I smile and look at his picture on the wall, taken in Indonesia in the Peace Corps—my Christmas present one year. It's now early April, I've got a small fire in the kiva fireplace, Ernest is snuffling. I crack Liza's little book.

Dear Diary:
Who writes that? Dear Dairy, I almost write. Mooo . . . If I don't laugh who will? Ricochet ricochet I was the girl who cut herself so deep she bragged to her counselor how she could pull out a vein. I was the girl guys copped a feel on at BHS and thought that meant I was appreciated. I was the girl . . . who . . . oh god oh god oh god DON'T FUCKING TOUCH ME and—a big

wrinkled blot stops all writing for four or five lines, as if she'd cried so much she drooled—*I am the girl. Replaced cutting with meth, with coke, with speedballs. Ángel conned me into believing he'd saved my life by keeping me away from smack but truth is what I really wanted to do was feel. Was. live. Meth did that a lot better. Not feel feel (I can barely stand that now), but feel something good anyway. Only thing that beat cutting. Ever.*

But Ángel could care. He could, really. Only guy who got what it was like to be raped. Only guy who when he was sane could, could . . . shit. When I'm insane I'm like this, curled on the floor in a corner, fetal, crumbled, non-existent cuz who I was Never. Fucking. Mattered. And when he fell apart? He sprung out of the corner like a slashed tiger, and he'd come at me and call me a fucking whore and punch me and scream at someone not me, and I go invisible again and I hit the ceiling and I punch my arm because it's Not. My. Arm and I just want to feel my ARM! My ARM! Where is my arm! I don't know anything and every woman is just boobs and butt and I think I'm supposed to kiss them cuz that must be what they told me to do at age four with Shelly Schultz the girl down the block. Funny I remember her god-damn name but nothing else 'cept—'cept—flashback. Fuck.

One thing I always forgave Ángel for was he didn't rape me. Never did. Never never never. But using Carmelina, using me as a mule, the beat-ings—enough enough enough.

God damn. Carmelina will find me once again on the floor, drooling and beyond sad, if I don't get up now. Don't make her dinner, don't don't don't . . .

I close Liza's journal for the night. I'm in my bedroom now, house bat-tened down. Things feel visceral, unsafe. I know what I just read. I know dissociation. The moment I felt the Octopus plaster all over me—*stop*. That place. I breathe. Reach down and touch Ernest.

The both/and of Liza's life, her strength and fragility. My own dad, the absentee con man who could paint and take photos and drank himself to death. The indifferent stepdad who nevertheless paid my college tuition— my pain is mundane compared to Liza's. I have, on occasion, back when I was twenty, twenty-one, been suicidal from loneliness and lack of trust, been sobbing in a corner like Liza, until I got pissed. And then I got up and threw clay, literally threw it. That led to intrigue at the splotches it made against the studio wall. Manic sunbursts, psychotic lopsided stars. Never underestimate the need for anger, I think. *You have to have experienced pain.* Luis's words. I peeled the stars off carefully, shaped them a hair, applied paint, put them in the kiln. I sold them all later at a co-op downtown, my first pieces that made me money.

I never looked back after that. I used clay as muse, savior, transformer, redeemer. I wasn't lonely when I could be with clay. How many damn men can say where their art emerged from? That it emerged from male abandonment, distrust, the vicissitudes of catcalls and sly looks from professors, and stupid choices?

I double-majored in art and sociology with an emphasis in criminal justice. Because my dad bilked people out of houses and, when he was down on his luck, made shady deals with cars and credit cards, I wanted to understand him. He was a master at economic crime. Stepdad hired me post-BA to do research for his law firm. And so began the dual track, the one foot in two worlds that only William, oh dear William, united. Mom married stepdad after he defended Dad in court. Christ. But she did okay—she did okay, and it was long after she'd divorced my dad, that crook. Now I'm weeping a little, here in the dark, sitting up in bed looking out into my walled backyard, my casita compound with its twin kiva fireplaces, one out and one in. Ernest moans in his dreams and stretches on his dog bed on the floor. The house is deeply quiet.

I close my eyes but the Octopus is there. It's only nine-thirty. Is Margot awake? I decide I'm too tired to talk, but I text her. *I need your shrink friend for a session or two.*

Then I turn off the phone. I don't want her alarming answer—*why, what's wrong?*—coming back tonight. I am not even sure she knows what happened. I haven't been able to bear telling her. She could call the land line—she probably will because no one uses cells to talk in Seco unless the one spot in the house where service magically shows up happens to be somewhere useful like the dining-room table. I take more Ibuprofen and my melatonin. I have to get some sleep.

Chapter 10

FRIDAY NIGHT FINDS ME in Santa Fe again, with an off-duty officer at the table behind me, thanks to Tom. It appears Tom approves of my budding relationship with Luis. Beefy Sleeves is nowhere in sight. I am still nervous as a cat but the show helps.

Luis is doing a special guest performance with a famous flamenco guitarist and the famous flamenco woman dancer (the one and only Rita Benavidez) who bequeathed Luis her business after she formally retired. She must be seventy, but she still has a thick mane of coarse curly hair that I am fairly sure she does not dye because there are occasional strands of unruly grey wires that up close—they are only visible up close—give her even more authority than she already possesses. She has an Aryan nose I can almost track from Rajasthan by way of the Caucasus into Romania, through the funnel of the Alps into southern Spain. In a tight bright turquoise dress with florid ruffles adorning the end of the long skirt, she looks regal, her slightly thickened waist somehow enticing, her hips commanding and voluptuous. I can only hope I look anywhere near that good at seventy.

"Damn," a voice whispers in my ear, halfway through the second dance set. I jerk about to find Larry at my side.

"What are you doing here?" I hiss.

"I have someone you need to meet."

"Now? We're in the middle of a show!"

Our whispers are harsh and we're getting dirty looks from patrons.

"Meet me outside after it's over."

"What do I tell Luis?"

Larry grins. "Bring him along. I need to assess the man." He turns back to the stage. Luis has joined Rita in a fierce pas de deux of slamming feet and "Allez!" catcalls. The noise helps cover our conversation. Luis's hair is a sheen of black sweaty curls, and as he whips around the spray goes all about, save, somehow, onto Rita. Larry stands up and squeezes my shoulder. "Lucky girl," he says, though I am unsure if he means me or Rita.

Beefy Sleeves is indeed working. *Fuck. Couldn't Tom scare him off?* I didn't see him until now, but then maybe he has been wondering what to do with me the entire first set. He sends me a dagger as he refills my water but murmurs, "I'm sorry," under his breath. If I'm not mistaken one of his eyes looks vaguely swollen. My heart is racing but I order a gin and tonic.

He looks at me with the gangster hooded look. "Sorry," he says again. He seems genuinely put out.

"You sure you should be talking to me?" I hiss. It seems pretty clear they beat him up too.

He looks at me with bafflement—who *is* this chick?—and I go back to watching Luis.

Twenty minutes later I sneak out to use the bathroom and come back to find a tiny straw cross next to my drink. I duck my phone under the table and cup my hands around its flashlight and look at the handiwork. It's beautiful. Cross-hatched designs, embedded tiny flowers of colored paper, the straw almost shiny. It feels both like an omen and a piece of gratitude. I look up, swiftly.

A faint nod from the rear of the room. Movement, like a ghost. I smile at him. He may or may not have smiled, ever so slightly, back.

Lew Wallace, the former territorial governor of New Mexico and author of *Ben Hur*, of all things, is widely quoted as saying that all that is based on experience elsewhere fails in New Mexico. I wrap my straw-art cross in a napkin and slide it into a side pocket of my purse. Lew, I decide for the thousandth time, is right.

I meet Luis backstage, Larry having shown up for the second time that night in that cop way of his by my elbow at the last encore. Luis has a small dressing room and is wiping sweat off his face with a towel, still breathing hard. He smiles when he sees me, taking an arm and grabbing my waist. I don't care if he's leaving a streak of sweat on the back my shirt; he kisses me fully and asks what I thought of the show. Then he sees Larry.

I have to say it does me a world of good to see Larry going bright pink with embarrassment. I will use this for weeks as office blackmail. Of course, poor Luis is a little put out too, but he has a performer's ability to recover and the joie de vivre of any good passionate Latin man. There will always be a piece of him, I see, perfectly happy to let another man see his woman swoon for him.

"Luis," I say, "meet Larry."

"Ah," he says. "I've heard about you."

"None of it good, I'm sure." They shake hands in awkward male fashion. "I need her for a bit, if you don't mind."

Luis looks at me. "Can you get to my house okay, *querida*? How long till I see you?"

I look at Larry for the assessment on time. "About an hour or so, I hope," he says. He looks at his feet, the shy boy on the playground achingly apparent. I want to knuckle the top of his head and tell him everything will be fine.

Luis takes Larry by the arm. "Come," he says, drawing him out of the shadow of the doorway into the little room. He procures a wildly good bottle of Spanish red and places it in Larry's hands.

Larry looks at him, baffled. Luis smiles that warm smile, the most sincere smile on Earth. "You have her respect," he says simply. "That's enough for me. Now take this and go fight crime, and as long as she is at my door by midnight, I will be a happy man."

"Christ almighty," Larry exhales when we are in the parking lot. "That man could seduce Attila the Hun."

I laugh out loud. "That's a lot, coming from you."

In the car Larry explains to me that we are going to meet one Rick Mucci at Evángelo's off the plaza. I groan. Evángelo's Greek Bar is a local dive, where archeologists and roadworkers and tourist-shop owners and all entrenched Santa Fe alcoholics go. The back tables carry on surreptitious craps games; men huddle in wheeler-dealer mode; my own father hung out here more than a couple of times, and I don't like the memory. Like Luis, I realize a bit jarringly, my dad in daylight could be ridiculously charming, and when he was on the up and up, he had a small successful gallery of his own work. But there was always the sideline, always the bottle, always the angle he worked. I hope Luis does not prove to have the sideline penchant, the con man at heart.

Rick Mucci, when I meet him, is this aspect of my father writ almost to caricature. He wears a shirt of slick material open to show a hairy chest and two gold chains—one a cross. His forearms bear a couple tattoos. He greases his hair back Pat Riley style and should talk with a Jersey accent even though he doesn't. If he has a daughter, I imagine she looks just like Snookie, a thought that makes me snort into the obligatory beer I have ordered. Larry shoots me a look and I sober up like a good schoolgirl. We're at a back table; the band is still playing, a kind of reggae version of Patsy Cline, of all things, and covers our voices.

"Rick does a little work for various law enforcement now and then," Larry says by way of introduction.

I bet he does, I think. I don't have to say, "Strictly under the table," because that's obvious. He's the type of guy who will off johns the cops can't touch; who stays just the other side of the law to swing bargains and keep a pulse on the backside of Rio Grande traffic.

"Hi," I say, extending my hand.

He takes it in a limp way, which surprises me. "Mucci," he says.

"Italian."

"First union miners of northeast New Mexico," he says proudly. "Raton, the mines near there. Railroads would advertise in shithole Italian towns about all the glory in America. My great-grandfather fell for it."

I sip my beer for appearances though I am up past bedtime and would rather crawl under covers. "It's hard to imagine there is a shithole Italian town," I say drily, thinking of the two trips William and I took to Italy.

Surely Raton would be a wee more shit-like. Who names a town Mouse? Mouse, New Mexico. But then there is Boca Raton. Mouse Mouth, Florida. Uh-huh. And I live at the foot of the Blood of Christ Mountains and am pretending to drink a beer in Holy Faith, New Mexico, the City Different and state capital. It all sounds so much better in Spanish.

I wipe my eyes. Larry is looking at me funny. I give him a rueful smile and let him lead the way. "Rick here might have some news about Chuy," he says.

Rick shells a peanut and pops it in his mouth. "Notorious in his day," he says.

"What do you mean?"

"Big dealer. Moved shit from Matamoros, Juarez, Chihuahua. A lot of it."

I make a face. "And how do you know this, Mr. Mucci?"

He looks over at Larry, as if asking, Do I really have to explain? But he straightens and decides respect is a good thing. "I do undercover work. I'm a PI."

"Okay . . ."

"So ten years ago or so I was doing a lot of work trying to figure out drug traffic for people like Larry here. This was after the feds made Sudafed hard to get and the meth market was, uh, realigning."

"And Chuy was moving meth? I thought Locos were mostly into coke."

Rick nodded. "They were. I thought I was staking out a meth deal one night down in the South Valley but instead it was coke." He kind of blanched.

"What?" I say.

"It was not even that. It was a deal gone bad. So they strung this guy up—" he turns away, swallowing. Mr. Tough Guy Mucci looks oddly human for a second and between that and having union miner ancestors I almost like him.

"Not pretty?"

"Medieval," he says.

"Like what? Flayed alive?" I remember being in Bruges once, looking at late Medieval and early Renaissance paintings. There was a wall-to-wall one depicting just that.

Rick actually nods. I pale. "And this was Chuy?"

Larry finishes his beer. "I thought they kept that shit south of the border."

Rick looks at him. "You can't be that naïve, hombre."

"Well, no, but still."

"Did Chuy have any kids?" I ask.

Rick snorts. "Most of those guys had twenty by twelve different women."

"But do you know about Chuy?"

He shifts, and in the shadows cast by low light I see the bags under his eyes, the flecks of gray at his temples. "Chuy grew up three blocks from me."

"Where was that?"

"Here. Off Agua Fria. Not far from Alameda. Skanky trailer park about to get gentrified like the rest of this town."

"So what was he like?"

Mucci looks away. "He was actually my good friend till seventh grade."

"Then what?"

"What do you think? Gang shit, being rolled in, me saying no. I had the crap beat out of me for that and it was Chuy who probably saved my life later on."

I let this sink in. It would be hard to reconcile the monster he'd seen in the dark in Albuquerque with the kid who had a heart. I try a different tack. "Did he—do you know if he had a mother named Leila?"

Mucci smiles. "Oh yeah. Leila is still around. He'd come visit a lot."

"You talk in the past tense."

He fumbles in his coat pocket and pulls out a day-old Santa Fe *New Mexican*. "Mira," he says, like the good barrio boy he actually is, despite Jersey appearances and Italian last name. He stabs at a story with his finger. "*Body Identified Off Relief Route.*"

I hold it up to the poor light and Larry fishes out his iPhone and hits the flashlight button so I can read: . . . *Jesús 'Chuy' Alarcon Martinez, age 46, was shot execution style . . . found lying under a juniper by a hiker's dog . . .*

"Forty-six and he's still gang banging?"

Mucci shrugs. "He's lucky he lived that long."

The bar becomes a swirl of feelings. I can't imagine what's running through Rick's heart, what with his childhood friend turned drug creep now dead; in my own lurks the ghost of my father, and a kind of grating sorrow I feel in any drinking establishment. I also need to get to Luis's but worry about collapse. I am in no mood for romance and ours is young enough that I am in doubt of its survival into the mundane.

Larry swallows and turns to me. "Make a point of calling on Ángel tomorrow, okay?"

"Why?"

"Ask if he has a funeral to attend."

I sigh. This business has no room for kindness, it seems. "Okay, Larry. But I am not going to be rude."

Larry smiles tiredly at Mucci, and we say goodnight.

Luis's small, elegant adobe is in a warren of streets southwest of the Plaza in the old Guadalupe neighborhood. It's twelve-thirty by the time I stumble in, reeking of dive bar and very tired. Luis smiles at me. He has taken a shower, and his black curls are wet against his forehead.

"Do you ever age?" I grouse. "You look twenty-five." I sniff my jacket. "Sorry. Larry took me to Evángelo's."

"A lovely spot," he says.

"Surely you have not been there?"

"Oh, but I have. Several times. Querida, Santa Fe is my home."

I regard him. It's true—I've placed him stomping his feet in the caves above Granada, Spain, more easily than I have placed him here. Maybe he is not that exotic. Why did I need him to be exotic? A twirl of earlier unease slides through my belly. I barely know this man. I like him too much; old, old distrust of my choices in men returns. Another ghost I thought William had exorcised for good.

"What is it?" he asks, seeing my face turn cloudy.

I flop onto his couch, right back where I was a week ago. "Oh, Luis." I put my head in my hands. "How do I know you are who you seem to be?"

"What do you mean?"

"Larry said you could seduce Attila the Hun. Is that what you are doing with me, seduction?"

He sits next to me. "I hope so." He has a small, impish smile and his hand strokes my hair. I swallow and go very still. I vaguely remember to breathe.

"Who scared you so, querida?" he asks. "You look twelve."

"I do?" I think about my long, graying hair, the crow's feet around my eyes. How can I look twelve? But he has nailed my emotional state. "My father," I say hoarsely.

"Ah. A traitor, then, of some sort."

I turn and look at him. "Yes. A traitor."

"I had one of those too," and leans in to kiss me.

I put my head into his shoulder. "My father used to hang out at Evángelo's sometimes."

"Yet you had a happy marriage."

I sit up. "I did, Luis. I did."

He smiles. "So trust yourself. You are a long way from twelve."

"What about you? Don't you ever feel twelve?"

He laughs. "Every day."

I take his hands. "Luis, can we—can we just go to sleep? And work out more romantic activity later?"

He brightens. "You're staying?"

I blush. "I—of course. I thought—"

He stands up in glee and holds out his hand. "Come."

I take it and follow him into a magical bedroom. There are candles lit, and a kiva fireplace with a fire in it. The bed is full of white pillows and a fat comforter. The tile floor has red Chimayo rugs over it, and a series of black and white photos adorn the far wall. I decide I will look at them in the morning. He presents me with a bathrobe. "Yours. If you want a shower, the bathroom is here—" and he flourishes an arm off toward a door on the other side of the bed.

I smile. "Thank you." Taking the robe, I lean in and kiss him. "Thank you." And before I am even in the shower I am thinking, *There is this hot man on the other side of that door . . . and I'll be damned if romance is not in the cards again.*

To sleep with a new man after decades of sleeping with only one—ah. Luis with his clothes off is somewhat of a relief, since clothes hide the way his own skin has begun to come away from his body, despite his dancer's fitness; his eyes tend to go grey under the lids when tired; I notice how the hands always betray age. So no, he is not perfect, and I feel less self-conscious of my own fifty-two-year-old body than I might have. He becomes fully human for me this night, and I remember then the real value of sex. It's not to lose ourselves in impossible fantasy but to drill down to our most sacred vulnerabilities. I don't know whether it is because I am exhausted from a late night that has brought up my father and the ugliness of murder, or that the candlelight works a buttery magic along with Luis's gentle hands; I don't know whether this is the consummation of five years of steady grief for my dead husband; I don't know if it is Luis's strange beauty and even stranger way we are attracted to one another—but I buckle. I slide into his bed, robe dropping, skin clean, hair damp. He slides in too, and becomes a brown chest with arms holding me, a masculine chin, lips that kiss my throat, eyes that look at and hold mine. He is liquid; the world is liquid—strangely fluid and intense. There are arms and curves and pulses and such a sweet pain when he enters me that I nearly convulse. And when it is all over, we are both silent in each other's arms, somewhat stunned. I swallow against tears; I see his own Adam's apple bob as if suppressing the same. I do not know his history but I know enough. I know we have both lived too long on this Earth not to know how rare grace is.

He gets up quietly to douse the candles and comes back. I am on my side by this time, and he spoons behind me, the brown arm with the defined muscles coming round to hold my hands in front of my chest. William was a master at this. It was his best contribution to us—this nightly wrapping around me from behind. I smile quietly in the dark as sleep overtakes me. Somehow, I feel William is coursing a little through Luis, and it is all alright.

"Querida," Luis whispers.

"Yes . . ."

He just sighs. And we both go off to sleep.

Chapter 11

ÁNGEL'S CELL PHONE, IN the manner of many a probationer, appears to be out of minutes. After a lovely morning with Luis, I say goodbye and drive home. Once out of the gorge and onto the plateau, where my own cell phone comes alive again, I will try calling. On second thought, I will just stop by. Always better to gauge responses to potential bombshells in person. He lives a little east of Ranchos, so it is more or less on my way. I really want to go home and run my dog and sit in the studio to brood and pull clay—what Margot calls "swamp work," that preliminary fumbling around to getting creative fires going. I am reeling a bit from Luis, bitten by guilt emanating from what I think is William's ghost. By Pilar, it's making me squirm, so I talk to him. I have learned it is okay to talk to ghosts.

"Okay, William. I am believing you hate me now." Darn, I really need to close my eyes for this. I pull off to a boat launch for the river, which runs close to the highway here. Rivers are very useful to me. If I am feeling stuck, I go to a river. Past Seco, up the ski valley road, it's the Rio Hondo, though the local acequia out the back of my studio does nicely for spot treatments. In town, upper end, it is the Rio Del Pueblo. But here I have the Rio Grande, albeit in mellow, early spring form. The snows have not yet begun their real melt.

I go right for the little beach, sit on a rock. It's early afternoon and warmish, the spring winds calmer down here, a feral apple tree going bright green with remnant white blossoms still clinging. A lurching adobe ruin of someone's hut can be seen past that, and the sky is that alacritous blue no one back east believes exists without a yellow filter on their camera lens. My heart sinks and seizes—how much I love my state! My New Mexico! That ineffable quality of air and silence and sad beauty, defined by adobe and piles of ancestral Puebloan ruins you can find everywhere if you know how to look, by the rabbitbrush and p-j level of elevation that really expresses the northern experience here. I blink back tears because joy and grief are the same and they come together in gratitude.

"William," I whisper. The cottonwood murmurs, the apple tree does a little dance. I close my eyes and breathe. I smell faint fish, river mud, the trace of cedar smoke from a local fire. "William."

I can feel him, that body. This time he looks at me from far away, maybe up on the Taos Plateau, maybe as far away as the Chama watershed. I swallow. He used to be so close. *Sweetie*, he says. *I am always close. Just because I'm not here does not mean I am not here.*

Well, so, then, how am I to proceed? Do I have two lovers? You and him?

He laughs, trickling it in with a clatter of ancient fall leaves swirling on rocks and sand nearby. I can't see them—my eyes are still closed—but I hear them. *Look!* he says. *You have fall leaves on the ground, new green ones up top. Both are here. Both are necessary.*

I sniff. What do you mean? I know what he means, but I want to hear it from him.

Without me there would be no Luis.

My eyes open. The river gurgles back, placid. The serenity just galls me. A slight movement catches my eye across the water. Two ears make their outline apparent from behind some willow. Coyote.

I burst out laughing. "William!" I say. The coyote hasn't moved. My voice should have startled it.

"William!"

He emerges from the brush. Takes a drink. A drink! Across from me! That audacious beast.

"You should be afraid of me," I say. "So you stay away from guns and traps."

He looks up, water trailing from his mouth. Shoots me a glance, as if to say, *I'm not that dumb, chica.*

"Well, okay," I say. I pause. Then say, "So, William, it's okay?"

Love, I want you happy.

That's what comes back. I look at the dead leaves, mulching into soil. Enabling the new leaves to be nourished.

I wave goodbye at the coyote, but he seems to have gone. Maybe I got the message after all because my eyes are cloudy with tears at the revelation—*qué milagro de todos los tiempos*—that I have been well loved and am loved now. It is a balm against all the other ugliness.

I get in the car and make my way north, to Ranchos de Taos, off 518 to one of the myriad divvied-up properties of New Mexico's old and fraying Spanish families. Loretta's mother's sisters and their husbands live in the front, in a combo adobe-doublewide compound. Several trailers list to one side, on about five acres. A small pen keeps three goats, and chickens spray off in different directions as I get out of the car. Ángel lives in one of the small trailers, is my guess. Probation officers have the luxury of "dropping by" unannounced, though we usually do it in pairs. I am not particularly worried about Ángel attacking me, however, and smoke from the adobe tells me someone else is home. Sunday morning is a good time to catch people off guard.

NM 518 past Talpa, where Ángel lives, narrows pretty quickly into thick p-j that climbs to ponderosa as you head east toward Pot Creek and Fort Bergwin. My archeology buddies on the soccer team work at Fort Bergwin, a.k.a. Pot Creek Pueblo, the largest prehistoric pueblo north of Santa Fe and ancestral grounds for Taos and Picuris people today, or so I'm told. Even though I am in what passes for wetlands here, with fruit trees and pastures, I look down at my feet when I get out of the car, because you never know in New Mexico. I did that once out back of the gas station in Abiquiu before they fancied it all up and realized I was standing on an enormous midden. Potsherds a-go-go, the crappy stone tools of four-teenth-century Puebloans. Once you get people past hunting and gather-ing and living mostly off agriculture, stone-tool technology the world over takes a dive. Nobody could work stone like those Pleistocene hunters. A well-done Clovis point is an act of grace, a work of art, an exercise in faith and hand control. The potter in me—who still has to learn what temper works best with what kind of fire, who cracks and destroys things on a regular basis—is in awe.

An old man with an impressive, drooping moustache has emerged on the little porch of the adobe. He just blinks at me, waiting for me to say hello.

I walk up with my hand extended. "Nina Montgomery," I say. "I'm Ángel's probation officer."

He takes my hand feebly and tilts his head to his right. "He should be home. That trailer over there."

"Okay," I say. "Thanks."

I start walking that way when he says, "Hey. You Loretta's neighbor?"

I turn back. "Yes. Why, does she talk about me?"

He smooths his moustache in the slow way old people do. He could be an absolute psychopath and I would, at that moment, consider him wise. It gives me hope for what growing old can do for a person's image.

He nods a little. "She said you were fair. A good PO."

I keep smiling. "Thanks."

He tut-tuts a little toward Ángel's trailer. "See if you can get that boy some sense."

"Will do," I say, though my belief in that kind of ability is nil.

The trailer is a dilapidated Airstream. Small. Airstreams can rake in lots of bucks if they are kept up right and I briefly consider suggesting to Ángel's familia that they should gussy it up, sell it, and put Ángel in a dumpy Winnebago, circa 1970. William and I had one when Jack was little. It was called "The Swinger." We bought it on the name alone; that and the fact it was cheap. Many a happy little camping trip took place with The Swinger.

A plastic patio chair sits to one side, and I see the ground around it is littered with wood shavings. The artist's perch. I knock loudly on the door, envisioning Ángel in the repose of the hungover. Shuffling occurs, the brief woof of a smallish dog. I wince, remembering the last time Ángel got close to a dog. But since it's *his* dog he probably wouldn't dream of hanging it from a tree.

The door creaks open and through the torn screen I see Ángel in white tee shirt and boxers, a little terrier at his feet. He gazes at me from a kind of stupor.

"Ángel," I say. "Your PO has arrived."

He runs a hand through his hair. "Why?" he musters.

"Can I come in?" I ask, though I am not sure I want to.

"Why?"

"Ángel, I am your damn PO. You want me to get a sheriff's deputy to help me out here? I can come in whenever I want. It's in your Terms and Conditions."

He sighs the sigh of the half-asleep, heavy and annoyed. I am reminded of Jack on school days when he was fourteen and loathe to wake up past noon. "Fine," he mutters. He opens the screen and the little dog sniffs my cuffs.

The trailer could be worse. I've braced myself for rotten milk smells, pizza boxes crusting over on the counters. But it's Spartan, with a dining table sporting five santos, all variations on the Scream one I saw in Santa Fe.

I nod toward those. "You getting a commission on those?"

He smiles a little behind hooded eyes. "Yeah. I'm 'pushing the art form,' see."

I laugh. "I know that one." I sit down in a chair with aluminum legs and a yellow plastic seat cushion that matches the dining table. I look him square in the face so I can see his reaction. "Ángel . . . do you know Chuy Martinez?"

He goes paler than he already is, his body tensing. "Why?"

"God, if you ask that one more time I am revoking your probation. Just tell me. Do you know him?"

"Know the name," he mumbles.

"Really?"

I let silence percolate into his veins. He fidgets, moves around his little kitchen, fills a tea kettle with water and a mug with instant coffee crystals.

He fidgets some more. Chuy Martinez makes him nervous. After my night of oversharing last week, I am not about to tell him I know he is his father.

"Ángel," I say.

He stacks dishes with anger. "Used to run shit for him back in the day."

"'Shit?'"

He sags. "I'm a Westsider, born and raised. You know that. Drugs, coke. It's on my rap sheet."

"So Chuy was an old drug connection?"

"Sí."

"How old?"

He shrugs, calculating a response. The water boils and he pours his coffee. "No sé. A couple years? Three?"

"Ángel, you're not that old. The years don't start mashing together until you are forty. Trust me."

My humor is lost on him. I try a different tack. "Ángel, you got anywhere you are supposed to be in the next couple of days?"

"What do you mean?"

"Family obligations of some sort? Say, a funeral?"

I swear I can feel his throat going dry. He tries to sip his coffee but he's shaking a little. "Why?" he asks.

I stand up, exasperated. "There you go again with that damn word. Cuz, Ángel." I pull out a copy of the *New Mexican*, folded to the article Rick Mucci showed me last night, and slap him with it. "Read this."

He takes the paper and does as he's told. He puts the coffee mug down because coordinating paper holding in one hand and sipping coffee from the other proves too hard. The paper shakes slightly in his hands. The light's dim in the trailer, but his little dog yips at him anxiously. Dogs know.

"Why do you think he's family?" Ángel asks after he's done reading.

My eyes widen. Does Ángel *know* this is his father? Or maybe Chuy isn't his father?

"Ángel," I say softly, "do you know who your dad is?"

At that Ángel's gone albino. "Please, señora," he says. I sense that if I were not his PO, he would have swung a punch at me. "Leave me alone."

I stand up. "Okay, hombre. But remember, you have court tomorrow at two."

I brush past him and the dog, shutting the screen door behind me. More than anything, what sticks is his hurt. The question about his father has skewered him and for the first time I truly can see the raw underbelly of Ángel. No wonder he does *Scream* santos.

Chapter 12

MY FATHER DIED AT sixty-nine from the accumulated ravages of alcohol and a life lived on the knife edge. I was thirty-nine. In college, he decided to get to know me better, calling from a payphone down the street from Poor Richard's Feed and Read, one of Colorado Springs's few establishments with a hippie sentiment to it. "Poor" Richard graduated from Colorado College twelve years before me, and his answer to Woodstock, LSD, SDS, and a philosophy degree was a hardwood-floor warren of mixed tables, vegetarian food, and used books. My predominant memory of the place is of wood—floors, lowish ceilings, round oak tables, farmhouse chairs, bookshelves. It smelled pretty good too, in that earthy *Moosewood Cookbook* kind of way. In his uncanny sensibilities, my father just knew that I would hang out there, reading late into the night or holding forth on Beat poetry (when I was a freshman and still trying to impress creative males) or radical feminism (when my rock band boyfriend and I had imploded, and I was disgusted with drunk romantics). So he would keel into town, usually in a vintage model car that had enough panache to convince some sucker he was an up-and-up art dealer or an artist. Mercedes was a popular choice. He made Colorado Springs part of his circuit; if rodeo men went from town to town getting paid to ride bulls, my father did so with his photography. He would ramble into galleries and coffee shops, put some pictures up on commission, ramble out again.

In that way that young people do, I confused symptom with cause, and I believed his career never took off because he never stuck around long enough anywhere to build stability, a network, or connections. But somewhere toward the end of my college career, I met him at Poor Richard's and could smell the alcohol on him. What jarred me was that we were meeting for breakfast.

All of my mother's swearing, her hurling of a whiskey bottle at a wall when I was four, the emphatic disgust at all things alcoholic, coalesced as I sat across from him on a Sunday morning with a stack of buckwheat pancakes in front of me. I stared at him, feeling as if the whole world were going down the drain. "You're drunk," I said.

He shook his head, salting his eggs. "Naw. I'm okay." He wouldn't look at me then, but when he'd come in, I saw how red his eyes were.

"You smell like a frat house."

He got impatient. "Here I come all this way to see my daughter, and this is the thanks I get."

Now, I would just roll my eyes. But at twenty-two I didn't have the insight or guts to call him out on his hang dog, guilt-trip behaviors, so I just backtracked. "Sorry, Dad," I said hurriedly, faking a smile.

He smiled back. But I remember distinctly feeling that we now had nothing to talk about. I picked at my pancakes and he swilled black coffee. The bottom had fallen out of whatever tenuous relationship had been attempted.

This was confirmed for me when he did not show up for my graduation several months later and, in fact, did not see me for five years. As with every other adult child of an alcoholic, I learned the lesson well: Speak Your Truth and Ye Shall Be Forever Banished from All Parental Love. It took years of crappy relationships that reinforced this and then several years of William's infinite patience with my paranoia and deep insecurities while I plodded and/or screamed my way through therapy, a few Al-Anon meetings, and my developing art, to mostly put this to bed. But that afternoon, the residue of Ángel brings up my father again.

I don't think Ángel is an alcoholic. But I think he's more shamed and hurt and failed than even my father. Unlike any other probationer—or maybe because of Liza's death and his art interests I am getting to know him better than most—he resembles some *felt* sense of my dad, like a lingering cologne. I am putting the finishing touches on my "Ángel-cum-dinosaur" piece as I ponder all this. It's a beautiful day, sunny, 75 degrees, the wind just a breeze for once and promising to die back a bit as it does in April. A few fruit-tree blossoms float by and I smile. Inspired, I make tiny flower shapes out of clay, applique one onto the bolo tie, another onto the belt buckle. I will glaze them a delicate white and perhaps add a touch of the faintest pink with a paintbrush after the piece is fired. Ángel is morphing from some sort of pure monster into my current statement about New Mexico. I put tiny turquoise studs in its stegosaurus ear plates. The cowboy boots I modify into full blown Mexican-style snakeskin, the kind that the immigrant boys wear on their night off when they put on their best jeans and their enormous belt buckles and parade around for the girls. I decide a feather is too cliché and then have to work the monster face a bit more, to get back to my original vision of menace.

"Good God, what's *that*?"

I look up. Margot is standing there, wearing, by God, a skirt Poor Richard would be proud of, and the infernal Birkenstocks.

I grin and hold it up—it's kind of an enlarged Woody size, a la *Toy Story*. "If I make a series, it might be titled New Mexico: Opus #1. But right now, it's sort of Ángel Martinez meets Dinosaur."

Margot rolls her eyes and comes over. "I brought you a gallon of my finest Earthship Mesa tea." She plops a sun tea container onto my worktable. Margot's teas are made from local bushes—odd, curiously effective mixes of things like juniper and sumac and serviceberry. "I'm using up my dried stash the next month or so. Then it will all leaf out again and I can pick new stuff."

"Cool," I say, and give her a quick hug. "I haven't seen you in a while."

"Well, ditto there, young lady. Did you go see Melinda?"

Melinda is her counselor friend I go to once in a while. I make a face. "No, not yet. I'm giving it three weeks. If I am still having nightmares I will go see her."

"Okay. Just promise me you really will go." She scowls. "I could be angry that you didn't tell me sooner about your attack."

I just look at her. She is so old and trusted as a friend I just let myself fall into her silently, the apology and surrender clear but unspoken.

"Oh, Nina," she says and holds me in the hug. "Am I going to have to watch out for you for the rest of my life?"

"Yes, ma'am." I squeeze her and let go.

She smiles. "Rumor has it you are now filthy rich."

I lurch inside. What voice in me is convinced all others will detest me for any real success?

I swallow. "You okay with that? If I was now rich?"

Margot peers at me. "Nina! Of course. Why wouldn't I be?"

But my chin is trembling, and I put down my sculpture for fear of dropping it. Luis, Rick Mucci, my father, Ángel, the slit throat of Liza Monaghan, my attack, all coalesce into a pool of tears. Shit.

Margot hugs me again. "Sweetie! I'm the rich girl, remember? You wanna know how to conquer feeling guilty for having what ninety-nine percent of the world does not, talk to me."

I smile wanly. She's right—just as she watched me fight off the demons of my father and wrestle with that other male role model, my stepfather, I watched her battle her birthright, which came with intense emotional pressure to be something she would never be—refined, cloistered, able to work a room and fundraise for some favored philanthropy, graceful in the way of debutantes. Her family actually possessed some very down-to-earth qualities—I went home with her on more than one break—and I especially liked her mother. But all that money seemed to lie heavy; it took years for Margot to learn what to do with it.

I sniff. "I don't know if I am rich, but I am blessed. Jade Kirchner is kind of cool, really. I would like you to meet her. If we ever get that chance, that is."

Margot nods and pulls two mugs off my rack to pour tea. "So I want to see the horses. For the gallery show."

The tea is sweet and sort of bitter all at once and I sense my liver thinks it's terrific. I can almost feel my bile ducts opening. "Well, that ought to cure me," I say, looking into the cup. "Come on."

I take her inside to a small storeroom. I haven't unveiled the horses because I want their debut to be Margot's event. Chiefly they are head and necks, arched or eyeing us sideways. I've raku fired some of them, especially the chestnuts; others I have used sawdust because I like the effect of the smoke. The paint ponies I find I can get the essence of by using sawdust. I use a slab technique with a lot of textural imprints—for manes, halters, the suggestion of muscle—and I usually start by watching the animals, making sketches. Seco has several local horses; beyond my backyard wall is a field with about half a dozen. There is one big black gelding I like in particular, and for him I have gone very traditional in my firing, glazing deep and shiny, almost like what the potters at Jemez Pueblo do only less matte in my finish, and fired so that I get crackle. I want him mythical, which the thick, black, shininess of the glaze gives me, along with the crackle—that imperfection—and slightly too-flared nostrils and eyes that I hope are a profound combination of wild yet wise. The last thing I wanted when I was working the clay was a banal rendition of the rearing stallion. Margot stops at the three versions I have of him.

"Wow," she says. "Can you make more of him?"

"Not in time for the show." I find that unique happiness only artists whose newest work has just won gold-star approval can know. I am tingling and excited. I grin like a prize child.

"Well, that's okay," Margot says, oblivious to the effect of her words. "The show's small. But let's front and center the black horses. And then put a couple of your others—she gestures to my roans and paints—around. Those are good—not too terrifying, perfect for people who want good art without being too hard on emotion—but man . . . *this* guy. . . . Wow."

I continue to be absurdly pleased. "You really like him?"

Margot walks around the biggest one. "Nina, I don't know what's going on in you these days—one minute you are delirious with flamenco sex and celebrity recognition, the next a complete puddle—but it's working. You ought to work on murder investigations more often."

I laugh. "I'll tell Larry."

Margot gets out her iPhone and starts taking pics.

"Wait! What are you doing?"

"Oh, Nina. I'm just getting the image for the flyer I have to put up. Show's in two weeks. Time to kick in heavy advertising."

"You are using a smartphone shot for the flyer?"

"Indeed I am."

"Aren't phone shots stupid? What happened to professional photography? This is the Horse Debut, after all."

"Don't worry. If I need to, I'll come back. But I want to play with this. Besides. You can get some good shots on a phone. Durango up in Colorado has a whole show on Instagram photography right now."

"Really?" I think of my dad, with his heavy SLR, his long, snout-y lenses, his rolls of undeveloped film we found in his motel room in Chadron, Nebraska, after he died. He was apparently backtracking to the country of his extreme youth, the Sand Hills. His liver was giving out, but thankfully he had a heart attack before the cirrhosis really went whole hog. I wonder if he would feel the advent of the smartphone camera was a sacrilege. I don't think he had the wherewithal to welcome it, to play with the newness. Margot takes several more shots, as the afternoon goes long and the two of us, friends for thirty years now, quietly work out how best to announce the show, and where we should put each animal in the room.

Monday finds me at work. In typical Taos fashion, the temperature has plummeted and snow threatens. This after a beautiful day yesterday. I attend our weekly staff meeting, then late morning court. I've brought a salad for lunch and have tried icing Margot's tea for a beverage. I'm itching for dark chocolate—I have acquired a taste for the eighty-five percent dark, dark stuff, which is supposed to be awesome regarding antioxidants and is low enough in sugar to justify biting off hunks of it. I'm mulling over a flash trip to Cid's in search of more of it when Larry raps on my door frame.

"Damn," I say. "I was just about to go procure chocolate."

He grins. "I'd go with you, but I need a desk and pen and paper and someone who was with me with Mucci the other night."

"Why?"

"I am trying to figure out Chuy's—and maybe Ángel's—family tree."

"Baffling, isn't it? I was mulling that over too, yesterday. I paid him a visit Sunday morning on my way home."

"And?"

"I showed him the news article about Chuy and asked if he knew him. After a little prodding he said he used to run drugs for him some years ago. I asked if he knew who his dad was and he got pretty pale. If I hadn't been his PO, I'm pretty sure he would've punched me."

"Touchy boy." He pulls out his iPhone. "Nice rendition of him, by the way." He flashes a photo of my New Mexico dinosaur man.

"Wha—?"

Larry is beside himself. "Your friend Margot."

I'm agape. "She sent it to *you*?"

"Hey!" He feigns offense. "Soccer buds. You know. I ran into her last night at Safeway."

"Margot shops at Safeway? Not Cid's?"

"You could use that against her in retaliation. I mean, what's with the Birkenstocks?"

I shade my eyes. "Oh, Larry. I've been trying for *years* . . ."

"Stuck in 1972, is she?"

"The sad thing is we were ten then."

"Yeah." He pulls up a chair usually occupied by probationers. "Hand me a pencil and paper, will you?"

I fish around for scrap paper and a writing implement, the latter kept well out of reach of potentially annoyed criminals in search of weapons.

"Ángel lives on his great-aunt and -uncle's property out in Talpa," I say. Larry just looks at me. "Huh?"

I realize he's been thinking about the Santa Fe line, whereas I live next door to part of the Taoseño band of his mother's. "Never mind. That's Loretta's family. We'll get there." I draw a circle and a triangle, with a line connecting them. "Okay, start here. How many kids do you think Chuy Sr. and Leila had?"

Larry's eyes glaze over. "This is Anthropology 101, right? Kinship charts."

I grin. "Damn straight. Serves you right for possessing a pic of my New Mexico dinosaur man."

"Fine. Question one for Rick, about how many kids he had. For now, let's just draw in Chuy Jr., okay? And add our speculations about Ángel."

Larry just gazes at it. Our chart looks woefully underdeveloped. "We don't know squat," he says. "Did Chuy Jr. have more kids? Did Lolo?"

"I can ask Loretta about Lolo but my sense is no. That Lolo had Ángel and got so strung out on drugs she had a hard time even with him."

"Well, that never stopped most people."

"I know. But Loretta's the type who probably would have tried to raise all ten of Lolo's kids if she'd had them. So I kind of don't think so."

Larry scrolls his contacts and dials Rick. His eyebrows go up in surprise when Rick actually answers. "You are awake, I see," Larry says. Something like a squawk emits from the other end and Larry asks him about Chuy Sr., Leila, Chuy Jr. He sketches in a sister from Chuy Sr. and two half-brothers from her other paramours. So Chuy Jr. had one full sibling and two halves. He draws a dotted line out on the other side of Chuy Sr. for a likely second mate and their children. More halves and steps. "What about Leila," he asks. "Is she still around?"

Rick replies, and I hear a "beside herself" and then a "tough old bird, *curandera* you know."

"Where can I find her?" He listens to Rick's reply, scowling. "Okay, sí sí. *Respeto.*"

He puts the phone on my desk. "Rick says there is a sister via Leila, rumors of an Albuquerque gang bird with other kids possibly there. I am to leave Leila alone until after the funeral out of respect. Chuy Sr. died in prison years ago."

"How?" I ask.

Larry squints at me, owlish. "You're thinking gang retribution, no?"

I shrug. "It's possible. Prison is a terrible place."

We're silent a minute. I don't think either one of us is very sold on our role in sending people there. It takes a real brute to want us to think there can't possibly be some other alternative. Most of the time I want to send people on a six-month Outward Bound–style test of endurance that does not exist or have a magic reset button I could push to start them all over down a different path. Larry finds it easier than I do to lock people up, but then he gets to deal with them during arrests, and people are easier to detest in those situations.

I sigh. "I have to go to court soon. Our boy will be there, I hope. But I'll ask Loretta tonight about her family, and what she knows of Lolo."

Larry smiles. "Can I take this?" He points to our crude genogram.

"By all means."

"My own family is one big sprawling mess. But we have a Bible with a lot of it filled out."

"Isn't Baca the same name as de Vaca, as in Cabeza de Vaca?" Cabeza de Vaca was a famously shipwrecked Spaniard who managed to wander from Florida to Mexico via Texas and New Mexico, and even lived to write about it.

Larry waves me off as he exits. "Yeah, yeah, Head of Cow and all that."

"The Spanish were weird!" I yell after him. "Whose family is named Head of Cow?"

I hear a snort from Roni next door, and then all goes quiet again in our little quad of the world.

Chapter 13

TAOS COUNTY BUILT A nice complex where our office, jail, and court all exist in the same compound. I amble over toward court at 1:55 and don't even have to go outside, which by now is full of blowing wind and swirls of snow. I have Ángel's file, along with two others. One is getting resentenced after revocation for failing three BACs and another is a new kid, nineteen, trembling and upset at throwing his girlfriend's phone out the window of a car during a fight where they both slapped at each other, and he ended up with a misdemeanor domestic violence charge. I've asked that he get a deferred sentence so that once he's done it will not appear on his record. I am fairly certain he will toe the line with religious attention to all Terms and Conditions, especially after his father, who could have perhaps afforded it, said he'd have to suffer the consequences and refused to get him a private attorney.

The Public Defender Office is generally run by young people right out of law school. Who else would work ungodly hours for crappy pay with an insane workload? It is the norm for defendants to have all of three minutes in the hallway outside to meet with their lawyers, after the initial meet-and-greet in jail or just prior to the preliminary hearing. I used to get mad at this. I used to think the public defenders did not care about their jobs; I was disgusted at the shoddy treatment for those too poor to afford a three-hundred-dollar-an-hour lawyer fee for a private attorney. And some of them—yeah. But over time I got to know a few, and I'd see how excited they were after attending Juvenile Justice conferences in Albuquerque, or how much they believed that they had to be there, in whatever form, to counteract the overwhelming power of the state as represented by the DA. Most of them were just as disgusted at the lack of money to hire more of them, and to provide better representation, as I was. This is the place where American justice cracks and completely fails—along the great fault line of money.

So it is that one of the more enlightened souls, Ángel's lawyer Bennie Garcia, baby-faced and probably no older than twenty-eight, comes running up to me just as I also see, behind him and in tears, Loretta. I know the game is off as soon as I see them. Ángel will not be present for sentencing today for beating his girlfriend and killing a dog.

"What's happened?" I ask.

"Ángel tried to kill himself last night."

"What?" I stare at Loretta. She's sniveling and nodding her head like an autistic child.

I look helplessly at Bennie. "Well, I guess you will ask for a continuance." My mouth feels as dry as the southern desert.

"I will. That's my job."

"I know. But this changes nothing about the facts of the case." Bennie and I look at each other. Is this cruel? Unfair? I shake that off. Ángel's had this coming. He knew the gig, agreed to the plea. Whatever this suicide attempt was about, it was not this. His plea had been in the hopper for months.

"I will argue to sentence him in absentia," I say.

"I would like you there in court if the judge wants to know why," Bennie says.

I look pleadingly at Loretta. "Mama, where is he?"

"Holy Cross," she mutters.

"What'd he do?" If he's in the hospital he is not in good shape.

"Tried to hang himself," Bennie says. Loretta moans.

I take Loretta's hand. "Mama, listen to me. This is not your fault. I need to stay here to get him sentenced. Then I will come to the hospital, okay?"

She nods. "How long?"

I blow out air. Court could take two hours. He's about fifth down on the docket, so I am hoping more like forty-five minutes. The other two cases I can get Roni to cover for me if I give her my files. "An hour?"

"Okay, bueno. *Mi tío y tía* are there. *Tío* found him."

I think back to my recent visit to Ángel's trailer, and the man on the porch. "The man with the moustache?" I ask.

Loretta looks blank for a minute, then almost smiles. "Sí. Refugio. He's had that moustache since I can remember."

I hug her and go into the courtroom with Bennie. My waiting is futile, however. The judge, upon hearing about Ángel's state of being, continues the case.

Refugio nods at me, a sentinel outside Ángel's door. He puts a weathered hand gently on my sleeve, catching me. "Mira, he don't look so good." His brown eyes regard me soberly from under their aged hoods. He is being a gentleman, giving me fair warning. Since it's a court day I am in a dress and low heels, my hair swept up in as elegant a chignon as I can get it. I find I appreciate his stateliness as much as he probably is glad for my feminine demeanor.

I pat his hand. "Thank you," I say, and take a breath before going in.

His face is purple. A deflated purple. He reminds me of an eggplant on the verge of going bad and I nearly laugh at the thought, nervous energy and revulsion careening to humor. Ángel Martinez's face has, for the first time in its life, some flesh on it, but it's distorted, ugly, bloated, unnatural. A tube plows down his open mouth, taped over by a mask to hold it all in place. An IV drip runs into his bony arm. His eyes, not quite able to close all the way, are little half-moons of red under the lids, blood vessels all broken from the pressure he inflicted on his neck.

I swallow, sit slowly down on a chair next to his bed, wondering what despair brought this on. "Well, Ángel," I say. "You, um, missed court." He heaves an odd sigh, which makes for a strange noise in his mouth, and suddenly, I realize I want to know what he would do next with his santos, where his art would take him. I forget the hung dog, Liza's twisted knee, her black eyes. I see Ángel's frailty, and stare at his hands that are toughened from woodworking, impervious in places to slivers. "Ángel. What brought you to this?"

The door opens quietly behind me and a doctor comes in. "Not a pretty sight," she says. She sticks out her hand and I take it. "Dr. Singh," she says.

"Nina Montgomery. I'm his probation officer."

She looks puzzled. "But aren't you the artist?"

I gape at her. "You *know* that?"

She laughs. "I go to your studio on occasion. I live up the ski valley road. I want to buy one of your pieces one of these days."

"What are you waiting for?" I, like all other idiots, assume she must be rich because she is a doctor.

She tucks a strand of glossy black hair behind her ear and I realize she must be all of thirty. "I have a year left of student loans. Then I tell myself I can afford art. My mother would still shoot me."

I smile. "And your mother is . . . ?"

"Back in Boston, waiting for me to marry another Indian doctor and have several grandchildren."

"Ah."

She turns to Ángel. "He'll probably make it without brain damage, but we're not sure yet."

"Brain damage?"

"From lack of oxygen."

Of course. I sit back down. What would I do if Ángel lost the power of speech? Or became a vegetable? Would I ever know about Liza then? Or Chuy Jr.? Or see another santo made in some renegade format that was already, no doubt, curdling the innards of the traditionalists? New Mexican religious art can be very strict in its form, and murmurs of sacrilege have probably already followed in Ángel's wake, smoky waiflike streamers emitting from the mouths of disapproving *abuelas* and lay preachers. Would Ángel be allowed in church again?

"When will you know? About his state of mind, his health?" I ask.

She looks up from feeling his pulse. "Another twelve hours or so, I think. He's very lucky. We would have airlifted him but for the storm, and I have some experience with this, alas. We had to intubate him, give him a solution of—" She breaks off. "Oh, there I go, speaking Doctor Talk. Basically, we had to get his heart rate down, induce a coma sort of to do it. Now we watch for pulmonary edema, take care of that. We're not out of the woods at all, though his heart's better now."

"How did Refugio find him? His uncle?" I tip my head toward the door, where I assume his tío is still standing guard.

"Oh," she says, "I think he heard a dog barking frantically."

Good lord. I can't imagine. The image of his grandnephew hanging from a tree, stretched long with his little dog yapping furiously at his feet, will linger with that man till he dies. I try to smile at Singh but fail. "I better go."

She nods, and in the hallway, I find myself gasping for air. I lean down and put my hands on my knees. "Refugio," I say, looking up to where the old man is watching me. "I am so sorry."

"*Por qué?* You did nothing."

"I don't know that." My voice cracks and I struggle not to sound hysterical. "What if it was something I said to him yesterday?" I keep going back to Ángel's pale face, the impact of Chuy Jr.'s name, and then the news of his death.

"You did nothing," he repeats. He's working his jaw.

I watch him, puzzled. "What's upsetting you about this? Besides finding him—I am sorry for that, so sorry, too."

He sighs and this time I see anger. "That boy. That boy had good family up here. Good family. And what did he do with that?"

The betrayal that suicide brings on becomes a party in the hallway, a sad ghost. "Not much, it seems. I know Loretta tried."

Refugio shakes his head. "That no-good sister of hers. Lolo. Lolo and Chuy. *Ahora hay un pendejo.*" Now there's an asshole.

"Chuy?"

"Yes."

"Was Chuy his dad?"

He swivels to look at me with those hooded eyes, head on. "*Claro.* Who else?"

I pause. "See, that's just it. That's what I did on Sunday."

"What?"

"I told him Chuy'd been murdered."

Refugio stares at me and I'm awash in all the guilt I knew I should have had on my shoulders from the beginning. But he shakes his head slowly, like an elephant annoyed with his trunk. "*No diferencia, señora.* Ángel had a choice." He gestures wildly at the door to Ángel's room. "And he chose like a coward."

I know there is no worse accusation, coming from a man like Refugio. A man who probably worked in mines and on railroads and in fields all his life; a man who did not back down from poverty or lack of an education. A man who stayed married, had many children, went to church, kept up the adobe on the local morada, believed that a man was as good as his word.

"I'm sorry, Refugio." I put my hand on his arm this time. "But one thing. I am an artist. And where I can find some belief in Ángel at all . . . it is in his art."

He eyes me. "You think those are good?"

"Yes," I say. Without hesitation. "They are original." I hold up a hand in preparation for an assumed defense. "And dangerous. I know they are not traditional. To think that maybe Christ screamed, even once, at all the suffering, *por ejémplo.*"

The old man rolls his lips, considering this. His moustache squirms a little. The crow's feet at the edge of his eyes crinkle upward even as his mouth can't quite grin. "Those *Scream* ones sure did piss off old Father Reyes."

I watch him. "I take it you find pissing off Father Reyes somewhat enjoyable."

He licks his lips this time, the moustache popping back out, a freed squirrel tail. "Never, never tell *mi esposa.* She worships any priest, señora. *Pero sí,* Father Reyes can kiss my ass."

I let out an unseemly bray. I'll have to introduce Larry to Refugio. They'd get along famously. "Thank you," I say.

He just nods. He has no intention of leaving the hallway, even if he despises the person behind the door. An honorable man, with a decorum I find endearing. I leave him to his vigil and wend my way out of the front door of the hospital.

I go over to Loretta's when I get home. She looks green. Carmelina is in the bedroom with Helena, who sounds exasperated.

"Is he going to make it?" Mama asks. "Carmelina can't lose both parents, even if she can't see him right now."

"He'll make it. But in what shape is still a question. I talked to the doctor."

Loretta sits heavily in a dining room chair. She looks more sunken than I have ever seen her. I sit next to her and take her hand. "It's not your fault," I say. "None of this is your fault."

She wipes her nose with a Kleenex. "Suicide is a sin. That's drilled in you the minute you can understand what the padre is saying, Nina. It's a bigger sin than beating your wife." She snorts a little at that, about as heretical as Loretta will ever get out loud.

"I know."

"So what drove him to that?"

I open my mouth to start to tell her about Chuy, then close it. I am not sure what she would say to that. Instead I ask, "Loretta, what do you know about the other side of his family? Chuy or whoever his dad was?"

She gazes off over my shoulder. "Lolo hung around Chuy, and these other boys. They would slink in from Santa Fe, big city boys to us. She was fourteen, Nina." For a second her gaze comes back to me. "Fourteen. I was sixteen and I was scared of them. But she wasn't. She wanted to flaunt them in front of me, her friends, our parents most of all."

"What happened?"

"My father was so angry. So angry."

I think a minute. "Maybe she was tired of being his princess. Maybe that's how she rebelled."

Loretta nods slowly. "That would make sense. When he drank—when he drank, he would ask for her and she'd come when she was younger and he'd put his arms around her and cry a little and stroke her hair and go *mija, mija, lo siento mija*. Made me sick." She looks at me. "He didn't

usually like to speak Spanish. Said that was for Mexicans, not us Spaniards. But when he was drunk . . ."

"Were you jealous?"

"When I was younger. I thought she got it all. Her dress at Easter was
always prettier in my eye, her Communion lace—ay! ¡Qué linda!" She's
gone far away again. "I had this round, round face. Always have, mira." She
grabs her wattles and shakes them.

"Mama, you didn't have a double chin as a teenager."

She smiles. "No, but you know what I mean. Lolo's face was round like
mine a little, but she had these full lips that took red lipstick on like
nobody's business. And wide eyes she'd make up like Cleopatra."

"So she starts to grow up . . ."

"Mi padre threw a fit." She closes her eyes. "'¿Dónde está mija?' he'd roar,
even with her right there. What he meant was where did she go? Where
did his little princess go? The little pretty thing now had a figure, wanted
to wear makeup. He wanted a little girl."

My stomach clutches. "What'd your mom think? How'd that make her
feel?"

Loretta sighs. "Probably not good. But she never said anything. She
didn't want him mad."

"So Lolo starts bringing home bad asses."

"Not so much bringing them home, just parading them around the
plaza, hanging out in cars, you know."

"Did you ever hang around with Chuy? Go down to Santa Fe with
her?"

"Once. She had me drive her. I was eighteen. Back then if you wanted
more school you went to De Vargas in Santa Fe, for community college.
They didn't have the campus they have here now. So I attended nursing
classes there for a bit, before I met Miguel. She had me drive her down a
lot, mostly to drop her off at the mall, or in the plaza. But once she had me
go to a neighborhood. Chuy's house."

"Anything happen?"

"Sí, Dios mío." She puts her hand to her chest. "This lady, jet black hair
piled so high on her head, a nose like Montezuma himself, these beady

little Indian eyes, long silver earrings with coral and turquoise set like a cross, wearing this floral dress full of reds and oranges—she comes out. Lolo's walking toward Chuy, who's leaning on this car, low rider special, all green with black flames, chrome rims, little chain around his license plate, and this woman starts screeching at her. Goes on about how Lolo had no respect, showing up like this when Chuy's dad's just been arrested, and what a *puta* she was—I just stared at her. I'd never seen a woman be so loud, Nina." She looks at me for understanding. I nod. She's just gotten done telling me how her mother never stepped up to her dad, after all.

"What happened?"

"Lolo just looked back at me and winked. She loved every second of it."

"Playing the bad girl."

"*La Princesa*. Sí, anything to break the rules. Chuy took her under his arm, said to Lolo, 'This is Leila. Mi madre. Leila, Lolo.' They just stared at each other, mad-dogging, I think the kids would say now. Chuy ate it up. Chewed on a toothpick and his eyes were laughing."

I have to laugh too. "Sounds like Chuy was dating someone a lot like mom."

"I guess you could say . . . So I sat in the car and then Lolo did this little wave, and I figured out I should just leave. I was going to be late for class anyway."

"Did you ever meet her again? Leila, I mean."

Loretta shakes her head. "*Nunca. Pero,*" and her eyes widen a little, "I think I saw her as I was leaving the hospital to come to court and find you."

"Today, you mean?"

"Yes, today."

I lean back, letting go of Mama's hands. Leila had to be at the hospital for Ángel. Why else?

"I think I need to talk to her," I say.

Loretta grunts. "Good luck, muchacha," she says. "Good luck."

Chapter 14

IN A FIT OF late-night curiosity, at home with Ernest Borgnine at my feet, some mint tea by my side, the remains of a languid phone call from Luis floating in my head and loins and (even, maybe?) my heart, I google "Curanderas—Santa Fe" and lo and behold, a Leila Candelaría y Martinez shows up, white skunk streak in her otherwise black hair, thick and piled high just as Loretta described. She is even wearing close relatives of the cross earrings mentioned by Loretta. Half the ad is in Spanish, for "sana de todos," "para el corazón, dolor, mal de ojo," you name it. Ulcers to cancer to curses, Leila could fix you up fine. I imagine a day in Santa Fe whence I meet with Gert Khan, Luis, and Leila all within the space of hours. I'd have to get a spa treatment afterward just to come down off all that arty, Spanish passion. I text Jade on a whim. Why not? She'd love it.

I have tomorrow off, and though I should be in the studio, this calls to me. Somehow, I think it will fuel this oddity that is happening with my clay, where my lifelong molding of animals is morphing into an interest in the human form. Ángel as Dinosaur may have Larry laughing, but it's the start of something new.

To my surprise, Jade texts back. *Oh yes! I'd love to.*

Are you sure? We are talking wild Santa Feans.

Perfect.

And possible party to a murder investigation. Are you up for that?

Cross my heart hope to die. Yuki can watch the boys. I have a script I should read but it's a money movie and stupid so I am uninspired.

A money movie?

Something I do for money, not art.

Oh. Do you wear a cat suit?

Sort of. A tight lawyer suit. It's not that bad. It's comedy. But still.

Meet me here at 9 am? I have to run with the dog first.

Where do you live?

Oh, right. Three blocks from the studio. 43 Calle de Lucero. Google it. A charming lopsided casita.

SQUEAL! See you then.

And so I go to bed with a smile on my lips, especially after Jack slips in the door, late, as my eyes are almost closed, and says he's home for a week or so before moving into a place in Albuquerque in prep for school in the fall. We hold hands, he kisses my cheek. "Love you," we both say, in that sweet little moment we'll forget while both of us are alive and miss forever when one of us is gone.

Ernest and I go up the ski valley road and run up the start of a trail in the pines. I have salved my hip with smelly goo and find a little jogging mixed with walking and stretching does it some good. It's cold and refreshing and Ernest happily barks after several squirrels. A mule deer does not interest him in the least, though the deer looks unhappy to see him and bolts off into a clot of aspens sprouting in a gully. At home I call the hospital and ask for Dr. Singh. She's off duty and I leave a message for her to call me. I think about stopping by Ángel's compound to see how Refugio is holding up but decide to do that later. I text Larry to tell him what I am doing, in case I don't come home, and Jade and I are killed by drug lords commanded by Leila the Curandera high priestess; he says he will let Rick know and Tom at the Santa Fe Police Department, though he doubts I'll need help.

He quits texting and calls. "Just watch your back. Last time you went asking about Ángel down there you nearly got killed."

"They would not have killed me," I say, though I am trying to convince myself more than anyone else.

"Still . . ." He hangs up and then texts again, saying he and Clara will be at my art opening. This is accompanied by a smirking emoticon.

Jade finds me finishing up a breakfast burrito and a cup of coffee. Ernest sniffs her and wags his skinny tail, a sure sign of acceptance. She has her Jacki O sunglasses on and an old pair of jeans with an embroidered top. She looks almost normal.

"You sure you won't be recognized?"

"Well, I have a head scarf if need be. We aren't going anywhere truly public, are we?"

I shake my head. "I don't think so. I'll warn you."

She smiles and we get in my truck. The day is warming up and promising a near-summer appearance. As I drive, I fill her in on the Martinez affair. She's quiet most of the way, listening.

"My dad was like Chuy, a little, I think," she says.

I look at her in surprise. "Really? How so?"

"He liked to steal things, just for the hell of it. He could be great fun, but he was no good to be married to and he smoked a lot of pot."

"So he was your best friend until—"

"Until he wasn't." Her face has gone stony. "He nearly died in a car crash when I was nine."

"I'm sorry," I say. "Where were you?"

"In the car, with him."

I let out a whoosh of air. "The sins of the fathers . . ."

"It's okay. I did some therapy for it about ten years ago, when my kids were born and all this anxiety came up. It helped resolve it."

"Well, that's good." By now we're down by the tacky strip that is Pojaque. Strings of casinos to our left, the turn for Los Alamos, then Camel Rock, the great uplift of the Jemez, to our right. I hate this stretch. It used to be dull, inhabited by low trailers and the rural poverty that is New Mexico, but now all that is hidden behind the bells and whistles of highway casinos, the promise of instant money that lures in those from the trailers to spend their last dime.

Leila has a tiny shop adjacent to tiny beauty salon off Agua Fria. This is not the Santa Fe known to the 1 percent or the tourists clamoring around the plaza. Low stucco adobes with cracks in them, chain link fences, tumbleweeds, half-eaten cars in grass-dead yards. Something happens with Hispanic hair in salons like the one we are near that I suspect would do my hair a lot of good, seeing as it is thick and dark and coarse like so many Latinas. I peer in the window out of curiosity, looking for alter egos, but I just see a couple of chairs occupied with the usual stylists—one guy and one gal, today—standing behind, teasing and blow-drying.

Jade tugs my sleeve. "Here," she says, pointing at Leila's door.

I take a breath. Her photo alone is enough to intimidate me, so I do a brief movie scene in my head and pretend she is just like one of my petulant probation girls, all grown up. It doesn't really work.

A little bell jangles over the door as we enter. The shop smells of a jumble of dried herbs and is saved from what I call Generic Weed Smell (and by weed, I mean Weed) via old cedar smoke emanating from a tiny wood stove in one corner, a table full of piñon pine products, and Mexican cinnamon, or canella, that wafts from a shelf to my left. A small, green cross sticker resides next to Visa and Master Card and so I know in her own discreet way, Leila dispenses medical marijuana.

Leila emerges from the back. She seems a little surprised to see two white women in her shop but hides it well by putting on a more formal mask. She doesn't look regal today; she looks beaten down, which is saying something for someone like Leila. The hair is still an intense updo with the skunk stripe, and she's wearing Cleopatra eyes and the heavy cross earrings (a third pair!) that seem to be her stock in trade, but she looks disheveled, as if she slept badly. Jade has gravitated toward a small display of jewelry on the counter, letting me politely do my business.

"May I help you?" she asks.

I take a deep breath. "Leila, right?"

She nods, suspicious, eyes narrowed.

"I'm, um, Ángel Martinez's probation officer." I take out my badge and lay it gently on the counter.

She goes very still. I can feel her chest going up and down in a highly controlled manner on the other side of the counter. I look up at her from the badge, which I had taken to staring at briefly as if it might provide some kind of anti-anxiety remedy. I am not on my own turf and I am potentially dealing with way too much grief.

She hands my badge back to me. "I saw you talking to Refugio, at the hospital."

"So Ángel is your grandson?" I ask, gently.

She nods. "Claro."

"And Chuy?"

She goes white. "Mijo," she murmurs, all of a mother's pain streaking through that single hybridized word—the word, when uttered by someone like her in a crowded New Mexican restaurant, would cause every man in the room to turn around with startled faces. She might be near seventy and Chuy forty-six when he died, but she is still seeing herself as the mother of a toddler. I know; I have a hard enough time with Jack growing up, much less imagining if he died. I have nights where I dream we are still at the hot springs in Ojo Caliente and he is four and I am holding him on my lap. I know that chest, its barrel shape, better than I know just about anything on the Earth.

Jade comes to my side. "I have two kids," she says. "Nine and eleven. I hope I never have to see them go." She has taken her sunglasses off and Leila is squinting at her.

"Do I know you?"

Jade just smiles and shakes her head.

"Leila," I say, "So Ángel is Chuy's son? I need to know."

"Why? Of course he's his son." She's back to finding some room for her usual sharpness, the eyes daggering.

"Did you ever know Liza—"

She howls, ripping the scented air in two. "So many dead! Claro, I knew Liza! Ángel came here weeping! Sobbing! I gave him some medicine—" she waves her hand out to her shelves of herbs—"and he calmed down."

"Why did he come here?"

She stares at me like I am some kind of idiot. "Why? Why? He's my grandson!"

I roll my lips and try to hold her gaze. "Was he—did he want to find Chuy?"

She goes silent. She aligns some homemade lip balm next to the register on the counter. "He did seem mad at Chuy. He was ranting something about him before he calmed down."

I wait for her to tell me more, but I suspect I'm out of the shared territory of maternal grief and into familial secrets that involve gangs and drugs. If she's going to be on my side in the future, I feel I better step back now. "Okay," I say. "Thank you."

Jade has selected a jar of pinon balm and a pair of earrings. "Can I—may I buy these?" she asks delicately, and it is a perfect turn of the play. The tension eases and Leila smiles diffidently at her from under a veil of sparkly tears that etch her mascara'd eyes. She pushes back an errant blot of hair. "Claro," she says.

Jade smiles her million-dollar smile, the one that has made her famous, and takes out her purse. "I love your shop."

"Thank you," says Leila.

"Do you grow your own herbs?"

"Some."

"I noticed a sign on the door saying there would be a workshop here on growing herbs in two weeks."

"Yes. My aunt, who is very old but knows a lot, is going to lead it. It's a rare event. She's ninety."

"Wow," Jade says. "I, um, could I come? I have a small bed at home I'm trying to develop. My mother-in-law would like to come too, I think. She is a Japanese gardener."

I look at Jade in surprise while Leila puts her purchases in a small bag. "You'd be the only white girl. And don't go bragging this to all those wannabe Santa Fe new agers about this, okay?"

Jade looks happier about a public outing than she has probably been in a while. This is perfect for her. No one will know her and if they do, they won't care all that much. "Of course. Can I have a flyer?"

Leila tucks one of those in Jade's bag and we begin to leave.

"Ms.—Ms. Montgomery?" Leila says to my back.

I turn. "Yes?"

"Will he make it? Ángel?"

I can't stand the layers of anguish I hear under that tough, flamenco exterior. "I hope so. I really do hope so."

I let out a lot of air in the car. "Whew."

"That whole shop had such a heaviness to it."

I nod. "Too much old smoke, too many herbs, her."

Jade asks, "Do you have a picture of Chuy?"

I look at her. "Why?"

She smiles. "There was a photo of some people in a frame behind the counter. You were too busy talking to notice. If Chuy's one of them I might be able to tell."

"You're a born detective!" I start the car and call Larry. He's not answering, but I tell him what I now know: Chuy is Ángel's father, and Ángel is Leila's grandson, and Leila knew Liza, Ángel was very, very upset at her death, and seemed to tie it to Chuy.

"Crime," I fume. "It always comes to this. Entanglements. Blurred lines. Leila's got a great little store, but how many people has she protected? How many pounds of coke has she held for Chuy at one point? Did she join a gang? Fuck." I bang my hand on the steering wheel.

"It's just a good story," Jade says, quietly. "All good stories are full of this kind of pain."

I look at her. "Is that what you look for in a good script? All this complication?"

"It's real, isn't it? It's how it all works. My dad with his stupid klepto habits, Leila's birthright into crappy socioeconomic situations, her brilliance as a healer nevertheless."

I nod. She's right. We drive down Agua Fria until she taps my hand. "Turn left here."

"Why?"

"Great burrito joint. We need lunch."

I can't help but smile. She's right again; I am ravenous.

Chapter 15

March 3

Dear Diary,

Ángel swears he didn't know them. But I can tell by the way their eyes cut sideways at each other that they've done deals before. I've been around too many bad boys not to know. Sometimes the deal was me. The deal was me when I was four. The deal was me in high school. I'd let myself be the deal and then cut and cut and take pills and drive my parents nuts. They hardly talk to me now. They don't know what to say. I've burned too many bridges. But I'm not letting myself be the deal anymore. Sometimes I want to write my mother that—the one who adopted me after her three miscarriages, the one with that Catholic background who couldn't ever understand. I want to tell her, Hey at least I stopped being a whore for drugs. But even the word whore—she'd flinch. Like I cut her. Like it was a knife.

Like I am a knife. Ángel treats me the same. When I stand up to him he hits me cuz somehow I've hurt him. Baby ass. Get a life.

After the men left, these cholos with thick black hair, tattoos all over their knuckles—WSL—gang shit—after they left Ángel went to the laundry room. What are you doing? I ask. I'm following him. Why are you in the laundry room? You need to leave. You need to LEAVE. I'm hissing cuz Carmelina is napping and I don't want to wake her.

Turn the corner, he stands up fast, whirls around. He feeds me some bullshit line about looking for a shirt he left when I kicked him out.

I glare at him. "You killed her dog."

We just stare at each other. The dog's silhouette comes back to me and I start shrieking, still in this kind of hysterical whisper. I can't stop myself. "You killed her DOG!" Poor Barney, the little Jack Russell. I feel so guilty for that dog every time I think about it I can't stand it. It's worse than any black eye I ever got. Worse than any blow job I gave out for drugs. Worse—well, almost worse—than what I did at four. I feel so bad for Carmelina. She loved that dog. Her dog. I got her the dog. We were going to start a new life with that dog. She named him Barney after that stupid purple dinosaur on TV, but she loved that show. And then asshole here blows a gasket and fucking hangs him. I never let her see. I said Barney must have run off. That he's in doggie heaven if he died. She wants another dog. I don't dare. Ángel's not even supposed to be here. He's violating the restraining order.

"Go," I say. "Or I call the cops."

He blasts past me without a word. I feel like he'll be back. Like he hid something in the laundry room. I know I'll be looking for signs he broke in when I get back from work for the next month. Jackass. Him and his West Side "brothers." I can tell he's been drinking, and he smells like weed. I smile. I like this. I'll call the cops and have him picked up. Violation of terms of release while he waits to get sentenced for the dog, for me.

Hah. New me. No more suck it up Liza. Fuck you. I turn off the light in the laundry room. There could be a ton of coke in there and I could care less. I don't want to know. Less I know the better. And I don't care anymore. I don't want any temptation, except to dial dispatch and have him picked up.

I put the diary down. This was the last entry. She must have run out of room because it was written on folded up notebook paper, tucked in the back. On the top fold was a shopping list. Even if you unfolded it the list went on for half a page. Then Dear Diary. Still. Did the cops miss this? Seriously?

It's after ten. Jack is happily asleep in his old room, which I've turned into an office of sorts. He's so proud he got into UNM's architecture program for the fall, and my mama pride is enormous. I called Loretta and

Carmelina and Helena to come over; Margot couldn't come but said congrats; Larry and Clara came over; I left a text for Luis, and even one for Jade Kirchner. What the hell. Maybe she'd like to be treated as if someone else was the celebrity for once. We ate tamales and drank red wine and Jack—for the first time in over ten years—did not seem to be embarrassed to be in the company of his mother's friends. Ernest stayed by Carmelina's side the whole night. Now I swallow at this, in light of what I have just read. Carmelina lost her dog. How does Ernest know these things?

"Old boy," I say, scratching his ears. He lifts up from his slumber on the rug, snorfles. No one snorfles like a Dane. I laugh a bit. "Maybe we should loan you out to Carmelina."

No. I need Ernest. Ernest is mine. "How about we get her another dog? Maybe another you?" I don't think a new Jack Russell is such a hot idea. Too much of a reminder of loss. "Do you think Mama would be okay with an enormous dog like you?"

The more I think about it the more I think she just might go for it. Danes can be the mellowest dogs on the planet. They are just large. I would be willing to subsidize dog food if it came to that. I sigh. Tomorrow is Saturday. Jack might stay, or he might go back down to Albuquerque. He's got a little job, some design work for Isleta Pueblo. He has a house, a typical Albuquerque stucco thing off Carlisle to the south, in a block that starts nice (toward Nob Hill) and gets seedy (toward Gibson) by the time it's done. Albuquerque, where every neighborhood is "transitional" unless you live in the far Northeast Heights (lily white, or at least upper-middle-class), or the deep South Valley (bird's egg brown, through and through, and poor).

I know Larry doesn't like to work on Saturday, but there's a laundry room we need to go inspect. I find myself irritated at him to the point of nearly trolling him on text. I blow out air. Stop that. I get ready for bed. When I come back, my phone has just buzzed. I smile. Jade Kirchner has texted back, offering her congratulations.

"Larry," I say. We are at Michael's, after an exhausting game against a surprisingly good team from Chama. Last year they were terrible; it's as if they instigated a draft and got rid of all the bad players. We learned three of the new ones were from Cebolla, south of Chama on US 84. Onion, New Mexico. I prance out a little comedy routine in my head: *Hi, I'm from Onion, New Mexico. Home of the Fighting Valencias. Or maybe the Walla Wallas. Our onions have performance-enhancing properties you vatos can only dream of* . . .

Larry is halfway through his blueberry pancakes, and now he's been corralled by me midbite. "What?" he asks before finishing putting pancake to mouth.

"What're you doing today?"

He sighs, chewing. "This can't be good. You want me to do something, don't you? On Saturday. My day off." He turns to Clara, who's trying not to smile. "Support me, wife."

Clara just lets the smile rip and pats his hand. "I'm sure you can handle Ms. Montgomery," she says sweetly, and winks at me before turning away to sip her coffee. I almost burst out laughing; there's a dry wit to Clara that is so understated you'll miss it if you don't pay close attention. But when you catch it—ah . . .

"Yes, Larry, it's true. I want you to 'work' on Saturday. But c'mon, I'm fun, so it can't be too much like work." I bat my eyelashes.

He grunts. "Fine. What do you want me to do?"

I take a breath. "I have a laundry room I want to inspect."

"What?"

I explain the diary but refrain from suggesting that he and his men might have been better at clueing into this diary and what it said, especially in the days before her death, when Ángel was clearly going nuts anyway. But it became one more piece of evidence in a sea of blood, a sea of other evidence. They thought it was Ángel who killed her, so not much else to think. Then everyone got busy and things got sloppy—or that's what I tell myself.

He sighs. "Fine." He tells Clara to take the car; he'll get Nina Pushy Broad to give him a ride home in her truck. Clara nods and asks if he wants anything from the grocery store. Larry mutters something about "the good kind" of coffee and allows himself to be dragged off.

I grin at Margot, who has brought this Richard dude with her this time, and she grins back. We are long overdue for a sister chat about New Men, Fine Art, and the State of the World.

Liza's place is forlorn. The weeds are getting tall in the yard and its tumbledown appearance seems more so than the last time I saw it. New Mexican adobe-style houses—those that are lived in, belong to locals, and are small in size—walk a fine line between enchanting and dilapidated. Cover them in two inches of snow and they all look enchanting, fodder for New Mexican calendar art. But today is warm and windy, and the screen bangs on the front door.

"Who's the landlord here?" I'm wondering when it will be rented again.

"Guy named Frank Garcia," says Larry. "We asked him not to rent it till we're done."

I open the front door. "When are 'we' done?" I ask. "When do you guys give up?"

Larry shrugs. "Thanks to you, it's maybe getting hot again."

"You sound dismayed."

He looks at me. We're standing in the kitchen, about where Liza was killed. "I just—hell, Nina, we missed some shit. I hate admitting that."

I sigh. "Well, it sure did look like an open-and-shut DV murder. All the hallmarks. Escalation, she finally gets up the nerve to leave—seventy-five percent of all women murdered in DV situations are done in then—you know that better than I do. But, yeah . . ." I sigh. "The diary is interesting."

"How's Ángel doing?" Larry asks.

I think of Refugio's worn face, his bitterness. "Not great."

"Is he gonna make it?" Larry looks alarmed, as if he didn't realize how serious Ángel's injuries were.

"The doc says yeah, probably. But we may be talking brain damage."

"Fuck." Larry doesn't swear much. I put a hand on his forearm. "Let's go to the laundry room."

We trot to the door leading to the private part of the house—two bedrooms, a bathroom, and a little laundry/pantry area off to the left. "Her diary said he was very testy when she followed him in here, probably hid something, but she was done with it all and I think she learned what all good learners learn in the criminal world—the less you know, the better your chances."

We open and close the dryer, the washer, the cabinets above them. I sniff the Tide box long and hard, rip off the top looking for what—baggies? A spot of pure white powder at odds with the blue speckled detergent? But there's nothing. I lean over sideways and look behind the appliances. I squint at the dryer hose. It's not on right, the metal ring lopsided. "Larry, help me," I say as I push against the dryer to move it out from the wall.

He grabs the front until I tell him to stop, the hose stretched as far as it will go and still remain attached. I squat down and reach in to touch the ring. The slightest residue comes off it, lint with a little white edge to it. I work the ring off, and the hose accordions closer to the wall, emitting a cloud of lint as it does so.

"Damn thing was going to overheat soon, that much lint," says Larry.

"I know. I wonder why it wasn't blowing it all out through the vent?" I fish around in there, fingers catching on something rumpled and plastic not far from the mouth of the hose. "Larry, you got any tweezers? Something like that?"

"Did you find something?"

"Maybe. And I already got a wee bit of my hot little hands on it, so I'd rather preserve what we can of what else might be on there."

"You really think you found something?"

"Christ, Larry, find me some tweezers."

He snorts and goes off to the bathroom, comes back with garden variety Rite Aid tweezers. "Here, O Queen."

I grab them and glare at him. Why doesn't he take this seriously? Using the tweezers, I pull out a half-melted sandwich baggie. I wiggle it in his face. "A *baggie*, Larry." I feel triumphant but the truth is it could just be, well, a baggie. I peer closer at it. "I swear there is fairy dust on here."

Larry sighs and inspects it. We plop it in another baggie to take to the lab. "You could be right."

"Wait," I say, and run out of the room, out the back door. Larry trots after me. "Now what?"

I kneel next to the vent coming out of the house near the ground. Sprayed around the New Mexico dirt, like frost, is an aura of white.

"Well, well," Larry says. "well, well, well, well, well."

I can't say he's not taking this seriously now.

We have to wait for an investigative unit to get here. The afternoon is slowing the world down. We're tired from our soccer match and the one o'clock sun seems to spread a blanket of sorrow over the weedy yard. I sit on Liza's front stoop and wait for Larry to join me. He seems agitated and has gone silent, pacing the dirt and periodically looking down the road whenever he hears a car.

"Larry, you know those guys will take at least half an hour."

He just nods.

"Larry." I sit up. "What's the matter?"

He glances over at me. "I didn't want this to be about drugs."

I swallow. "Well, it turns out to be about drugs. Is that better than a DV murder?"

He shakes his head. "No, of course not." But I see his throat tighten and I watch a small trail of fear, like a ghost-snake, swirl across his face.

"Oh . . . you're thinking of Eva." I thought Eva was clean, going on a year now, but as I think about it, I see that Larry was preoccupied the whole soccer game this morning, not his usual aggressive self and missing a few plays.

"Did she relapse?"

To my surprise Larry's blinking back tears and working really hard not to let me see. "Probably. She disappeared."

"Disappeared? You mean, you can't find her?"

"Yeah."

"Jeez, Larry, you should have told me." But even as I say it, I know when a child messes up how quickly the parental wagon train circles—how much we fear judgment; how afraid we are that we've done something irreparable to our kids to make them behave as they have. I stand up and put a hand on his shoulder. "Larry, it's not your fault."

He shrugs and walks off, barely able to contain his anger. "I didn't want to see all this. I gave you the diary because Liza is too close to Eva's age, too close to her life with the shitty boyfriends and the crime." He's openly weeping now, in that silent way men do, tears running down his face into the warm April sun. "And it probably cost me catching Liza's killer." He kicks a stump and says "shit" under his breath, but I can't tell if that is because he hurt his toe or because an investigative van has turned into the driveway. He rubs his eyes with the palms of his hands, sniffs, gives me a hard stare as if to say *be cool, sister,* and shambles over to the lab people getting out of the van. Even in his postgame sweatpants, in my mind's eye Larry is always wearing cowboy boots and his boot-cut polyester dun-colored sheriff pants that are a half inch too short. Larry is always my cop hero.

Chapter 16

THE NEXT MORNING DAWNS so pretty my heart aches. The leaves are out on the cottonwoods in that rare shade of spring green, and the air is cool but not cold. A light little rain passed through the night before, leaving everything fragrant—at least until the sun rises higher and burns it off. I have to go to town for groceries anyway, so I pack Ernest into the truck at 7:00 a.m. and head to Upper Ranchitos Road. Like most Taos roads, it's semirural, with El Rio del Pueblo running along one side of it until it bumps into Millicent Rogers Drive. Millicent Rogers was a wealthy patron of the arts whose house is now a decent museum. I take visitors there and always find a book or two in the gift shop. People don't know I am a lifelong student of the Southwest; that I minored in anthropology and have, throughout the years I have lived here, found myself invited to Pueblo dances and homes, and hovered, rarely, in the backs of moradas stuttering along to understand the odd Castilian Spanish that still abides in pockets in northern New Mexico. Mostly this consists of old verb forms (*hiaga* instead of *haya*, etc.) and slurring of words together (*nomas* versus *no más*, though in my experience everyone does this), as well as mashing Indian with Spanish. The Pueblo have seven different languages, Tewa and Tiwa and Towa and even Keresan words inflecting all life in this great crossroads of a state.

I usually prefer trails for my church, for that silence nature demands, where the pips of squirrels are prominent, and the slight noise of the breeze causes me to stop on my jog to listen and simply breathe. But another secret to Taos is that town jogs can provide similar immersion in the senses through the smell of woodsmoke, the small noises of humans who are awake on a Sunday morning, and, for today, that combination of happy cottonwoods and wet earth beseeching me toward awe. I come here maybe three times a year, a route I keep in the back pocket of my Coat of Dreams, my Sacrament Bag. I have many of these routes, depending on whether I need the desert (the Rio Grande Gorge is good here), the mountains (the ski valley road, higher up), the cottonwoods, or what-have-you. This is one of the great beauties to the Taos area, this access to different accoutrements of worship.

Today Ernest and I find old bear poop from last fall, two *descansos* replete with loud plastic flowers and the usual crosses marking where their honorees lost their lives along this road; silver roses stuck inside the gnarl of a cottonwood at eye height. Artist that I am, I stop and probe these a bit for materials—they look like they're made of something flexible and plastic (mylar?) and spray-painted silver. But getting paint to stick to plastic is an art in itself, so I wonder about papier-mâché, but it looks more metallic than this, its edges sharper. I smile. Only in Taos.

A large olla, reddish and tilted on its side, marks the entrance to a long low ranch house that likely harbors a transplant with a little money; in an adjacent yard a field away two trailers and an unassuming stucco house announce the more traditional Hispanic arrangement, similar in all likelihood to Ángel and Refugio's set-up—generations and extended family sprawling on a single plot of long-held family land. Another New Mexican hallmark lurks in the yard of this place—an old pickup (Ford F-150, circa 1979) with a campaign sign from last fall still rigged in the back. RODRIGUEZ FOR DISTRICT NINE it reads. The paint is starting to peel and if I remember right Rodriguez lost, but it doesn't matter—pickups carrying homemade wooden signs in the back of them, usurping their usual tasks of hauling firewood or carpentry tools or hay, are part of what I covet about this place. The Koch Brothers and other Citizen's United oligarchic crap can't make much headway here. In one sense, maybe no one cares enough about New Mexico on a national stage to throw money at it, and in another, old nepotistic family ties make New Mexico famous for more tribal levels of political corruption. Ten to one, Rodriguez's cousin lives in the compound I'm jogging past. So what if it's not clean? None of it is ever totally clean. But it's its own form of local magic, like finding silver roses stuck in a tree.

I'm a bit sore from being brutalized yesterday by the Cebolla/Chama bunch, my hip squawking, so I jog and stretch and walk and stretch some more, doing the kind of "jog" I permit myself more and more in my fifties. The thing is how enjoyable I find this, and I curse myself for not allowing myself something less than gonzo-all-out-cardio-this-is-the-only-way-you-do-fitness workouts earlier in my existence. Middle age teaches a person many lessons in how to really do life, and with that comes regret for years wasted on trivial matters such as fear of fat, what other people think, and similar narrow definitions of How To Be. In this mood of quiet repentance, a church tolls distant bells toward early service, and Ernest and I get back to the truck for water and the organization of shopping bags. Safeway is next. Ernest will remain curled up on the front seat while I go inside, and he'll expect a treat for his behavior when I return.

A faxed report from the Santa Fe County Sheriff's Department awaits me on my desk Monday morning. I've arrived with a cup of local half-caf (*Au lait!* So much like ¡*Olé!* Or, in honor of Luis and flamenco, *Allez!* Heh heh. I boggle my own mind with how easily I am amused). I also have a nongluten chocolate brownie to nibble on later. I see the fax is the initial report on Chuy's homicide and force myself to put it aside long enough to organize my day. I check e-mail, my Outlook calendar, and phone messages. Court today at ten. Two revocations, one early termination for being a good kid. Three probationers paying a visit this afternoon. One's a guy so I will have to get someone else—maybe Jerry—to monitor the pee test for him. That is perhaps the most undignified aspect of this job, monitoring people through a one-way mirror as they pee into a cup. The litany of creative ways people have tried to work around giving us a sample of their own pee is truly inspiring.

I prep the documents for court this morning and shoot off a PSI to my supervisor to read and hopefully accept without too much ado. This gives me an hour to settle into the homicide report before trundling over to court. Roni's already texted me to have my phone ready for a serious round of Words with Friends should proceedings bog down.

The police report on Chuy is fairly bare bones. County sheriff's office received a call from a morning jogger along an informal trail near Las Campañas Drive west of the Relief Route. This is a ritzy development unaccustomed to dead Hispanic males showing up under juniper trees. A whiff of connective tissue floats by, a flashback to Ángel's art opening and Larry's syringe with remnant China White to it. The cognitive mind, with its biases and snap judgments, doesn't put two and two together, but my more intuitive brain—the limbic, as the addiction folks say—feels as if the same file folder has opened up. Why? I take a sip of my au lait and know immediately. Rich people's turf, poor Latino gang banger association with said turf. Man, I'm smelling some interesting rats though I try not to let my head get too far with a CSI plot involving movie stars, exclusive heroin, and socializing with the West Side Locos.

Male, midforties, overweight, scar on left side of face, another old bullet wound in abdomen to match the new one that left a hole in the back of his head. Prison tats. A once-lanky build with the potbelly of starving Suda-nese children or excessive years of beer hanging off him. Our man did not lead an easy life, but, well, he must have died fast, which also interests me. No signs of gang torture prior to execution. That was the term, "execu-tion-style" killing. In an odd way, that spoke of some sort of respect. Chuy was not some vato in need of serious realignment, his skin boiled off or his fingernails pulled or his hands hatcheted. He was worthy, simply, of a deal gone wrong. Either that, or the job needed to be quick and silent.

Ballistics, angle of shooting, all this will be added to the final coroner's report. Same with the formal autopsy. Next of kin, a Leila Candelaría y Martinez, mother, notified. Next of kin hysterical and claims no knowl-edge of why this death might have occurred.

I shut the file. I can just see Leila going prostrate with an admixture of genuine grief and her penchant for drama. It probably worked to get the cops away from her as fast as possible, so she could be alone in the safety of her shop. Maybe she would call her sisters and abuelas; maybe she would find the right marijuana edible to take the edge off all of it. She was one proud woman. And somehow, knowing the kind of pain that pride masks, my heart crumples for her. What would it take for that woman to stop holding up the world with her big hair and loud dresses and fancy silver? What would it take?

I am leaving the building at 4:45 when a tug on my sleeve finds me looking at Larry.

"Lab report's back. On our dryer baggie."

"That was fast."

"I called in a favor." He puts his hand up to stop me from what he knows will be a snide remark about cops and favors. "Don't even go there."

"Fine, deny me my fun. So, what'd the report say."

Now he's looking like a schoolboy with one juicy secret.

"What?" I say.

"You are gonna love this."

"I am?"

"Yup."

"Well—for chrissake, Larry."

"China White."

"What?"

"China White."

I blink. "Not coke?"

"Nope. Not coke."

"Well, well, well."

We're both silent a minute, looking out to town as the last of the sun disappears and the adobe-colored walls in the foreground take on a faux alpine glow. I breathe in deeply, catching a whiff of cedar smoke.

"What now?" I ask.

"Dunno. I called around to my Drug Task Force people. I had already told them about the syringe. They're looking into it but it's new to them too."

"What about Mucci?"

He looks at me. "What about him?"

I shrug. "I dunno either, Larry. But Chuy was shot in a wealthy area. The Westsiders of Chuy and Mucci's turf center around the 700 block of Alameda and San Francisco in Santa Fe, bleeding out to Agua Fria. Or that's one place anyway. They fight with the Hopewell/Mann version of the same gang, which is light industrial and out by St. Michael's. Not as 'nice' compared to the old Alameda area. That's being gentrified."

Larry's gaping at me.

I sigh, exasperated. "You know, that area behind the old Guadalupe church."

"Yeah, I know it. But you've been doing your research."

I strut a little. "I have! Besides, I have gangbangers on my caseload. Mostly Barrio Small Town, Taos local shit. But still."

He beams at me. "Go on."

"Well, Jade and I drove back toward Alameda from visiting Leila to find a burrito joint Jade likes, and I was amused to see gated adobe walls hiding sweet little casitas next to sagging houses with bars on the windows. There's even a manse along the river there that looks just like a Mexican cartel house. High walls, barbed wire, a kind of weird silence. A black dog looking out at us from the gate. Next to that house is something out of whatever the Santa Fe version of *Town and Country* is."

"*Pendejo Bonito*," Larry offers.

I whoop. "Oh, that's good."

We grin at each other.

"Jade," Larry says after a minute.

"What about Jade?"

"We-ll . . ." He squints into the cooling air. "Ask her if she knows any heroin-addled celebs, will you?"

"Good idea. She'd love it. Besides, she hit it off with Leila and is going to do an herb class with her in a weekend or two."

"That's rich."

"Isn't it?"

We shake our mutual heads and go home.

Get a Twitter account. This is from Jade.

Why?

So I can give you updates on Leila's class coming up.

Can't you just text me? Like you are now?

I suppose. But so old-fashioned. Besides, you can be #jackalope.

Huh?

Combo of your son's name and the antelope. No one will know! Whereas your number is traceable.

Jade is a born PI. I hadn't even thought of my handle, much less terms like "traceable."

What'll you be, then? #wannabecop?

Very funny. No. #barnpainter.

Ah. Like your disguise at Gert's.

Yes. I figure if it worked to evade the paparazzi it might be good enough for Santa Fe gangs.

It's possible the latter is smarter.

Possible. But I doubt it. They don't get paid to sniff me out like creeps in search of a photo op.

Tru dat. Oh, Jade, do you know any rich heroin addicts?

Wow. Now there's a question.

Sorry.

No, it's ok. But not offhand. Not my crowd.

I figured. But I had to ask. I'll fill you in before you go to Leila's.

Cool.

We don't text for a minute. I go brush my teeth. When I come back, I see *Night, Nina.*

Night, Jade. I text.

My light goes out. My bed is warm, a little lonely, but warm. The silence is deep, not even a snorfle from Ernest. Sleep falls fast.

Chapter 17

MODERN COMMUNICATION CONTINUES TO greet me in the office the next day in the form of an e-mail. It is from the Bayfield School District, office of the high school principal.

Dear Ms. Montgomery:

I hope this finds you well. I am writing in part on behalf of Liza Monaghan's parents and in part for myself. It has been over a month since her death and we have essentially been told that it is either "a cold case," or, as of yesterday, possibly a federal one. I am also writing on behalf of myself. Liza, when she felt safe enough to come out of her shell, was a force of nature. She had the lead in Hello, Dolly, *if you can believe that, and loved to act. I think acting gave her a way to express herself without fear of exposure. She was also a stellar scholar and writer. She was a National Merit Semi-Finalist and we had high hopes she could make Bayfield proud in college.*

You are the only contact I know. I assume you were Liza's probation officer, but I don't know. Her parents have expressed their heartbreak and failure to find closure for her murder but are demoralized by the lack of response from Taos area authorities. It does not take much to do them in these days.

Can you help out? Just FYI, they found a scrap of old journal before she disappeared. She had started hanging out with an older Hispanic male

*who was up here working a temporary construction project. There was a
younger one too. Anyway, I am in possession of this scrap, if it helps. Any
information would be useful, likewise, for us.*

> *Sincerely,*
> *Dave Schaefer, Principal*

I feel my throat constrict. Training on matters such as these does not
exist at Probation Academy. All I can see is the forlorn face of her two
parents, utterly flattened, at her funeral. My eyes are welling up, and I leave
my desk in search of a cup of tea. Jerry's in the break area, regaling Charles,
the roving sex offender PO, about his son's possible signing with UNM for
football. In his big bear linebacker way, he glances at me and says, "You
okay?"

Jerry has a heavy DV caseload and Charles sees things on people's computers I have no compulsion to know about. He has a PhD in psychopa-
thology (anthropological lens, officially, which I appreciate), and beetles
around Taos County and other parts of northern New Mexico in a Prius
armed hilariously with a machete, mace, hammer, and—most lethal of
all—the "Doohickey of Truth," which he plugs into people's computers
and discovers all manner of clandestine activity. He looks like an over-
grown hobbit, but his clientele learns to respect and fear him. He knows
more about sex offending than any person alive, I am sure of it. When he
retires, I anticipate a spike in sex crimes and a total inability on the part of
the authorities to know how to deal with it.

So am I okay? I smile. "Yeah," I say. "Congrats on your son."

Jerry can't help but strut a little. Football saved him, along with a grandmother and his wife, from a life of alcohol. He's the kind of Christian that
drives me nuts at the polls and in my heart, but his openness and gratitude
for simply being alive are lovely.

"Thanks," he says. I heat tea water and listen in on football talk. Jerry
loves coaching the Taos high school team and they have improved notice-
ably since he's been on the staff. It's spring now, though, so there is a lull in
game activity, which means he focuses on college recruiting and the NFL
draft.

Office small talk sometimes saves us more than we realize. I go back to my warren feeling lighter and give Larry a call, because I don't know what I can and cannot tell Dave Schaefer about Liza's case. I have to just page him as he appears to be out and about, saving Taos County from mayhem. I finish up a PSI and call the DA about charges in one case as I am confused as to why someone was pled down. Then I call Larry's wife to request the victim's statement for a file where that particular item is slow in coming. Then the phone rings for me and instead of Larry it is Dr. Singh. I sit up.

"What's the news?" I ask.

"I just wanted to let you know I think Mr. Martinez is going to make it."

"Meaning live, or have a brain?"

"I think—we're not out of the woods yet—but both. Preliminary testing looks good."

A giant slab falls off my chest. Shit. This just proves that I have living, breathing feelings for an artistic sadist. Loretta and Refugio slide by my eyes too. She will be relieved of guilt, and he will be glad if only to figure out how to beat the living shit out of him to teach him a lesson. "Is he awake?"

"In and out. Mostly out. But reflexes are good, he actually mumbles, vitals are strong."

"Wow."

"Yeah. Some people are lucky. I had an uncle who had a heart attack and no oxygen for twelve minutes. You would think he would have been a vegetable. But no, he's alive and kicking and developing software code to this day."

"Qué milagro," I say softly.

I can hear her smile again. "Yes. No other language says it quite so well."

I decide I am done for the day. I will come in tomorrow, but I have no court, no urgent PSIs, no afternoon clients. I e-mail my supervisor to let him know where he can find me and go home to my studio after stopping at Cid's for a tub of kale and chicken salad with pine nuts and sundried tomatoes for lunch. I let Ernesto out of my backyard, and we waddle down the street to the little studio. The sun is out and warm.

My statuette of Ángel-as-Dinosaur greets me. Today he reminds me of Howdy Doody. He appears to be dried but I will wait a day to fire just in case. I feel a tad sacrilegious about him now, but Ángel's screaming Christs come back and give me permission. I can do a series of Ángels, I decide. The next one will be forlorn, with a dog and a noose. Crap. I sit down and snivel. Why does everything set me to tears these days?

It is always a good idea to have two or three different projects going in my case, because one artistic mood will be too much to bear whereas another one will feel lighter, joyous. For this reason I switch back to my animals and get busy sketching out ideas for—of all things—mountain goats. William and I saw a small herd of them while hiking in Glacier National Park twenty years ago and they have the right level of humor for me this afternoon. They are not the funniest animals nor the cutest—no cat video material today, no adorable sea otters—but they look to me as if their sun basking on high shale mountainsides comes after an intriguing night at a goat bar where they held court without getting ripped and have come away after years of this with the wisdom and humor reserved for high lamas. Margot thinks I am snorting crack when I talk like that, at least at first. But then she slides into Art Appreciation Mode and gets it. We usually become hysterical pondering the karma of various beasts after this; in our twenties this hysteria was often fueled by pot.

I have moved on to considering how I want to arrange my pieces for Margot's show when the bell over the front door tinkles. I come out. Larry's belt squeaks as he adjusts his waistband and not for the first time I wonder if cops get heat rash at their midlines from all that leather and assemblage of tools. I couldn't stand having that much stuff on my waist.

"You rang?" He spies my black beauty of a horse and goes right over to it. "Wow," he says. "How much?"

"Seriously?"

He's nodding his head at it. "Yes and no. I can't afford it, you know that. But that's a good one."

I grin. "Thanks. I'll jack up the price by a couple hundred based on that appraisal alone. Margot wants it to greet people as they come in the door next Friday."

"Good plan. So . . . what's going on?"

"Hold on." I find my phone, pull up my work e-mail after punching in the requisite remote password and show him Schaefer's e-mail. "What can I tell him? I would like to call him back."

His brow furrows as he reads it. "Dammit, I'll call the Monaghans myself. Sounds like we haven't been keeping them in the loop much."

"Hard to when she is from a different community."

He nods. "Yeah. Albuquerque PD was never very good at letting us know about Eva when she was in trouble down there."

I put a hand on his upper arm. "Have you found her yet?"

He sighs. "We got a text. *I'm ok. Home soon.* She says she's in Isleta. I don't know what she's doing in Isleta."

Isleta is a pueblo south of Albuquerque. "Well at least she let you know where she is."

"I hope that's actually where she is."

Larry and Clara are long past the Control Freak phase of being the parents of a sometime addict. He assumes at all times she could be lying, without accusing her of it. Larry told me once he now and then checks his hopes at the door and assumes she'll be found dead one day so as not to get his expectations up. He goes to Mass every morning but from what he tells me it's more of a Heart Sutra practice of letting go, repeatedly, melting it all into the Christ at the altar. Clara is part Taos Indian and so sometimes he goes to the church there, because the Corn Mother up on the wall in front of him seems more appropriate, more about life than death. He has a good relationship with the Pueblo as a result, better than most county cops.

I turn things back to Liza. "Larry, Schaefer says the feds are involved now?"

"Maybe. The China White alerted them. That, and oh, Chuy's body was found just inside BLM land. Or just outside, depending on which map you use."

"You're kidding."

"Would I kid you?" He smiles ruefully. Like my office small talk, Larry is searching for lighter ground. Jurisdiction is a nightmare in New Mexico, between all the federal land, the tribes, the state, and private property.

"So does that mean we give up our case to some guys in crew cuts and ironed pants?"

"I hope not."

"So you'll call Schaefer? What are you going to tell him?"

"I'll tell him it may be drug related. That, at first, we thought it was domestic violence but now we think differently."

A thought occurs to me. "Oh, Larry . . . Carmelina is their granddaughter!"

We just stare at each other. How have we been so callous toward her family? And how have they not asked to see that child? Do they even know Carmelina exists?

Larry clears his throat. "Maybe someone should meet with them in person."

"You?"

He shakes his head. "Ramirez would never okay it. Any budget item not accounted for by his notion of what Taos voters deem appropriate will be shot down."

"Day off?"

He looks at me helplessly. "No," he simply says.

"Sorry," I say, thinking of Isleta Pueblo and the miles in between, and about Liza and Eva and wayward beautiful daughters. This will be too much for Larry, too close to the disaster he tries to prepare himself for every day at Mass.

"You?" he asks.

I sigh. "I could take a day of PTO. I have a lot of it."

"Okay, then. Tomorrow?"

"Christ. Call Tim and ask him for me. Otherwise I will have to feign illness or family emergency."

He unsnaps his phone from its thick, squeaky leather case and calls. Tim says okay. Then he calls Schaefer, who is not in, but whose secretary tells him it would be fine if Ms. Montgomery came in at 1:00 p.m.

tomorrow. Meantime, he says he'll give the Monaghans a courtesy call, so they warm to us and don't feel so helpless.

I brew him a cup of coffee and we go outside to the clay mess. Ernest lifts his head and thumps his tail three times at Larry before resuming his nap. Larry looks at the mountain goat sketches. "Nice," he says.

"Thanks. You done for the day?" The afternoon is stretching long and the shadow from the cottonwood over the arroyo behind my studio fence is shading part of the yard.

He shakes his head. "No, I'm on till seven."

I put my hand on his arm for the second time. "Larry, I forgot. Ángel is going to live."

"Really?"

"Yeah."

He finishes his coffee. "Well," he says slowly, "I hope he can tell us something sometime."

Chapter 18

IN MY BOOK, APRIL is the weirdest month in the southern Rockies. Drive south, and the fruit trees have all lost their blossoms, turning bright green in the strong winds off the mesas to the west. Spring in Albuquerque is six weeks ahead of the high valleys at the foot of the peaks. Taos is nearly two thousand feet higher than Albuquerque, and it often refuses to maintain truly warm days or bring trees into full leaf until May. It only gets worse driving up into Colorado. I head west on US 64, across the treeless sage plain and into the ponderosas that begin to show up at Tres Piedras. I'm now out of Taos County proper, into the gigantic mishmash that is Rio Arriba County. Tres Piedras (Three Rocks!) is one of those little spots in the road where if you are white of a certain generation you went to get lost; if you are Hispanic your family might still raise sheep in a multigenerational attempt to scratch a living from a land of high summer pastures and tumbledown winter barns. If you are lucky, you have enough feed to get them through winter. Much of the rest of the county is owned by the Forest Service with a big chunk of its western half the Jicarilla Apache reservation.

One of my favorite parts of this drive is the sudden shift out of Tres Piedras: where there were few trees, now there are many; where the road was straight and sunbaked and relentless, it now begins to curve and climb. I am up in the forest, winding my way up over a road that in winter is never open. It is not the highest road I have been on nor the most treacherous (Red Mountain Pass in Colorado takes that award) but in Poor State New Mexico a fairly nonessential highway like this one is not worth the upkeep. I pass the creepiest ranch gate in the state—a high wooden frame with a hanged scarecrow and threats of gun violence for trespassing attached to it. These people live in the middle of nowhere, so perhaps a shotgun by the door is not completely ridiculous, but the idea of regular marauders strikes me as a bit paranoid.

The top of the pass is almost treeless, not quite above timberline and graced with aspens on either side, although the aspens are sick, and have been for some time, with a fungus. Here, though, it is still winter, with remnant snowbanks and aspens that are still trying, full of bud but no furl. The bald top affords a terrific view down into the Chama Valley and up into the dramatic sweep of the south San Juan Mountains. Whispers of grizzly bear curl around these high palisades, the hidden meadows, the rarely seen brooks. The human population here has never been large, and the south San Juans are still a bit of a well-kept secret for backpackers. Terrifying thunderstorms hang up in the cliffs in summer, and for me this landscape speaks of Tolkien, holding both great beauty and the promise of malevolent intent.

Tierra Amarilla on the other side of the pass does nothing to dissuade this. It's known for a famous courthouse raid in the seventies by Latino agitators on behalf of local land-grant holders whose land was being sold out from under them via application of Anglo law that in no uncertain terms did not recognize land grants as viable entities. And it's a place where being white never felt particularly comfortable. I went into the Phillips 66 gas station there once when Jack was a baby, and because Jack was really, truly, an adorable baby, and because I was a proud mother and babies are usually universal conduits for favorable cross-cultural rapport, I smiled and jostled him as I paid for gas. The woman at the cash register held nothing but a cold stare. The other woman, younger, emerging from the restroom, just ignored Jack and me. I got out of there as fast as I could and, I must admit, I have never gotten gas there again.

If I had turned left down the Chama Valley instead of up, I would have found Cebolla, home of the Fighting Onions! I salute their soccer prowess and open into a smile as the valley spreads itself in front of me. I am heading north now, the grasses beginning to think of green, the river birch still bare but furred with a green nimbus. In Chama I stop for a burrito and coffee and then keep going through the forests into Pagosa Springs and finally to Bayfield. A narrow stretch between the north end of the Chama steppe and Pagosa embeds travelers in a close canyon of that remote country, and a part of me always wants to abandon the car in some small turnout and walk into the mountains, never to be seen again. A rare wildness encloses the road, reaches out and touches me even inside the steel of my modern conveyance, even at 60 mph.

Pagosa lures with its hot springs, but I promise myself a dip on the way back and keep heading to Bayfield. The high school is easy to find, just north of US 160 with the chunky gym and angular fascism of all modern public-school architecture. Home of the Wolverines. I park in the visitor slot and go inside.

Dave Schaefer is actually milling about in the reception area, an all-purpose venue full of attendance takers, parents picking up kids early, kids needing the nurse, visitors like me, and two competent women managing the whole mess behind a high counter. My guess is they know everyone and everything about the kids and their families. Dave is taller than I remember, a lanky Germanic sort with a ruddy complexion and unruly blonde-gray hair he keeps short. The goatee is gone. He brightens when he sees me and ushers me into his office a short walk down the hallway behind the reception desk. He thanks me for coming, offers me water or coffee, and asks how my drive was.

"Thank you for your e-mail," I say in return. "It jolted me and one of our investigators out of our narrow mindset."

He sighs wearily, tossing a file aside as if clearing a space on his desk might also clear his mind. "I understand that. Day-to-day business tends to overwhelm."

I smile. "That, and in Taos, so much of what happens stays there—local families who have been there forever . . . even the hippies have settled down. So it's a little insular."

He nods. "We have that too, but also a lot of retirees, and Texans who think they want to live in Colorado but have ties elsewhere, and recluses up at Vallecito Lake."

"And Hispanic construction workers—?"

He raises his eyebrows. "Yeah." He rustles his desk some more. "Here." He hands me a battered composition book. "This was really her senior English notebook but in the back are some journal notes."

A commotion ensues in the hallway, and I think I hear one of the reception women say something to the effect that Mr. Schaefer would call them when he was ready, but the door bangs open, and the ghost faces of Mr. and Mrs. Monaghan stare down at me.

Schaefer clears his throat. "I was—uh—going to say they would be joining us in half an hour, but, um, well, here they are."

Liza's mother extends her hand. "Patty Monaghan," she says. "This is my husband, Ralph." Ralph nods, shaking my hand far more limply and looking more or less as I remember him from the funeral.

Dave pulls up a couple of chairs lurking in the corner and we form a half moon around his desk. "I thought it might be a good idea if they talked to you directly." His voice is dry, and I wonder if they have been pestering him for a good long time now to the point where this is how he figured to best get them off his back. If so, he knows I am a sucker. But also, perhaps, a good soul. I shoot him a conspiratorial smile and turn to them.

Patty Monaghan leaps directly into the burbling cauldron. "What happened to her? No one will tell us anything. Some nice cop called us yesterday to apologize and I do appreciate that, but he didn't say much."

"Larry Baca?" I say.

"What?" She looks blank a minute, the crushed lines of her mouth turning down further. "Oh, yes. That was his name." She twists her hands in her lap and Ralph simply puts one of his on top of them. The hands settle a bit.

I try to reassure them with a smile. "Larry is the lead investigator. He is a good friend of mine. He knew I was coming up, so that's probably why he did not say much." Inwardly I throw Larry a snarky, *Thanks a lot, bud. Leave it all up to me why don't you?*

"Were you her probation officer?" Ralph asks.

I shake my head. "I am her—her boyfriend's. Ángel Martinez."

Patty goes pale. "Ángel was her boyfriend? Still?"

"Yes. How did you know him?"

"About a month before she disappeared, she started hanging around him. He and some relative? Older than he was? I met Ángel twice. He came to dinner. We—we were trying . . ."

She breaks off, crying. Ralph's own eyes well up and even I am doing my best not to start weeping. Patty takes a deep breath and says, "Did he kill her?"

I swallow. "We thought so at first. He, um, had a history of domestic violence with her." I see Ralph wince, Patty sigh, the latter not surprised anymore by this, the former still wounded. "So we thought it had escalated the way they do sometimes. She was doing her best to leave him."

"But now what do you think?" Ralph's voice is a pancake, monotone.

"Larry has said I can't go into details, but we think now it involves drugs."

"Apple doesn't fall far from the tree after all," Patty mutters. Dave sits up, offers her a tissue.

"I don't think she was doing them, Mrs. Monaghan," I say. "She was doing better than she had in a long time, since probably leaving here."

Patty Monaghan turns a beaky glare on me, all hawk and wariness. "How do you know, if you weren't her probation officer?"

I sigh heavily. I hate this. All the family secrets I hold in Ángel's several PSIs and court history, and now Carmelina's face dancing before me. It appears it is up to me to unshoulder these burdens and drape them on their laps. "Patty—can I call you Patty? You have a granddaughter."

Patty and Ralph go very still while Dave's ears rotate like a fox sniffing prey. I pull out the two pictures I have brought. "Her name is Carmelina," I say softly. "She's four now, and a delight."

Patty and Ralph look at the dark-haired girl with the big brown eyes and round cheeks. She has Liza's freckles and her curly hair with a hint of red where the sun touches it. I've chosen smiling pictures, ones I took two days ago and printed off my phone. Ernest helped me immensely here.

"Whose dog is that?" Patty asks, as if this is all she can muster.

I almost laugh. "Mine. Carmelina and Ernest Borgnine—that's his name—are in love with each other."

Dave guffaws. "You named your dog Ernest Borgnine?"

"He's huge!" says Ralph. But he also sees Carmelina reaching up and draping her arms around his brindled neck, and Ernest turning to lick her.

"He's the most harmless beast on the planet. Looks like a tiger but has the heart of a lamb. Carmelina is staying with a neighbor of mine, Ángel's aunt."

Dave leans over to look at them. "Is Ángel's aunt—?" he asks, not wanting to wade into offensive territory.

I put my hand up. "The best mother creature you could imagine. She is sick over Ángel. She tried to care for him when he was young, on and off, when her sister couldn't. Her sister . . ."—my brow furrows—"I think her sister was probably a lot like Liza's birth mother. Drugs, bad parenting, bad men."

"So Ángel was a foster kid too?" This is Patty.

"Yes, in and out. But no permanent placement like Liza had with you. Loretta—that's my neighbor—would care for him, then Lolo, Dolores, his mom, would take him back, then she'd fall off the wagon again, and Loretta would take him, or the state would, and so on till he was in his teens. And then I think he just ran away. Lolo died three years ago of a drug overdose."

Ralph sighs. "Same story, isn't it? Same damn story."

I attempt a smile. "Yes. But I feel—I want you to know—Liza really was doing better. She had a job with Head Start helping little kids, which meant she could take Carmelina there with her. And she'd left Ángel. She was clean and making it on her own. I think she has you to thank for that."

Patty Monaghan buckles, the hard prairie face crumbling. Ralph's own chin is quaking. "We tried so hard," she whispers. "We tried so hard."

In their own way, I know they did. I try to keep at bay the questions about why they did not follow through on more family therapy, more skills building, but I know the answer. Patty Monaghan has more stiff pride than an Arabian horse. Ralph more stoicism than a mule. They were going to trust their willfulness and good intent to carry the day. Having read up on Reactive Attachment Disorder, having seen several women in my office since who probably fit that bill as toddlers, I know they had no idea what they were up against. Liza had healed herself more than they realized.

Ralph looks at me. "So, if she wasn't doing drugs, then why was she killed?"

I hope Larry doesn't shoot me, but he did say the bottom line was just not to mention the China White angle. "We found a stash in the dryer tube."

"The exhaust?"

"Yes."

"What led you there?"

"Liza. In her journals. I think Ángel pressured her into keeping them. The drugs, I mean."

"Crap," says Ralph, flashing anger. "I want to kill him."

I close my eyes. "Well, he nearly did that for you."

"What do you mean?"

And then I have to go into the hanging, and his current condition, and my growing belief, despite all his hideous behaviors, that he truly had a heart for Liza.

After it's all said and done, a dense silence descends in Dave's office. The football trophies gleam incongruently on the window behind his desk. His PhD in Education diploma squats on the wall to my left. An office plant says nothing.

Patty finally turns to me. "When can we see her? When can we see Carmelina?"

Some ray of hope glides through me. I am envisioning a Loretta Family Picnic production full of tamales and horchatas on a warm day. Then again, Mama could be wary they would take Carmelina from her. I sigh. I'm going to have to negotiate. "Soon," I say. "I hope very soon."

I give them my card, promise to keep them updated, and leave them to their smashed hearts, there in Dave's office in one small town in southern Colorado.

It is only later that I read the scrap in her composition book. It's at the back, dated two months after graduation. *Ángel Martinez and his dad, Chuy. Ángel Ángel Ángel. Working on the road up on Wolf Creek Pass. Mom has invited them to dinner. Ángel! Muy guapo, as he has taught me to say. He wants me to go to Taos with him. I want away. He showed me a shrine up the pass, all plastic flowers and the Virgin Mary. I love it. Love the Spanish. Love his dark skin. I want away. I want away from this stupid white world.*

Don't we all, I think. Sometimes I feel that colonial white b.s. has so permanently disfigured the world that it is hopeless. I'm now in my favorite 104-degree tub at the hot springs. The river mists by. I remember the rumor about the springs being a money-laundering operation for some Florida drug ring. The DEA has flown in a couple times. I roll over.

Can't get away from it, Liza. It's everywhere. Wherever you are now, has the brown world become just as bad?

Chapter 19

THE REMEDY FOR DESPAIR is always time outside. Home from Bay-field, I find Margot and we go out early to explore the Gorge. Here I (at last!) learn about the mysterious Richard and am revived by simple walking and good company. I am driving down to Santa Fe to see Luis after his rehearsal tonight—he told me to just let myself into his house until he gets back. Having left a hiked-out Ernest with Loretta and treated myself to a fine repast at Dave's Burgers (hey, I hiked six miles today), I now take my laptop into Luis's. I find in my inbox a forwarded video attachment from Rick Mucci labeled "Chuy-funeral." Ah, I think. Good show, Larry. Mucci is the perfect neighborhood spy. I curl up on Luis's comfortable sofa and start watching.

The first thing I think is how quickly New Mexico can go from completely enchanting to just poor in every way—poor in water, poor in soil, poor in human wealth. Outside the church the wind sprays tumbleweeds and even though the cottonwoods are green not much else is. Patches of grass grunt into being at the base of the trees but the lot around the church is desolate. The camera cuts and shows up next at a dusty cemetery. People are not as dressed up as I would have thought. White shirts and jeans seem to be the costume for most of them. The pallbearers wear suits, and Leila is of course in deep finery. She can make a black dress look like Carmen Miranda's show outfit. I scan for the purple colors of the WSL. I don't see any. The women have straight mouths and take their teens almost by their ears, and I get the feeling that one wrong move by some hapless fifteen-year-old son would have had him shining his mom's shoes till the cows came home. Still, if it had been gang related, I don't see how the abuelas could have stopped things.

Who are the pallbearers? They are built like Chuy and Ángel, lanky and slight. Leila leans on them and then I see then the resemblance—the Aztecan nose, the fierce gaze. Her other sons. I lean closer, stop the video when I can get a clear shot of them. Larry says the Santa Fe cops are blowing up stills from the funeral tape and will get them to him. There are a few cops outside, just to convince any gang member loitering around not to act up. One cop stands next to Mucci. He has the rotund build of Pueblo mixed with old Spanish (conquistador Juan de Oñate was short, I tell you) and I figure he was a neighborhood kid too, another playground acquaintance. It is amazing how strong those ties are, ties made when we are seven or eight and have so little in the way of maturity going for us, so much growth left to do. Maybe that is why they are so strong—it is what we have at that age, period.

The camera pans to two men on the left of the coffin, in the first row surrounding it. The pallbearers are taking red and white flowers, one at a time, from grieving audience members, and putting them on the coffin. I sigh. This slow floral build-up will take a long time. I squint at the two men. Older, sixties? Haggard faces. Tattooed teardrops out of one eye. Broken nose on one, knife scar on the other. They are wearing leather jackets with patches on the front. I stop the film to look at the patches. I see the unmistakable yellow bar with red stripes and green trim that says Vietnam vet. Both of them. Then another, diamond-shaped, that says "1%" in black letters on yellow. I will have to wait for the blowups from Mucci for more detail, but I'm intrigued. Who are these guys? I rewind to their faces, looking on their necks to see if there are prison tats. Maybe. Hard to tell. I can't see their hands, because people with flowers keep bending over in front of them, getting in the way.

The women have started to keen as the last of the flowers are laid on the coffin lid. They are leaning over the casket, sobbing. Leila leads the way, but there is another woman, younger, who keens with her. Leila's daughter? How many aunts and uncles does Ángel have on this side? A couple men wipe away a tear. The two men in leather jackets remain implacable. Finally, the procession of flowers ends, the coffin is lowered by the men into the pre-dug hole. I am puzzled—I guess Mucci didn't film the actual service, with the priest and the eulogies. Maybe that isn't done. I don't know. Or maybe holding up a cell phone during Mass is just too obvious. Here he can pan around as others are doing, taking photos.

With five seconds left to the video the two older men in leather jackets turn their backs to the camera. The full regalia of the Bandidos outlaw motorcycle club hits me in the face, stitched into the leather of the jackets. I groan and stop the film again. The top, curved patch, or "rocker," says Bandidos. The middle patch is a fat Mexican in profile, with bandolier, sombrero, serape, boots, one hand holding a machete, the other pointing a gun. I've heard shady talk regarding the Bandidos but never had one on my caseload. Now I am going to have to research just what drugs the Bandidos run, and who they are, and what their gig is. The "1%" niggles at me—something about living outside of the law—and the bottom rocker on the back of the jacket clearly says New Mexico, a claim of territory these guys take ridiculously seriously.

I text Larry. *Bandidos???*

I stare at my phone, but Larry is silent. Like a sane human being, he is probably at home watching baseball with Clara and trying to forget about his day job.

I take my cue from this, settling in to read a book till Luis comes home. I'm fast asleep when he finally does.

It occurs to me with a jolt on Sunday morning that Gert Kahn might throw a fit if she finds out about Margot's show. I did agree to let her represent me, after all. I relax a little when I realize I have signed no paperwork, but I am due to deliver Jade's antelope later this afternoon (or rather, Jade's "men" will come pick them up) and it would be common courtesy to let her know about the show. It is a bit disconcerting to realize I am not quite a lone operator anymore. My admired black horse head floats by and I groan. Gert will drop me like a hot potato if I don't give her first dibs, or a cut.

Luis rolls over and nuzzles my ear, murmurs, "*Buenos días, señora.*"

"*Hola*," I say, my Spanish lurking in the part of my brain that is distinctly unawake. I am staring at the ceiling.

"What are you thinking about?"

I tell him about the show, and Gert Kahn, and how odd it is to feel some success.

"You know Gert Kahn?" he asks.

I turn my head and look at him. "*You* know Gert Kahn?"

He laughs. "All of Santa Fe knows Gert Kahn. She's one of those City Different icons."

"So you don't *know* her know her."

"Not really. We have met." He props up on an elbow. "Now I remember, we met after my show was first well reviewed."

"She makes it her business to keep tabs on things like that."

He puts a hand on my shoulder. "I know what you mean about success. It's strange. Flamenco is really an obscure art form by an oppressed people. My aunts danced in the caves of Sacramonte above Granada."

I roll over and face him. "Luis, why did you come to America?"

His face darkens. "I was a child, *querida*."

"Oh. So your parents came."

"Yes. My father was a dance professor, if you can believe such a thing exists. My mother was haunted by something in Spain she never talked about. They were both children in the Spanish Civil War. I don't think some things, some—how would I say—parts of themselves, their families—survived." His language halts not because he doesn't know English but because the rift between that and Spanish and what his emotions want to convey is too strong.

I smile gently. "Did your father teach flamenco?"

He nodded. "A bit. But mostly modern dance with a Spanish twist."

"Oh. But someone in America wanted him."

"Yes. In New York at first, then New Mexico."

"Wow. So you came to New Mexico—when?"

"I was fifteen."

"Oh!"

He smiles. "So much for my exotic Spanish appeal, hmmm?"

"But you still speak English with a, um, ESL style, if I can say that." I figure if he went to an American high school, he will know what ESL means.

He seems to as he chuckles. "Some people keep an accent all their lives. Linguists think this is an 'identity posture.' Too, I went back to Spain and married there, stayed for twenty years."

Now my face clouds. "What happened to your wife, Luis? You know what happened to William."

He turns bittersweet and kisses my forehead. "She had breast cancer. Ten years ago."

"I'm sorry," I say into a small silence. The room ticks, the cream-colored walls and red rugs in muted morning shadow.

He shrugs. "We married so young. I was twenty-two. I wanted to go back to Spain. I felt there was unfinished family business there. I was a young man who wanted an identity and that was where I felt my parents had left my identity behind."

"The United States is bad at making people feel as if they can have identity."

He nods. "In a way, that's true."

I snort, remembering a joke. Before I scowl at myself for always deflecting to the defense mechanism that is humor, I begin telling it. "What's the difference between yogurt and America?"

He smiles. "What?"

"One has a culture!"

I laugh hysterically at my own bad pun, and Luis manages to show he thinks I am funny too. We end up in a flirtatious bout of wrestling before I realize he is in way too good a shape for me to keep up with him for long. I flop back on the pillow, and he starts kissing me. I close my eyes and let him. It is magnificent.

Breakfast in Santa Fe is never the same for me after the Guadalupe Café more or less closed, but we make our way to an obscure veggie place off Agua Fria that turns out to be quite good. I have gone for a morning run along the river, passing by the house I am convinced harbors drug lords, the graffitti'd park benches, the drizzle of water crawling down the streambed below me that is the remnant of the Santa Fe "River." I remind myself that snowmelt has yet to happen in the high country and that the drizzle will pick up. On my left, running upriver toward the mountains, across Alameda, the outskirts of the plaza creep up, with the faux adobe flanks of large hotels haunching in the morning sun, and import stores run by Pakistanis lining the sidewalks. Back home at Luis's, I shower, and we head out, arm and arm, to our repast. I admit it is fun to be romantic again, to feel I have a partner. I think Luis feels the same way.

Afterward we swing by Ohori's for coffee I can't get in Taos, and then bother to see if Gert Kahn is in at her gallery up the street. It is eleven, and the gallery on Sunday is barely open. But Gert is not in, and I just figure I will call her. We end with a nice walk along the old rail tracks near Site Santa Fe, take in the art there, and agree Luis will come up next week to Taos. This is beginning to feel almost too comfortable, but while driving home, instead of guilt I feel that our mutual long experience in marriage has made it easier for us to slip into a partnership state—as if William and Luis's wife (Rosalinda, I learned) have given us an odd sort of blessing, a teaching on the arts of subdued loving that do not involve drama, hardship, or a replay of abandonment fears we worked out with them a long time ago. I find myself crossing my fingers as I drive past the spot where I saw the coyote in Pilar. *Please, Trickster Dog, don't pull any shit.*

I realize with some trepidation that what Luis and I are likely scared of the most is that our significant other will get sick, will die. This is the abandonment we must now heal together, if we continue as we are. Like the fallen leaves nourishing the next layer of soil, the cycle never ends. This has, at times, exhausted me. But today I simply feel an odd poignancy, a kind of grace. William lightly pats my shoulder, and I smile through the increasingly familiar arrival of small, strange tears.

Jade shows up at my shop at 4:00 p.m. with two burly men, a pickup truck, and a child. The two men have their own truck. The child looks to be about nine and is a shy boy with brown hair and slightly Oriental eyes. I seem to remember something about Jade's husband being Japanese or some such. I give a low whistle and Ernest dutifully emerges from his dog bed behind the counter. The boy's eyes grow wide.

"This is Ernest," I say, squatting to his level. "Who are you?"

"Ray," he says, his voice a scratch.

"Named after my husband's father," Jade says. She bends down to him too. "Ernest is a Great Dane."

"He won't hurt you," I tell him. Ernest has sat on his back legs and is patiently waiting for instructions.

Ray reaches out to him. Pets his ears. He looks up at his mom and smiles just a little. "Methuselah is half his size!"

I arch my eyebrows at Jade, as if to say, *Methuselah?*

"Definitely not named after my father-in-law," she laughs. "He's some kind of large terrier."

"Oh dear," I say, turning away before my cackle turns into full-fledged laughter. Jade and I run the danger of hysteria again.

"Would you like to meet him?" Ray asks, saving us from ourselves.

"Methuselah? Sure!" I say. I look at Jade. She nods.

"Help us load your art and come eat dinner with us."

"Are you sure?"

She looks annoyed. "Of course, I'm sure. I am not made of porcelain just because I'm a famous movie star."

"Sorry," I say. "I just—um—want to respect privacy and all that."

She stops all motion and looks at me. "Can we please—*please*—just be friends?"

I blush. "Of course. I would love nothing more."

I have BubbleWrapped my antelope and the men are securing them in the back of the pickup. They have brought packing blankets and are now wrapping them in these and securing all of it with bungie cords and nylon straps. It is an odd thing to watch three of my pieces leave my studio and shop at once. It is even odder that this sale is changing my entire artistic existence. I hover like a mother hen as the men work. To my relief, they seem to care for the pieces as if they themselves were artists and mothers. I learn they are Nando and his nephew Chris, and that Nando and Jade's mother-in-law do something with gardens, with landscaping, in some sort of joint love-hate venture that nevertheless produces gorgeous outdoor spaces.

"You'll see," says Jade, watching the two gently lift an antelope head, unrecognizable in wraps, into the bed of the truck. They position the bungee cords around it, then the nylon straps, securing it to the little hooks built into the side of the truck for activities like this. This being Taos, Jade will live down a dirt road with a dirt driveway. I anticipate some forty-minute drive up toward Hondo or something, but to my surprise she gets on Rim Road above the Rio, turns right up the valley, then right again into a (dirt) lane that takes us to a gate. It's a fine New Mexico gate, coyote fencing gone upscale, with insets of willow weavings that in turn have sandstone insets of horned gods and other figures from petroglyphs nearby. Blissfully, no inset sports a bastardized Kokopelli. I need to know the artist who does the willow weaves. I love them.

Beyond the gate immense cottonwoods line a lane, undergrown with clematis and wild roses. I squint. They look like sand plums, which usually only grow in river bottoms. This is also true of cottonwoods, and clematis does best around here on north slopes. I turn to her in the driver's seat. "Where do you get your water? It's like living in the bosque here!" *Bosque* means river bottom, the vegetation in low wet places. Other parts of the country have coulees and bayous and creeks. We have bosques.

She smiles. "I learned long ago from my con man daddy that the one thing you look for if you have any money at all to spend on land in the West is water rights."

I smile. "Right. Fuck the house. Do you have first ditch rights?"

"Correct. The house was a rotting adobe when I bought it twelve years ago. I was pregnant with Sheila—that's my daughter . . . you'll meet her—and so Yuki, my husband, he did most of the work."

"He's Japanese, right?"

"Part. His mom's side."

"Ah." I run up against my reluctance to pry once again. This is so unlike me. One thing probation work teaches you is to cold call everyone, ask questions, dig deeply into people's shit.

She maneuvers the pickup over one last rut and the road opens to a beautiful two-story, territorial-style adobe with a pond out front and sculptures strung like jewels out on a meandering lawn-rock garden that flows around the entire house. "So lovely," I say. "You've done a fantastic job."

She smiles. "Remember what I said about Nando and my mother-in-law. She was a Japanese gardener. She lives here now, is the caretaker when we are gone to LA or New York."

"I get to meet her too?"

Now Jade blushes. "Of course. She keeps Ray and Sheila in line, right?" She tousles Ray's head, which is stuck between ours from the back seat.

"Yes, ma'am."

"So you don't have a personal chef and your own masseuse and a trainer and permanent make-up artist on staff?"

She rolls her eyes. "Not here." And then she snorts. "I have a chef in LA because when I'm there I'm making movies or meeting with execs or otherwise completely overworked 24/7, so it helps. And the kids have a nanny there; it's true. But they only come out to LA when there is no school."

I turn to Ray. "Where do you go to school?"

He gets all shy again. "Montessori. In Taos."

"Excellent!" I say.

The truck stops. The men get out of theirs, having followed. Jade tells them to take her truck with the antelope and drive cautiously around to the back of the house. She'll meet them there.

Jade and Ray and I go in the front door and straight out the back through what looks like a magnificent living room I will have to greedily consume later. The back opens to a wider lawn and gravel space that makes use of water wisely but provides ample space for garden parties or family frolicking. Lilacs line the fences in places, a huge cottonwood dangles over the largest lawn expanse—smart use of shade to preserve greenery, I think—and roses bask off the heat of the back of the house. I am smitten. She has an elaborate sculpture made of broken terra cotta pottery, full of holes and half-arcs and little burrowing opportunities. "Bee house," she says.

"Huh?"

"That's designed to attract bees."

"Really? Wow." It's the most elegant bee house I have ever seen. Not that I understand bee housing beyond stacked white boxes in the middle of fields that to me always seemed ridiculously susceptible to bears.

There are several Buddhas strewn about, in prayer or serenely gazing, and I am sure they are worth a fortune, as well as a wind chime from the local general store (I love them); a line of Day of the Dead skulls and skeletons laughing and dancing along one wall above the roses, and lovely wrought-iron benches made into vine-backs and aspen leaves and sunflower arm rests. A venerable juniper in one corner hosts a small tree house for the kids, and at its base a gravel area with slide and one swing. Three quaking aspens guard the northeast corner, along with combed gravel and a solitary rock here and there—a Zen garden within a garden.

I find myself breathless. "Where do the antelope go?"

Jade sees the men at a side gate and nods to them. "Nando," she says, "what do you think?"

Nando, overweight with beautiful, weathered eyes, looks out at the garden. "One here," he says, pointing to one side of the patio.

Jade nods. "I was thinking the other two may be a pair, as if they were talking or grazing or something. Not far from the other one."

Nando nods. He walks silently over to the opposite side of the patio but in sightline of where the other antelope would be. He steps slightly off the stone onto some gravel, a small pinon and a mountain mahogany just behind him. "Here."

She grins. "Yes!" She turns to me. "Meet Nando," she says. "Nando, Nina. Nina, Nando."

His eyes remind me of wise dog eyes. His brow moves from one woman to the other, slightly worried, assessing, nodding. "Nice pieces," he says.

"Nice placement ideas," I say.

Jade smiles. "Nando and Mika—that's my mother-in-law—get in garden spats all the time. But they love each other. Right, Nando?"

Nando grunts as only men with bellies and a certain age to them can grunt. But there is a shy smile edging the corners of his mouth. He licks his lips. "Let's get these set up."

I sit back while Nando, whom I learn is the formal gardener, and Chris, who turns out to be his (somewhat errant) nephew, and Jade place the antelope. A small, silent Japanese woman comes to the patio doors and just watches. Ray plays in the tree house with Methuselah at his feet (a rough version of an Airedale, it seems). Ernest, who has cautiously stepped into this with me, sits at my side. The afternoon sun is long, the day cooling. Nando arranges the antelope so that they look like part of a herd, as if they all know each other, two of the heads in a pas de deux with each other on pedestals, the other one on stone plinth gazing at the others.

I swallow. This is brilliant. Then the small Japanese woman comes out onto the patio and ever so slightly moves the solitary antelope. It makes all the difference. The entire tableau falls into place—these antelope have turned the garden into their meadow, their home. Nando and Mika exchange glances. Ernest pushes his head up into my hand. A magpie flies in and chirps loudly at Methuselah, who is suckered in and runs after it, barking.

We all laugh.

"Come inside," says Jade. "Let's eat dinner."

Jade in "real life" is a small woman with bird bones. She tells me most movie stars are small. Somehow the camera likes them better. She is lanky by small-woman standards, so the effect is tall and thin even though she is 5'4" or so. Her wide smile transforms her face in a profound way, and it is there I see what compels people to watch her on screen—it is as if her heart had unfolded itself in front of you. That sweet vulnerability, that prettiness, combined with a no-nonsense set of eyes and a way of wearing vintage dresses and wedge sling-backs, harkens back to the supple tough-ness of forties stars, of Bacall or Bergman. Today she has no makeup on, her hair is back, and she is almost plain.

The table we eat at is a long, rustic, picnic-style wooden beast. I feel we are eating in Tuscany, especially with the French doors leading out to the garden and the vines overhanging the back porch, looping around vigas and down the carved wooden supports. Mika and the kids produce udon with a sweet ginger broth, seaweed, mushrooms, and chunks of fish. My eyes widen. Now I could just as well be in Tokyo. Yuki is a handsome Japanese American hybrid, and they explain they met fifteen years ago on a movie set.

"I was the cameraman," he says.

Jade rolls her eyes. "He was second in command behind the cinematographer."

"Do you still do cinematography?" I ask him.

He glances at Jade. "Now and then. When a friend asks me too." Jade purses her lips and smiles a small, pert little smile.

"Would that 'friend' be your wife?"

He nods. "We work well together."

"I like . . . he does things with a camera that I haven't seen with anyone else." She's blushing a bit.

"Are you feeling vain?" I ask, in my usual cop-humor way. I have slipped into assuming I can talk to her like Larry.

She giggles. "Exactly. Like you would think I was a total egotist to give a crap what a camera does for me."

Sheila, who is eleven and on the brink of sassy adolescence, smirks. "Well, duh," she says.

Yuki shoots her a laser. "Watch it, honey."

Sheila rolls her eyes and slurps noodles ostentatiously.

I put a brief hand on Jade's wrist. "I saw a movie once—*My Week with Marilyn*—with Michelle Williams as Marilyn Monroe and Kenneth Branagh as Laurence Olivier."

Jade nods.

"That taught me a lot about the art of acting in front of a camera versus stage."

Yuki nods. "'Specially Michelle."

"I was far more interested in that than all her sexuality," I said. "As an artist, I mean. And I completely felt for Olivier." I blush. "Sorry. I may be out of my depth. But I like talking about other art forms because it helps me see my own better."

Jade smiles. "That is right on. But yeah. I have always worked better with cameras than on stage."

"It was as if the camera is its own animal. And you have to know how to work with it."

"You train it; it trains you," says Jade. "And then you have to have someone like Yuki behind it."

I flash on a video I saw on Facebook about a guy who works with lion conservation, lounging with them as one of them decides to roar and take over the video for a bit. Yuki is the lion tamer. I turn to him. "So . . . if you don't work except for a 'friend' anymore, what are you doing now?"

Yuki's face crinkles up in that cute-rugged way only certain Asian men can pull off. Both he and Jade must be early forties, the age when laugh lines are charming. "You know the Taos School for Film and Camera?"

I cock my head. I'd seen an ad in the local independent but because I have no school-age children anymore and they don't offer free training for probationers, I had not been paying much attention. "Is that you?"

He nods, beaming. This seems to be his great pride. "We sent three shorts to the Durango Film Festival last year. This year we have one in Telluride! All by kids!"

Sheila, done with her bowl of noodles, turns to him excitedly. They sit next to one another, and like oldest girl children everywhere—hi Jade, hi me—she is clearly daddy's own. "Dad and I are making a feature length! It's so cool!"

"So even though he tells you to watch your mouth, you love him." My own mouth is twitching. I am pulling coyote magic.

She looks at me with cool eyes, appraising. She can sass, I can sass right back, is what I am saying. She decides to get that. She smiles the same pert smile as her mom and twists her shoulders up and down in some kind of updated disco move designed to taunt. "Duh," she says.

Ray scowls, fed up with his sis. He seems to take after Mika, who is quiet and deeply observant, at the end of the table. I wonder what she has suffered given her exodus from Japan and her widowhood. Ray Sr. apparently died three years ago. Later, on the back patio, the night feathering in, I ask Jade if her own parents are still around.

Her expression constricts in the dusk. "My mom is in DC, where I grew up. We don't have much to say to each other. I don't know where my dad is. I think he is old and not doing well. But I don't know where he is."

"What happened to him?"

She faces me. "Nam," she says simply. "Nam and heroin."

I go still. Bandido men flash before me. That and the fact that I had glibly asked if she knew any rich heroin addicts the other day. I swallow.

Her turn to put a small hand on my arm. "It's okay you asked about heroin. You didn't know."

I turn to her. "I know. But I didn't mean to cause you pain."

She gazes at the antelope off to her left, barely discernable now in the oncoming dark. "You didn't. Your antelope make for far greater joy."

We smile at each other and then she takes me and Ernest—who as always has made himself at home with the kids—home to our little casita.

Chapter 20

MONDAY MORNING LARRY SENDS me a photo of the Corn Mother at the Taos Church altar. He texts, *She is looking especially fine today. Eva came home.*

Glad, I reply.

Then he sends a picture of the creek that cuts through the middle of the Pueblo, dividing summer people from winter people. He leaves it wordless.

The other goddess, I write.

Yes. Water is life. Me too glad re Eva. Re: Bandidos. Let's get a late breakfast. Pretend you are gathering motions for Ángel.

Ah. And you?

Detective work, before they file Liza's murder off into a dungeon.

I hate the sound of that. *Ok. Lead on McDuff.*

We go to the Taos Diner and split a massive burrito smothered in green chile. He orders his usual double macchiato and I get a decaf latte because this morning I don't need coffee. We are at a tiny corner table that provides a bit of privacy, though anyone walking in the door could see us and probably know us. Such is small-town life.

Larry takes out a manila envelope and scoots it over to me. "Stills from the video."

I smile. "Are these my copies?"

"Yes."

"Thank you. You didn't have to do that."

"I know." He shovels a bite of burrito into his mouth. "Bandidos usually run meth."

"That's what I thought."

"So I don't know if they have anything to do with Chuy dying or Liza."

I lean forward. "But these particular Bandidos are also Vietnam vets." I tap the manila envelope with the stills from the video.

Larry scowls. "So?"

"China White was their drug of choice in Nam. Most of them stopped when they came home. Using, I mean. But some didn't. And they got exposed to a big drug trade."

He swigs his coffee and ponders this. "Interesting."

"And I looked up Chuy Sr.—Ángel's granddad, Chuy Jr.'s father. The one who was in prison a long time."

"And—?"

"Vietnam vet."

"Really?"

"Yes. Involved in some heavy fighting. Wounded. But two tours. Who does two tours?"

"These days, people do five."

I blink. "Yeah, well, different wars." And a whole lot of basket cases uncomfortable with anything but the rush of combat.

Larry clears his throat. "What'd he go to prison for?"

I grin. "Get this. Heroin distribution. Accessory to murder with a drug deal gone bad."

I think I have played my ace card, but Larry slaps another manila folder on the table.

"What's that?" I ask.

"More on Chuy Jr.'s autopsy."

"And—?"

Time for him to grin back. "Traces of China White on his right front jeans pocket. Like he had a baggie. That wasn't there anymore."

"I'll be damned," I say softly.

"Yeah. What we do with all this . . . I have no idea. We've picked up no activity on this in the task force. But then, we have such a big Mexican tar and prescription opioid problem, not to mention the usual meth and cocaine, that we may have missed it. I think it's really a niche thing."

I can only agree.

"I don't like where he was killed," I say, after a minute.

"BLM land?"

I frown. "No, just outside ritzy private property."

"Like designer drug territory?"

"Something like that. Remember the syringe you found in the bathroom at Ángel's reception?"

He nods, wiping his mouth with a napkin. "Yeah."

I snort. "Soldier's drug gone upscale."

He sighs. "I guess if you are rich enough you are bored enough to go after shit like that."

"Maybe," I say. I hate how wealth fucks things up. Jade is so human, her family so lovely. But I think about her compound, the trees and fences and isolation. And how she has to work very hard to use her money for growth, not superfluity. Something pulls off in me, as if a stitch in my spleen were tugging toward that refuge. *I'd like a family*, a voice says.

I must look pained because Larry is peering at me. "You all right?"

I come back to the table. "Yeah, sorry." I shake my head.

We stand up. "One other thing," he says. "The 1% badge? That's the one percent of Bandidos who live outside the law, or at least brag they do."

I sigh. This confirms my memories of said badges. "Excellent," I say. "Just great."

The empty feeling around family clings to me all day. When I am feeling uncertain, as if the ground beneath my feet has just turned to Jell-O, or I am on a raft when the seas decide to swell too much beneath me, I get back to basics. At the office, I call Margot, asking if we can do dinner tonight. I am used to Margot being single and available at the drop of a hat, but with Richard now, and my current mood, I feel afraid of displacement. But she hears my tone and says of course.

The seas steady a bit. Then I call Jack, who actually answers.

"Hey, Mom. Whassup?"

"What are you doing?"

"Working. I got a nonprofit job with New Mexico Housing Solutions."

"You did?"

"Yeah. And I can go down to part-time in the fall when I start school."

Did he tell me this? I can't remember. The silence stretches.

"Sorry if I didn't tell you. It just started last week. And I've been moving in to my new little place." I can hear the guilt in his voice, the kid who wants to take care of his mom after his dad died—but he needs to move on.

"That's really great, bud. That's awesome." I wince. I can't keep the loneliness out of my voice.

"What's Luis up to?"

Luis feels so new and tender the seas start upwelling again. What month is it? April . . . choreographing the summer season and down in Jack Land as a guest at UNM in the dance program there. I swallow. "He'll come up in a week. He's teaching where you are, at UNM."

"Oh."

"Go visit him in the Dance Department."

"Really?" Now Jack's turn to be uncertain.

"I think he would like that." And I know I am right.

I crawl through the afternoon, sitting through court for two hours, burying my nose in paperwork to avoid office coffee klatches or even other eye contact. When the time comes, I slip out, go home and feed Ernest, whom I hug prolifically, and go to Margot's.

She has prepared an old college dish we used to make that I got from my mother. It's a kind of cream cheese spaghetti sauce that is so rich I don't know how we ate it so often and did not gain thirty pounds. I don't do much pasta anymore, but the minute I see it I grin. "You knew!" I say. *You knew in the way only old friends can know!*

"Yes, Sweet Pea." She chuckles and puts down a red Fiesta Ware bowl full of the slathered noodles next to an elaborate salad. "Dig in."

We wash this down with wine direct from Margot's dad's vineyard ("Private Estate") and she asks, "What's got you down?"

I tell her about Jade and her family. The idea of family. The emptiness of my own little house. I tell her I wish I'd had ten kids. I tell her I am in my fifties now and for the first time I worry I will die alone. I nearly wail, "Who will take care of me?"

She leans forward. "I will, I promise."

"But you have Richard—" I stop, flushing.

She takes my hand. "Ah. Are you afraid I will run off with Richard and leave you?"

"Ye-es." I hang my head like a ten-year-old with her hand in the cookie jar.

"Can I tell you something?"

"Sure."

"I have had the same fear about Luis."

We regard each other. The raft stops flailing and the Jell-O disappears, rendering the earth solid again. My shoulders drop out of my ears, and I take a healthy swig of wine. "Thank God," I say, letting the rest of the fear crumble into silence.

She swigs wine too, and we listen to a crow squawk out her open window.

The moment passes, the crow hopping on Margot's adobe wall, and I say, "Now tell me about this man of yours."

So it is I finally hear about Richard, an environmentalist and social-justice type who works up and down the Rio Grande corridor trying to keep methane leaks and old gas station spills and other industrial nightmares out of poor neighborhoods. They met at one of Margot's meetings, but it turns out she knew his sister in graduate school. It's funny how, anymore, we care about connective tissue like that, how it renders things more meaningful. In our twenties we would have run screaming from it.

"Can I meet him sometime?" I ask.

She nods. "Of course. Friday night, remember?"

I balk. Fuck. I forgot about the gallery show. My shoulders go up again. She laughs. "You'll do fine. Just wear that little blue dress you have that makes your Rivendell eyes pop out. And stand by the black horse." Something funny strikes her about that and she snorts into her wine. "My God, you won't have to say a word!"

Tuesday morning, I call Refugio. Ángel's case is before court and I am sure he will be granted a continuance, but I want to be on top of his health situation so I look like a competent probation officer. It's an old Taos number with a venerable prefix. No cell phones here. I imagine a rotary phone ringing in a kitchen full of yellow linoleum and a stand-up mixer in one corner.

"'Lo!" Refugio is nothing if not declarative.

I introduce myself and he remembers me from the hospital. "Good to hear from you, señora," he says.

I blush. Respect from Refugio matters a lot. "How is Ángel doing?"

Refugio lets out the sigh of the long-weary. "Okay. He's home."

"Can he talk?"

"He can whisper like a sick goat."

I chuckle. Once again, I think Refugio really needs to meet Larry. Or rather, Larry needs to meet Refugio.

"Well, I need to talk to him sometime soon. But he has a court date this morning and I need to tell them his status, or at least be on top of it so I know his lawyer is doing his job."

"*Gracias para usted*," he says. "Never trusted lawyers. Anyway, yeah, he still is pretty weak."

"Okay, thanks. When would be a good time to come see him?"

Refugio chuckles. "Anytime. Cabrito ain't going anywhere."

I smile and hang up, armed for court with the latest status on my client from his esteemed great-uncle. I am about to text Larry for an Ángel meeting when he texts me.

Santa Fe? Mucci can arrange a meeting with those Bandidos.

Ooh! But how do I justify that?

You can't. And you have to do it alone.

Huh?

They won't meet with cops.

Well, screw that. Can't cops insist?

At this point my phone rings. "Texting is too stupid for this," says Larry.

"Okay, so what gives?"

"So my buddies in Santa Fe brought those two in but they sat there like, and I quote, 'two fat potatoes' and said nothing."

"That's pretty eloquent for cops."

"I know! I patted them on the back for that by laughing."

"Good for you. Continuing to make friends everywhere, I see, right Larry?"

He snorts. "Anyway, so then I called Mucci."

"And—?"

"He worked an angle with them. Told them about Ángel being up for the murder of Liza only we don't think their poor great-nephew had anything to do with it, and in the interest of his innocence would they agree to chat. With you. The motherly, caring probation officer."

"But we're trying to find out if he had anything to do with Chuy dying! And China White. More serious biz than DV, at least to them." I roll my eyes.

"I know, but they don't know that."

"Fine. So what do I do? Go to that biker bar out on the highway east of town with Mucci as my bodyguard?"

"Naw. Just Evángelo's. Neutral turf. Dark back room. At 3:00 p.m., not midnight."

My stomach flips. "I have tomorrow off. I was going to do art. I have to get ready for Friday's show."

"I know. I'm sorry. But this would be a great favor, fingering these guys."

"Ewww! Larry! I am not 'fingering' anyone!"

He sighs. "You take everything to extremes, muchacha." But I can hear him cackling before his phone goes dead.

Chapter 21

I DECIDE TO MAKE the most of this. I get up at five. Brew tea. Go on a dank run with Ernest looking puzzled the whole way as to why we are running in semi-darkness at the coldest point of the day. I work in the studio until nine. I eat bites of a hastily made burrito and sip coffee and leave instructions for Margot's team, who will come for the pieces later in the day. I text Margot this. I stare at mountain goats and throw a little clay around. All I seem to be good for is pulling little pieces into mountain goat horns. I etch in spirals. By themselves they are sort of intriguing. Are they shells or horns? Miniature cornucopias? Hmmm . . . maybe I am moving into an abstract phase. I do manage to lose myself in this idea for a couple hours, making hooves in the same manner, little noses. They all could be shells, flowers, seed pods, or animal parts. I like the ambiguity. But does it work? I decide that is a question for another day.

At nine I shower quickly, throw on unassuming jeans, my pseudo-cowboy shirt with the cool gold embroidery and Victorian dresser-drawer buttons, and Santa Fe silver. I emphasize my graying hair, since I assume this is what Larry meant by "motherly." God forbid I carry a whiff of sexuality. If I put it up in a loose hair clasp—a chignon ladies of the nineteenth century would shudder at—my gray sides stand out. Unwashed and grumpy, this can age me ten years. Now, however, I work on formidable elegance, using age to my advantage. My hair clasps William once called "salad tongs" in that hilarious way of the uncomprehending male. The fortunate thing is I have a lovely silver hue that accents my dark blue eyes and so I combine the two with highly polished silver and lapis earrings I bought from one of Margot's connections on the Navajo rez years ago. The shirt is a boutique purchase and, ergo, I figure I am also hip enough for a check-in with Gert Kahn. I adjust small things in my oval stamped-tin mirror in the bedroom. Should I put on makeup? Okay, fine, a little black around the eyes. But don't cry like you usually do, Nina girl. Mascara must be the single biggest reason women suppress their God-given emotions. That and stupid men.

In Santa Fe, the Kahn gallery is bustling, and I am hopeful I will catch Gert in. I park next to a Jaguar with an immaculate just-washed look that no local partakes in because we all know it's fruitless. Actually, we wash our cars in droughts because then it will inevitably rain or snow and ruin the gleam. It is a way of invoking rain gods.

Inside, people with the studied look of money in casual attire mill about. What I mean by this is strategically distressed jeans that sell for at least $250 a pair, big watches (male) and buttery leather purses (female). Gert's husband, Reza, is at the back in an animated conversation about, as far as I can tell, a piece of Spanish armor. He probably knows where it was smithed, what small town in Spain suffered through the mining and heat it took to hammer the thing out, who in what conquistador's party likely wore it. You had to hand it to the man. I had never seen him look more animated.

I skirt my way to the back to a little side door that leads to a small hallway of offices. It appears to be open so I go in. "Gert?" I poke my head around in her office. The Tiffany lamps are on, but the room still carries a kind of dim depression to it, the mustiness of grandmothers' attics that you think ought to be fascinating but for the moths eating the wedding gowns and the musty smell of age.

A small circle of light shines down on her desk. Her elegant head is bent over some invoice or other. When she looks up, I am surprised. She looks haggard, run down.

"Is this a good time?" I ask. "I wanted to let you know about the show and discuss our contract."

She smiles wanly and motions toward one of the high-backed chairs. "Have a seat, Nina. Good to see you."

I sit down and wait uncomfortably. Her motions seem slowed down, as if underwater. "Are you all right?" I ask.

"Getting over a cold, I fear."

"I'm sorry to hear that. I, um, sent you an e-mail about the show—"

"Yes. The horses are lovely. I will want to represent them, of course."

A slow snake slithers in my belly. My conversation with Luis about the hazards of artistic success floats up. I sit forward. "So, Gert, I have never hit the big time before. I have read up a bit on art contracts. I've had a couple in my day. It was one reason I decided to open my own space."

"Nina, my hope is to take a select few, triple the price, take forty percent of whatever I make, and give the rest to you. You made a smart move by opening your own place. It has helped with exclusivity, from my perspective. I want to keep that sensibility."

I have to smile. "Meaning I am rare and endangered and therefore I must be worth more?"

She livens up a bit. "Exactly."

"For an artist I must seem positively left-brained." I am trying to make her laugh. It's one of my techniques, learned all too well in the face of my unpredictable father. If he laughed, he might like me.

She manages an upturn of her mouth, but her eyes are mostly flat. I remember that she found my humor unrefined, to say the least, the last time I was here with Jade, but I'm not sure that's what's going on here.

She opens a drawer and pulls out a boiler plate contract. "Let's make this more specific to you and me." She holds up her hand. "Remember, you don't have to sign anything; you can take it with you and have a lawyer look over it first, if you like. I will make it to the opening Friday, I promise. But here is where I would like to go."

I lean in and we haggle over details. I apply my criminal radar, remaining skeptical of all suggestions, but for the most part I feel oddly comfortable with Gert. She and I would never be friends outside of this office, but in a business sense she seems to get me. She wants the horses, large animal series especially, as they are worth more and are the kind of thing wealthy people like. It's hard to think of my black beauty being handled by someone other than me; he kind of makes a balking noise in my heart. I soothe his mane. *It's okay, boy. I'll get you someone who will pay what you are worth.* He settles down a bit. Still, his mama is a bit reluctant to let him out of her financial hands. And then there's the pressure to continue to make large animal series. What if I want to make seed pods modeled after the cloven hooves of mountain goats? What if that tickles my artistic brow more than making the whole critter? And what about New Mexican People-o-saurs? I must look pained because Gert stops talking.

"What's the matter?"

I shake my head as if to clear it. "Nothing. Just thinking like an artist. It, ah, changes my relationship to my work, all this potential income."

She neatens the paperwork and hands it to me. "Indeed it does," she says. There is not a whiff of sympathy. She is a businesswoman through and through.

I waddle out into the bright airiness of the gallery. Reza Kahn has emerged from a unisex bathroom discreetly located in one corner. This makes me aware that I need to pee. He nods at me, as spaced out now as his wife. What is with these two? The vibe is off today.

In the bathroom I find the requisite Mexican tile and custom ceramic sink basins. The lighting is comprised of artistic sconces, and little lizards, brightly painted, make their way up the walls. Oy vey, I think. I towel off, stuffing the paper into the woefully inadequate trash bin that is the lower half of the towel dispensary. A swab of cotton with a prick of blood peeks out. Eww. I do my best to seat the towel into the trash without touching anything else. On my way out, I catch Gert and Reza in a kind of tense standoff, like hyenas over a kill.

Oh for God's sake. Evángelo's will seem downright exuberant next to this.

Evángelo was a Greek war hero. Or rather, he came to America as a teenager but went home to fight the Nazis after his family was slaughtered by them. He then came back to America, was granted citizenship, and did what good Americans do after all that: opened a bar. He had a face a photographer liked, and he even ended up on TIME magazine and a postage stamp. Those photos are framed and over the bar, Evángelo looking like

Ernest Hemingway in his ambulance-driver days, or some Spanish Civil War partisan. I pay homage and walk to the back.

Mucci is sitting, rat-like, with his back to the wall, hunched over the remains of a taco he must have brought in off the street. Half a beer sits in front of him. I scrape a chair to announce my presence and sit down. He looks up at me with his jaws open around the taco.

"Don't let me stop you," I say. I am about to ask where our two Bandidos are when a tinkling of chains and the heavy clomp of boots behind me announce their presence. Evángelo's has just opened for the day and is otherwise fairly empty. I have a moment of feeling vulnerable, but there is a side door immediately to my left that I test surreptitiously. I discover it is behaving according to fire code; that is, it's unlocked. I take a slow, deep, Zen breath, unnoticed by my male companions. One Bandido sits next to me, the other next to Mucci. They nod at Mucci and seem not to know what to do with me—as with so many tough men they're masking intense shyness, crippling insecurity, and, worst of all, a tendency toward sweetness that they have to bury in order to survive. I think women like me are hard on them because we drill right down to the abandoned three-year-old most of them are.

Mucci swallows and helps them out. He swings a hand at me. "This here is Nina Montgomery. She's Ángel's probation officer."

This here? He sounds like a Texan.

I extend a hand, working hard on what I think passes for respect. Being *respected* means everything to this ilk. "Disrespect" is what leads to murder, usually. "Nice to meet you. And you are—?" I play the somewhat baffled sort, like Peter Falk in Colombo.

Their handshakes are limp and rubbery. The one next to me is chubbier, more haggard. "Bennie," he says.

"Bennie. And you?" I turn to the guy sitting next to Mucci.

"Mac."

Bennie and Mac. I know from their files their names are Benito and Maclovio. Fantastic old New Mexican names. And so here they are, disowning their heritage by turning their names into Velveeta cheese and then expressing it sideways and in a perverted manner in the form of a motorcycle club with a fat Mexican for a logo. I just love this country.

The waitress comes by and I order an iced tea. "I have to drive back to Taos," I offer by way of explanation, as if on any other ordinary Tuesday, I would, of course, be slogging back Crown and Cokes at three in the afternoon. Ben and Mac restrainedly order two Coronas. I turn to them. "Tell me about Nam," I say.

This is not what they were expecting. They shoot glances back and forth at one another, their brows wrinkling like basset hounds. "We came here to talk about Ángel," Mac says.

"Ms. Montgomery is concerned for her probationer's welfare and any information that would help clear his name from his girlfriend's murder would be helpful." Mucci has finished his taco and beer and is now downright eloquent.

I shift in my seat. "See," I start. This is hard. What do I want to say? How do I want to play this? "See, the thing is, I am wondering if his dad's death and his girlfriend's are connected. His dad was your nephew, right? Ángel your great-nephew?"

I look at them, with my maternal gray hair and winking earrings, trying for the I'm-a-woman-so-the-family-angle-is-important air. "What I mean is, um, I want to know about your generation. About Ángel's granddad. About you. I know you served, I know his granddad did."

"Why do you want to know?" This is Bennie, voice crushed by years of cigarettes. These guys have to be pushing seventy.

"Because I think there's a drug connection to Liza's death, and to Chuy's."

There, I've said it. The iced tea and Coronas come and still the silence is heavy.

"Why would this have to do with us?"

"I think it has to do with Nam."

They look puzzled. "Nam? Why Nam?"

"Why'd your brother do two tours?"

Bennie and Mac seem frozen. They sip the beers. Mucci interjects, "Ángel's about to get pinned with a domestic violence murder. But it looks more like an execution. As does Chuy. So she is confused."

Yes, the poor little woman. I sigh, watching the freeze, the way the word Nam paralyzes them. I realize their clamming up has less to do with drug wars and much more to do with what happened over there.

I go soft. I've had Crisis Intervention Training. Freeze means their nervous systems have fritzed out, like sticking a fork in a light socket. I pray no one slams a glass down on the counter or backfires their truck outside. "Look," I say. "I, um, had a cousin in Iraq." I am lying through my teeth, but I've had enough probationers with this profile to do it justice. I keep my voice low, steady. "You don't have to talk about it. I just want to know what happened to Ángel's dad. Because I feel like his son—and now grandson—have carried on some business he never got to complete."

Bennie sips a beer. "Chuy Sr.—we'd call him Big Chuy—he—the war did something funny to him. He was the oldest."

Mac does the wrinkled dog brow again, to Bennie. "Yeah. He tried to protect us."

"You were over there together?" This never occurred to me.

"Yeah. And one other brother."

"There were four of you?"

"Yeah. We were all a year or two apart. Bennie and me are twins."

God bless their mother, I thought. "Four of you? Wow."

"The other one—he died."

I don't have to say much else. It's as if someone had let off a smoke bomb, the pall is so heavy. "Chuy Sr. was point man, wasn't he?" I say, softly. I've heard this story before. Taos Indian whose cousin-brother got snipered under his watch. He never forgave himself.

They look startled. "How'd you know?"

I shake my head. "Doesn't matter. So . . . what happened?"

"Tranny stepped on a mine. Bouncing Betty. Fell forward into another one. Poof!" Mac does this almost elegant thing with his fingers, like an origami flower exploding and collapsing.

"Were you there?"

They shook their heads. "Kind of. We were bringing up the rear."

"Tranny is short for—?"

Mucci lets out a sad sigh and closes his eyes.

Bennie wipes foam off his upper lip. "*Tranquiliano.*"

"He was the nicest kid."

And there you have it, the big-picture reason why Chuy Sr. went back to war, found China White, and destroyed his life. I clench my jaw and close my eyes.

Chapter 22

MUCCI, NOT A MAN comfortable with emotions, toys with a swizzle stick and won't look at me. Bennie and Mac have left, their time with the female PO thankfully over. I had tried to veer back to the more present-day realities of their grand-nephew's plight, but they were clearly agitated. It was as if a Huey were landing outside and they had no idea if they would live or die. I clear my throat and finish my iced tea, rattling the ice to draw Mucci back to the present.

"Well, that was informative, in its own way," I say.

"Yeah." The swizzle stick flops onto the table.

"Rick, what do you remember of Chuy Sr.? Big Chuy?"

"I was just a kid," he mumbles.

I scowl. "For fuck's sake, I know that." I lean forward. "Sorry. Look, no one talks. It just amazes me."

"He sat on the porch all day, zoned out."

"Excuse me?"

"Chuy Sr. He'd sit on the porch all day. Gazing off somewhere. We'd see him walking home from school. Chuy—my friend, Chuy—would kind of slink off without saying goodbye. He hated that everyone saw his dad on the porch like that. Usually with a beer."

"Anything else?"

He shifts in his seat. "Yeah. Sometimes yelling from inside. Leila screeching. Things being thrown. If he wasn't on the porch, it was usually a bad sign, unless he was off in jail. Sometimes Leila would stay with us."

"Any black eyes when she came over?"

He shoots me a look.

"Sorry," I say. I have my own reasons for not wanting to imagine that proud cockatoo of a woman with black eyes, but the great shame of a poor barrio seems to be spilling out all over Mucci's face. It sucks living up to everyone's stereotypes.

"He was a disturbed man," Mucci concedes. "I see where Chuy, Chuy Jr. I mean, went off the rails a bit."

My sense is Mucci barely holds onto his own rails. I decide I don't want to know about Italian fisticuffs or the mother with too much wine in the larder or any of his own heartbreak. I've asked enough of him today.

I get up to go. "Thank you for arranging this meeting. I know that wasn't the easiest."

He stands up too. "Welcome." Again, he won't look at me. Diffident, suddenly, which is an odd experience in a man with slick hair and gold chains and an Al Pacino roughness to him. He says, "I turn favors for Larry. He's a good man." He offers me a limp paw, which I take. I watch his back as he walks out of the bar, sloping with an air of defeat he will get rid of as soon as sunlight and the eyes of the public hit him.

The Good Man calls my cell phone not five minutes after leaving the meeting. He is glad he caught me because he wants me to pick up a file on Chuy Jr.'s case from the Santa Fe County Sheriff's Department. "We can look at it together," he bribes.

"Okay."

"How was the Bennie and Mac show?"

"Heavy. I think I now know why China White if nothing else." And I tell him about Vietnam and the four brothers.

Larry doesn't say anything for a minute. The silence stretches between here and Taos.

"Jade says it always comes down to this," I offer. "'It's just a good story,' she says. If it's good, it's about family and failure and love far gone. That's how she knows if she has a good movie script."

Larry sighs. "Yeah, I suppose. You lose sight of that arresting people for the same shit over and over again."

"I know."

"Bring the file. I'll get takeout and we'll look at it when you get up here."

"Should I come to the Prison for Midgets?" This is the loving term the deputies have bequeathed upon their squat building a block behind and down a side street from the grand newer edifice I inhabit.

"You bet," says Larry. And my evening at the Taos County Sherriff's Department is set.

Song's Chinese Food awaits my presence in Larry's office. It is not half bad for Rocky Mountain Chinese, which is to say those from the Pacific Coast would probably wrinkle their noses. But I am glad for beef with broccoli and some moo shu pork. The file sits in front of us until we have eaten, so as not to sully the contents with soy sauce or hoisin.

Larry finishes first and opens things up. Three things stand out once it is all laid on the table: a map of the neighborhood adjacent to where Chuy Jr. was found shot under the juniper tree, a narrative of Chuy Jr.'s last known whereabouts, and Chuy Sr.'s prison records.

We start with the last. Apparently, in 1978, when little Chuy Jr. was nine years old, Chuy Sr. got busted for possession of heroin. Deep in this report is a mention that it was not Mexican tar, though in those days apparently China White was more available anyway, even in New Mexico, due to all those Vietnam vets coming back and using it. Larry and I look at each other.

"See?" I say. "Goes all the way back. We can thank the US government for this here case."

I am being facetious and Larry scowls. He doesn't like it when I get sarcastically left wing. I roll my eyes and we read on. Two years later, Chuy Sr. got busted again, and finally, in 1984, when Chuy Jr. was fourteen, he was named as an accessory to a murder and sent away to prison. His son was twenty by the time he got out. When he went back again, he died there, shanked but dying anyway of diabetes and kidney failure. Chuy Jr. was twenty-five.

"1995," I whisper. "That's what our records say too."

"The file you found in probation?"

"Yeah."

What I see there is a litany of paternal abandonment. How many times have I seen juvie boys fall for the bad life because their daddies are in prison, and this is the way they find to finally have something in common with them? Dads who never gave a crap suddenly are sending little Johnny one-hundred-dollar bills in jail, going on about how "now you're one of us" like some alcoholic who has made a convert. I just love this kind of thinking. When I see a kid like that, who is in love with this fantasy absent dad, it's all I can do not to throw up my hands. No justice system can conquer that longing.

Did something similar happen with Ángel and Chuy Jr.? The pattern of absentee fatherhood certainly continues on. Larry and I move onto the narrative of events leading up to the shooting. According to one Leila Candelaría y Martinez, mother of the deceased, Chuy Jr. was with her earlier in the day that he was killed. Helping her rearrange her shop, along with her daughter, Maria, and grandson, Ángel Martinez. I sit up. Larry and I look at each other. Really? Leila reported to have been happy that the son and father had reunited.

"Somebody needs to talk to Leila more," Larry says.

"Sound like the Santa Fe Sheriff already did."

"Yeah, but my guess is she has dealt with local cops for years. Is related to half of them. She needs a different person."

"Maybe Jade," I muse.

Larry looks at me. "A movie star? Really?"

"Leila's running this herbal workshop coming up. Jade can't wait to go, and Leila seemed happy she was that interested. I dunno," I shrug, "but she can act her way out of a box."

Larry considers this, making one of those questioning faces that an emoticon would capture with a raised eyebrow. "Intriguing idea," he finally says.

"Well, glad you think so." I take a sip of jasmine tea and Larry unfolds the final item, a folded, taped together compilation of Google Maps satellite views, blowups of the two arcing streets of wealthy, set apart houses that abut the BLM land to the west of where Chuy Jr. was found. We missed takeover by G-men in pressed slacks by five feet. We wrestle the maps open, and I put my tea down.

From Google's drone-like perch the houses are large, squat, one- and two-story adobe-stucco manses, arranged in a meandering way around a golf course. Though they face roughly east toward the course, they sport large patios and sliding glass doors to the west, so one might view the sunset over the Jemez Mountains in the far distance if one so desired. The accompanying report reveals that doors had been knocked on by the Santa Fe deputies, inquiries made about gunshots, knowledge of Chuy. General denials all around. Names in fine sharpie adorn each house on the two streets. Kavanaugh, Venn, Reichenbach, Turner. White names, all. One Garcia. Carlson, Vetch, Grumann, Kahn, Wildman, Roach, Ramey, Campbell, Hunt. My eyes dart back. Kahn.

Really? My finger halts on the name. "Shit."

Larry looks at where my finger sits. "Same Kahn?"

"How many Kahns can there be in Santa Fe?"

"It's a pretty common name in Iran."

I snort. "We do not live in Tehran."

"And not just Iran! Think of Genghis! Maybe all of Reza's brothers migrated over here too. You don't know."

I have to smile at Larry. Forever the historian. "Okay, okay. Let's google Kahns in Santa Fe and see what happens. But I'm willing to bet this is them. It's a wealthy neighborhood, they have money."

"A little modern for such artistic mavens," Larry says.

"Maybe. Or maybe since creating the Santa Fe fantasy is such a big part of their job, they'd rather live a bit away from it."

"Could be."

"Who knows? Maybe Gert likes golf."

Larry chortles and flips open his laptop. Cops have access to databases the rest of us don't want to know about since Orwell's 1984 will doubtless invoke itself for anyone who made it past ninth grade. He snoops around briefly, enough to ascertain that (1) it is that Kahn, and (2) Reza did not migrate, it appears, with other Kahns.

I don't know what to make of this information. Three connections immediately lead to one common denominator—the syringe at Ángel's Young Artist party, the cotton ball with the drop of blood on it at the Kahn Gallery, and the location of what I presume is the Kahn house. The common denominator is Gert. Shit. I don't want to think this. I flash onto my contract lying on the dining room table and think it's good that I haven't signed a thing.

Larry senses my mood shift. "Still trust her to sell your stuff?"

"Oh, Larry . . ." I tell him about the cotton ball in the bathroom at the gallery and ask him to remember the syringe in the bathroom at Ángel's gig.

He just nods and folds up the map.

We're done for tonight.

The need to see Ángel, now that he is out of the hospital and can talk, grows. Refugio is out stacking wood in a little shed next to his house when I drive up. I've spent the morning in ordinary probation officer pursuits, and after lunch I scrawl where I am going on the white board in the office so that should my body wash up in Pot Creek my supervisor, Tim, and colleagues will be able to trace what happened more easily. Tim doesn't want me going alone until I tell him about Refugio and his wife Maria, who will be there, and the state of Ángel's health. At that point he decides Ángel is too feeble to aim a gun or stab me and gives me the go-ahead. We're supposed to be back in court Monday.

"Hola, señora," Refugio says, putting a hand to his lower back and unwinding his spine into a more upright position. He's got an old plaid cowboy shirt on, the kind with the snaps on the chest pockets and snaps for buttons. He wipes his brow with one sleeve and offers me his hand.

"Hola," I say. "How is he today?"

Refugio shrugs. "Very quiet. Maria feeds him soup and a little chicken. He can't eat a lot of solid food yet."

"Okay," I say, and troop back to the Airstream.

Ángel is sitting on the stoop staring at an array of woodworking tools. There must be ten awls in a treated canvas tool bag, each awl with its own slot. I think you could roll the whole thing up, as chefs do with their knife holders. I pull up the rickety old kitchen chair he seems to use to aimlessly whittle in the great outdoors and sit next to him.

"How are you doing?" I ask.

He shrugs, won't look at me.

"Ángel . . . how's your throat?"

"Sore," he croaks.

I look at it. The bruise is fading but he nevertheless sports a bathtub ring around his entire neck.

"Don't ever do that to your family again," I say.

He just sulks and says nothing.

I try again. "So, we gotta talk."

"I can't seem to want to work on anything," he blurts. "No vision, señora." He looks up then, eyes droopy as a basset hound, the rest of his face as gaunt as I've ever seen it.

I do appreciate the artistic vulnerability. There may be no one else in his world who can empathize. I take a breath. "I've learned that when I've been through a lot emotionally, I produce really bad crap or nothing at all. Eventually this will settle and you will make something else." *If you're not in prison*, I want to add but don't.

"I can't even make really bad crap."

"Well, it's okay. And actually," I try to brighten, "maybe if I help move this along, you'll get unstuck." I take a big breath. This isn't totally fair—in fact it's devastating to compare what I am about to say to his artistic needs, but I tell him, "Getting unstuck usually means facing a lot of shit you'd rather not."

"What do you mean?"

"Ángel, you're not gonna like this, but in Liza's diary she mentions 'vatos' of yours, and we found the China White baggie in the dryer hose." I've decided to go for the jugular, no pun intended. I can't do much more damage to it that he has already done.

He actually does reach for his neck. It's funny how we will protect our most vulnerable spots even if they have nothing to do with the issue at hand. His color, such as it is, drains.

"You didn't kill her. I know that. Her throat was cut clean through, ear to ear."

Now he kind of collapses onto the stoop entirely.

I stand up, go around him, and find a glass of water for him in his trailer. Coming out, I hand it to him and sit next to him. I have such mixed feelings. Part of me wants to mother him as I do Jack—they are not far apart in age—and the other part cautions me to keep my probation officer detachment and cool. Then another part remembers the cruel kid who bent his lover's knee into a pretzel.

I start talking. "Look, I know you grew up West Side. I've met Leila. I've talked to your uncles, Bennie and Mac. I know you saw your dad the day he died. You live here now but your dad's roots are Santa Fe."

He sips water, slowly and somewhat painfully, and just stares vacantly at the tree where he tried to hang himself.

I pull out his rap sheet from my handy giant Kenyan woven bag, the kind that was all the rage in the eighties and has echoes of sixties romance with all things ethnic. Margot would be proud. "Your rap sheet has some early issues with gangbanging. As you've said, you would get asked to do things." I frown. "Here's a possession charge, coke. Four years ago. Then a dismissed Attempt to Distribute."

He's still staring ahead.

I risk putting a very gentle finger on his wrist. "Who asked you to push China White? Who are these vatos Liza talked about?"

"Friends of my dad's," he whispers, and I swear he starts to shake.

"Chuy."

"Yeah."

I let that hang there. A pinon jay squawks and I can hear the cluck of chickens around the corner in their coop. The day is warming up and the air smells of bosque and fruit trees. The small, tight beauty of New Mexico bottomland surrounds us, and it could almost make me weep.

"He's dead too," I say.

"I know."

"You kill him?"

He turns to me and just crumbles. Insofar as his ruined throat will let him, he starts to sob. His head plows into my shoulder and, despite everything, I know he is asking for what he never had: a mother. I put a tentative hand on his hair. He actually smells clean, showered.

"Ángel . . ."

He keens.

He's probably needed to do this all his life. Maybe he will never twist another knee or hang another dog now. It is with this hope I let him stay buried in my shoulder, my hand on his head. I even find myself rocking us a bit. I swallow and listen to the jays talking.

Finally, he sits up. He looks exhausted. "Are you asking for prison for my current charges?"

I blink. "Ye-es," I say, my mind flying back to the PSI I wrote. "You've had too many—too many DV charges, and—and . . ." I stop, flailing. What's relevant here? If he knows I am asking for prison, will he finish what he tried to begin with the noose? His crimes against Liza are awful, but now we are up against two unsolved murders.

"Do you think the judge will listen to you?"

I snort a little. "Maybe."

"How much prison for that?"

"What?" I realize he's whipsawed from dejection to calculation.

"How many years?"

"Two." I stare at him. The DA stuck an F3 on him, which is technically good for up to six years, and a rarity in DV cases. But it's probably better as an F4, which gets you eighteen months. I figured I was being generous in asking for two years. "What're you doing? Striking bargains in your head?" I am angry. My heart bled for this kid a minute ago and now he's back to con man. I have only myself to blame. "Ángel, you need to come clean about the China White. About everything."

He shakes his head and just gives me a wan smile. "That's for me and Bennie Garcia to discuss."

"You're gonna confess to your *lawyer*?" I don't know why I act as if this is unheard of, but I do.

He just smiles ever more cagily. "Depends. Depends on what you and the cops find out."

A chill runs down my spine. "Are you going to have your vatos off me too? If I am too close to the truth?" *Is one of your vatos an enormous Octopus?*

He manages to stand up and I make sure I am right there with him. I don't want him towering over me. A streak of rage is back across his face. "I.did.not.kill.Liza."

"Did your dad?" I edge away from the porch, taunting. These pas de deux are exhausting.

He fences one more parry. This time his face is a mask of fury. "No . . ." he says, but it trails off without conviction. He gathers up his awls and glares at me. "He killed me." And into his trailer he goes.

Chapter 23

MARGOT'S GALLERY, EARTHART, IS just off the plaza in Taos, in a little cul-de-sac filled with an independent bookstore, a gourmet cooking shop, two other arty establishments, and a bakery-coffee shop. This is not lowbrow barrio territory.

The reception starts at six, part of a Taos Art Walk night, where people are plied with wine at various galleries and inveigled to buy pieces they can't afford. I show up at five-thirty, wearing the little royal-blue sheath Margot told me to, flat black sandals, and shiny silver jewelry. If I get cold, I have a little black cardigan, though Margot thinks I should go total Taos and buy a white sarape with the same blue in it and wrap it dramatically around my shoulders for effect. I admit this might look good, but as ever, when it comes to my public appearance, I crumple at being the center of attention.

As I step into the gallery, I'm immediately aware of a handsome man in a startling maroon dress shirt—vaguely shimmery yet somehow understated, as only Latin men can pull off—standing across the room. He turns and stares at me. For a minute we don't recognize each other. Then I burst out laughing. "Luis!" I am not used to seeing him outside of the dance floor, his casita, my kitchen, or our bedrooms.

And then a woman winds around me like smoke, holding a tray of tapas. "Dios mío, muchacha, is he guapo . . ." and I find myself gaping at Loretta.

"*You're* doing the catering?" I ask.

Luis has sidled up to me, nibbled my ear, and told me I look alarmingly attractive. I grab his hand much the way I did the first time he cooked at my house, to stop myself from swooning and wanting to take him right there on the gallery floor.

Loretta smiles sweetly. "Yes, I am. Your lovely friend contracted with me weeks ago."

I see Margot out of the corner of my eye, touching up pieces, arranging brochures, making sure the small drink station looks tidy. "So this is a giant conspiracy? You and Margot? You kept this from me, both of you!"

Loretta's eyes flicker with a tiny piece of concern. "You're not upset are you, Nina? We thought it all should be a surprise. For you. For having had your success."

I let go of Luis's hand and give her a hug. "Oh, thank you! I love you!" And she's back to beaming again, offering Luis tapas, and flirting unabashedly with him. Christ, what an evening this is going to be.

EarthArt sells with the goal of simply paying the bills and then offering any leftovers to three worthy environmental action groups affecting the northern Rio Grande corridor. Margot vets each group every year to determine if they should be the recipients and if they don't muster up, she drops them cold turkey. What passes for "leftovers" is not insubstantial, and, as a result, she's made for healthy competition among groups. Northern New Mexico is thus blessed with nonprofits run as tight ships beyond most others of similar ilk. The joke is she single-handedly got the Rio Grande Gorge National Monument established, as if the president would not have had the faintest idea why this was worthy without her backing. The truth, as she puts it, is that without strong local leadership from some of our female soccer mates and their daughters (who ran away to UNM or Highlands and obtained sociology degrees), nothing would have happened. Still, her money matters.

My black horses—I have three—are front and center and dramatically introduce the casual art walker into a whole new world. They do exactly what good art is supposed to do—muster you awake, make you think, gape in beauty or ugliness or at life itself. My red, raku horses, smaller but with a kind of agony befitting their firing, are to the side of the black ones, and several of my other pieces are scattered around. A table hosts my twenty-dollar bunny rabbits and squirrels. Framed sketches that I have turned into prints line two of the walls. Overall, I am pleased.

I find Luis walking slowly around one of the raku horses. Subconsciously, he twists his hands in that slow way flamenco dancers do, India and gypsy fires and an almost palsied pain palpable in each twist. I see then the parallel, the way my raku horses' necks are twisted, their manes flung, their eyes a mess of fear and love. For a minute I am stabbed with horror that I have made 3-D versions of Picasso's *Guernica* horses, but that passes, and I see instead some small elegance and grace shining through despite their tortured passion. They are my flamenco horses, and there is my flamenco man, now beginning to almost strut, ever so slowly, as if circling a partner, around the horse.

"Good God," Margot says, coming up beside me. "That's perfect. Can he just do that all night? I'll sell them for sure."

I give her a hug. "The gallery looks beautiful."

She smiles. "Thanks. I've sent out enough PR. Hopefully you'll have a good crowd."

A shadow crosses my face. "Is Gert Kahn coming?"

"Of course. She said she would, right?"

"Ye-es . . ." I think back to our conversation in Santa Fe.

"What's the matter?"

I sigh, shake my head. "Business stuff."

She gives me a squeeze and saunters off.

By seven the gallery is a buzz of people, drinks, tapas, circulation. My black horses sell in half an hour, for the ridiculous price I dared to suggest. Jade had texted me she'd let movie people know where she'd gotten the antelope, and sure enough one director, two producers, and some kind of marketing guru have swooped down upon the gallery. New Mexico harbors pockets of movie lords thanks to tax breaks the state offered, then rescinded in a fit of stupid political pique, then reinstated. *Breaking Bad* sealed the deal. I chat with them, though trying not to do what one of them—an alpha-male, psychopath type who probably fucks twenty-year-old wannabes/starlets and smokes cigars in his convertible while navigating the 405 freeway—clearly wants me to do, which is be awed by Hollywood glamour and go all obsequious female on him. I work hard to hold to adult strength. Christ. Why is it still so hard? What is it about that kind of male energy?

Gert and Reza have come in and my attention toward my buyers disappears. My blood drains. What am I supposed to do? Go up to them and ask about how the heroin habit is going? Pretend I am stoked still to sign the contract? Larry! Where is Larry when I need him? I find Loretta, eat three tapas, and feel her maternal solidity next to me until she moves away to make the rounds. With relief I finally see Larry and Clara come in, and I excuse myself from the next movie guru who wants to talk. I make noises about "my agent" and flee.

I nod to Gert, telling her I will talk to her in a minute, and drag Larry off to a corner.

"Muchacha," he says. "What's up?"

I pull him outside to a little back courtyard where small parties are sipping wine and speaking in low tones. The gravel crunches under my flats and the evening is cooling rapidly. "How do I talk to her? What do I do?" I am literally wringing my hands.

He just looks at me with benign eyes. "Well, you can't avoid her."

"No." I sigh. "I am just so lousy at pretending everything is fine. I hate that kind of fake."

"You'd make a terrible actor."

"I know."

Larry is clearly not going to offer sage advice on handling potentially drug-associated art agents. I give up and switch subjects, swilling wine to dampen my anxiety. "What have you found out on your end?" He was going to look into vatos and WSL politics.

"Interesting . . ." he says, "Bennie and Mac are old-timey vatos. First gen Westsiders. So it's a family thing. Ángel was blessed in."

"What does that mean?"

"It means he didn't have to have the shit beat out of him to be considered a member."

I wince. I hate gang crap. "So what does that make Chuy?"

"Oh . . . Chuy was in it way deep. All his life. *Was* his life."

"So he was used to drug running."

"Yeah. Last stint in Grants he met some Mexican Mafia and, um, MS-13 friends."

Grants is a prison west of Albuquerque, set amid a tundra of black lava from old volcanic flows, and near the town of the same name where, in Cold War innocence, local uranium miners built backyard patios with radioactive slag slabs leftover from the mines. They glow from space. Needless to say, cancer rates have been alarming at times.

"Great," I say. My blood drains further. "Larry . . . I hope I'm not in danger."

His face constricts, his voice tight, the nearest thing to cop-fear he'll let me see. "What do you mean?"

I tell him about my visit with Ángel, and the last bit where I asked him point blank if his vatos would come after me. Larry's shoulders sag. "I don't like this," he says.

We stare out at the chattering masses. Another world. Margot swirls in front of me all of a sudden. "There you are! I've been looking for you! All the big pieces have sold!"

I kind of just gaze at her, the way cows do at cars passing by.

"What's the matter?"

I sit down on a bench behind me. "Oh Margot," I say. Larry says nothing.

She pales. "Does this have to do with your day job?"

I just nod. She looks at Larry. "Be careful," she says, "both of you."

"Thank you for the good news," I say drily. I look at her, pleading. "I really mean it."

She leans over and kisses my cheek. "I know, sweetie. You'll bounce back." And leaves Larry and me pondering fates on her back patio.

It is my delight to see Refugio and Dr. Singh and some of my colleagues and soccer buds show up. Refugio says he's there for Ángel, who knew better than to come and was still pretty weak anyway, but still he wanted to offer congratulations. I just shake my head. That kid will have to go to Social Rehab School the rest of his life if I am going to ever believe in what passes for manners from him. Refugio is not entirely comfortable in Taos's higher-end plaza settings, but he moves with the quiet confidence of a man who knows he is home no matter who moves to town. On a whim I show him a phone pic of my New Mexico Ángel Dinosaur Man. He laughs and tells me it's perfect.

"Mira," he says in return, "my granddaughter sold these at the state fair last year. Huge hit." And out of his wallet he takes a squashed photo of a display of—brilliance upon brilliance!—orange barrel jewelry. New Mexico has been plagued with orange barrels since time immemorial. They are the chief weapon and traffic tool of the New Mexico Department of Transportation. We don't use cones or big arrows. We use orange barrels. They are everywhere.

I see orange barrel earrings, orange barrel crucifixes (!!), orange barrel charm bracelets. I am smitten. Only in New Mexico. I tell him I want a pair of earrings and to talk to Marta Gomez, our soccer team member who owns the shop in the main plaza. "Your granddaughter needs to sell these there."

He flushes with pride. This man, who might just believe it when Jesus shows up in a tortilla (another New Mexico legend), also totally gets orange barrel jewelry. I drag him over to Larry.

"Meet," I say to them both. "You are perfect for each other." And then flee before I have to witness the awkward hemming and hawing of aging males trying to socially navigate at the behest of an obnoxious woman.

"There you are!" says the voice I have been dreading all evening. Gert Kahn is back, dressed impeccably in pencil skirt, red silk blouse with an enormous ruffle, her hair pulled into a dramatic bun. In her stilettos and with Reza next to her, she makes me feel like I am in the presence of Boris and Natasha. I dimly wonder if they came in on a Ural motorbike replete with side car. I am surprised Reza is here, as he does not usually come to social gatherings. Crowds overstimulate him, and in situations like this, he seems to cope by falling ever more deeply into connoisseurdom. With a start I realize he was the vaguely familiar face behind Ángel when Larry and I went to the Mariposa Gallery. He gazes at one of my bunny rabbits as if it were the Holy Grail, wanting to know about glazes, clay sources, tools I used. He starts talking about Native clay sources throughout New Mexico, particularly proud, it seems, of a prolific layer of it in the Galisteo Basin that produced most of the pottery for the Pueblos there in the late 1400s.

Gert rests a hand on his arm. "Reza, honey, can I speak to Nina for a moment in peace?"

He stops talking and puts my bunny rabbit down, blinking a bit like a small child. "Of course. Nina, can you tell me where the bathroom is?"

I adjust to the change in conversation and point toward the back of the gallery. "There," I say.

Gert just sighs as she watches him saunter off. "I'm sorry. He is not socially adept."

"Does he have Asperger's?" I ask.

She winces a little. "Is it that obvious?"

I chuckle despite my nerves. "Oh, Gert, that's been the suspicion for a long time in the lower art circles I hang out in. It makes him really good at the detail of all that stuff he sells."

"Yes, I suppose it does."

I don't ask what it's like to be married to that, since my limited experience with it seems to point to some difficulty with empathy for others coupled with a penchant for tantrums when senses are overwhelmed. Jack had a friend in elementary school who suffered through it, and I clearly remember the times he came over to our house. I maneuver us back to a corner to say what will inevitably have to be said. She is going to ask if I have had a chance to look at the contract; she is going to gush about all that I have sold this night; she is assuming the beginning of a lush and fruitful business relationship.

"Marty Langdon bought the first black horse you see coming in," she says.

My shoulders fall. "Is he the guy who looks like a caricature of every Hollywood mogul you've ever seen?"

She chuckles. "Probably. Yes."

I send a silent *I'm sorry* to my beautiful stallion. This selling-to-rich-assholes bit is beginning to grate on me. Maybe I should just remain a middle-of-the-road state employee who sells bunny rabbits and ceramic roadrunners. I let out a kind of brrrr noise along with a sigh.

"Nina, you can't be picky. And you have to admit, the stallion is full of alpha-male energy. Maybe the stallion will dignify him a little, instead of him degrading the stallion. Besides, I happen to know he has one of those brilliant infinity pools that looks as though it spills straight over the edge into Topanga Canyon. Fabulous deck, modern, all planes and angles. The horse will look terrific there."

I stare at her. "You go to LA often?"

She laughs. "I've been in this business a long time, Nina."

I feel like crying. I really like this woman, in all her updos and high heels. She could give Leila a run for her money. Or vice versa, though Leila is more lowbrow than Gert would ever cop to. Not for the first time I wonder what humble origins Gert is compensating for. "Gert, we have to talk."

She blanches in that way one spouse does when the other one issues those four deadly words. "What about?"

Reza is out of the bathroom and pondering a piece by another artist tucked into a corner of the gallery. He seems different somehow, relaxed yet oddly alert.

I stare at him. "Excuse me a minute," I say abruptly and run to the bathroom. I lock the door, wildly anxious, and search the trash. Lo and behold, a cotton ball with a drop of blood. I fish a little more, but I don't want to disturb what by now is clearly evidence. If there is a syringe, I want it found too. I close my eyes and try to remember to breathe. I realize I have some relief that it is Reza, not Gert, who has the heroin problem. But really? And China White? But the word *connoisseur* floats back in, and I go "Ah," in the back of my throat. I grab a paper towel and gently cradle the cotton ball in it. Out I go, make a beeline for Larry, whispering in his ear. "Go find the fucking syringe," I finish, and gently hand him the paper towel with its treasure nestled inside. "It's Reza."

His eyes bug out, but he excuses himself from Refugio, Clara, and Maria, the four of them having no doubt discovered they are all third cousins or that their offspring hung out with the same crowd in high school. "I'll be damned," he says under his breath.

I go back to Gert, who is looking baffled and somewhat insulted. I can't seem to stay presentable in front of this woman to save my life. I offer profound apologies and steer us to Margot's back office, where no one will hear us. I shut the door and slump on the edge of Margot's desk. "Gert . . . I know about Reza."

She looks puzzled. "What do you mean? That he has Asperger's? We just talked about that."

"No. That he has a heroin problem."

She goes about as white as someone with her olive skin can. "*What?*"

It seems abundantly apparent that she had no idea. This evening has just been too much, such an odd mix of delight and success and sadness and depravity. "Oh Gert," I blurt. "I really like you. I need to say that. I know I can't hold a candle to your elegance, and I botch every social interaction we have, but I think I trust you implicitly with my art."

She looks somewhat relieved and if I am not mistaken the chin of the mighty Gert Kahn trembles a bit. "Thank you," she says drily, waiting for the rest of it.

"But . . . well, you also know what I do for my day job. And we've run into a highly unusual drug case involving what around here is a rare strain of heroin."

Now she really reels. She has to know that "rare strain" and Reza would come together like moths to flames. Reza can't resist the esoteric for, in this case, literally the life of him.

"Oh my God," she says, and stumbles her way back to a chair with books and papers on it. She swipes these off to the floor and collapses into it.

"You had no idea?"

"None. Though he's been odd, not himself, the past few months."

I nod, thinking back to the tension in the Kahn Gallery when I visited with her earlier in the week. "I noticed things were tense the other day."

"Yes," she says simply and pales further. "So has he—has he committed a crime?"

"Well, if we find he has it on him, then that's a possession charge for sure."

"Shit," she says, with eerie elegance. It's as if shit were a lacy butter cookie she was nibbling. She pats her bun then looks up at me. "What do I do?"

I sigh a huge sigh, thinking. "I'm not sure. If you can, for now . . . maybe nothing? I think I can get my sheriff friend to discreetly take him aside. Reza is not the big cheese here, not by a long shot. But his use probably led to a murder—or two—and there are some high stakes in this, clearly."

Her eyes go wide. "Murder?"

I nod. "You know that guy they found shot out on the edge of your neighborhood?"

She cocks her head. "You know where I live?"

"I—I think so." And I explain the Google map and Chuy's death and the white residue in his pocket. I refrain from talking about Ángel or Liza's dryer hose, but I do mumble something about a Taos connection.

Tears steal out of her, smearing her mascara. "What do I do about Reza?" she asks, her voice scratchy. I lean in, wanting to take her hand but thinking better of it. We don't know each other that well and her dignity would not permit it. "Gert, we can get him cleaned up. It doesn't sound like it has been going on for that long. And if he has Asperger's, it sounds like he's partly just fascinated with its esoterica—"

"Yes but, you see, he struggles so much with some things. Some things send him over the edge like fingernails on a chalk board, to be trite. I wonder if heroin helps with that." She looks up at me. "So it would be hard to get him off of it."

"Has he ever tried something else? More, ah, appropriate?"

"Like what?" she asks, and I am stricken with the burden of an older generation for whom autism and other developmental disorders were never on the radar when they were children. All their lives they have had to fend for themselves.

"Well, even Prozac," I say. "Temple Grandin swears by Prozac to take the edge off that chronic sensory stuff Aspies deal with."

"Who's Temple Grandin?"

I smile a little. "A really brilliant, weird, autistic woman who has single-handedly revolutionized the cattle industry. I can give you a book of hers."

Gert snorts. "So cattle to Temple is like historical artifacts . . . or art materials, to Reza."

"Exactly. She can get into a cow's brain better than a cow can."

"I'm not sure that's saying much."

I allow a little laugh. "I dunno. She's been amazing with slaughterhouses and dipping baths and such."

Gert just shakes her head. She looks very tired. "How did we get to cows?"

"Temple, I guess. Esoterica."

It's dark by now and I've turned on a low wall sconce. We sit in an almost companionable silence. The thick walls of the gallery begin to smell like cold dirt, the way the backs of cliff dwellings do on a summer evening. Everything in New Mexico comes down to dirt, dust, and the odd perfumes of piñon, juniper, chile roasting.

A kind of cockatoo shriek pierces the room. Gert sits straight up, deathly still for one second, and then bolts. My shoulders slump further as she runs out of the room.

I know exactly what's happened. Larry's asked Reza for an accounting.

When I emerge on Gert's heels, I see Larry steering a struggling Reza out the front door of the gallery. In a matter of seconds, it seems, Larry's gotten backup from two town deputies, and I seem to recall they do a fair duty on weekend nights downtown. Larry's doing his level best to keep the drama from infecting the rest of the gallery despite Reza's clear inability to cope. He and other cops in the area get some training in dealing with mental issues and de-escalation, and in my mind, this is money well spent. Gert flies over to them. Reza's system overload has led to flapping hands and the Tourette's-like shrieks, especially as Larry tries to touch him. But when he sees Gert, he buries his head in her shoulder. His hands go still and his voice silent. I have rarely seen something so tender and desperate, and in that moment of total trust—of one human being so needing and loving another—I understand why Gert stays with him.

Things are winding down. Low hums of satisfied people sink into my ears. Luis is chatting animatedly with a young man over by one of the raku pintos and I realize it is Jack. I flee to them and wrap my arms around both.

"Oh, thank God!" I say. A flood of familial gratitude launches into my veins.

"Mom, you okay?" Jack looks at me, pulling away from my clutches.

I shake my head. "It has been a very weird night."

"Well, I wanted to surprise you—"

"And you did! It's lovely! It's the best thing to happen, to end this night."

Luis keeps a light hand on my waist, and it serves to calm me. "Querida," he says. "What if we all go to your house and have a nightcap."

"Yes, let's do that," says Jack. "I was talking to Luis about his dance thing at UNM I went to the other day."

"You actually visited?"

"Yes, he did, querida. It was wonderful to see him there."

Chapter 24

WHEN I AWAKEN, I smell canella-perfumed coffee. Ernest is whining because I usually am up and about an hour earlier, and he can't figure out why I'm not out running with him. I get up, scratch his head, and find Luis and Jack looking at photos on Luis's phone. I peer over their shoulders and am greeted with a picture of Luis in the middle of two beautiful young women, an arm around each stunning waist.

"Who's that?" My mouth shouts out, it's owner apparently a jealous hag. I clearly have not had my coffee yet.

Jack laughs. "Relax, Mom. Those are his daughters."

I throw Luis a "WTF?" look. Daughters? How many? I hate how much we seem to love each other on so little information. Is all we are just pheromones? Or have we merely bonded in our mutual grief over dead spouses?

"You'll meet them soon, I promise." This is Luis.

"How come I haven't met them before?"

"Well, you've seen them before." He's stood up to his full height, the photo forgotten. His hand rests lightly on the back of one of my dining chairs, like a matador loosely on the lookout for the bull.

"I have?"

"Sure. At rehearsals. They are part of the troupe."

"Oh," I say, deflated. "Fuck."

I plop into a chair. Jack brings me coffee and switches the subject. "So, um, grad school."

I am in the weeds more than ever. "Huh?"

"Don't we have a, um, family nest egg for that?"

I take a giant swig. It goes down like a drunk needing a martini. "I thought you got a scholarship."

"I did. But it doesn't cover all expenses."

"Oh." Just then my phone lights up with a text from Margot. I gape at this too. I appear to have made a small killing last night. "Jesus H. Christ." I close my eyes. "Jack, yeah, you're fine." For some reason Margot's admonition from our boy-meets-girl soccer game comes back. *Stay present.* And maybe this is what Luis and I are doing by not delving too fast into past families and lives. Staying present. I give into it and blow a strand of hair out of my face. "What are we all arguing for?" I ask.

Luis laughs. "I'm not! Come on, let's make huevos and greet the day."

Damn that chirpy dancer. And just like that we're even more family, having navigated our first encounter with the choppy water of small misunderstandings that only families can blow up into monstrosities. Luis opens the patio doors and ushers Jack and me out back to the table. It's just warm enough for an outdoor repast. He goes back in, humming, and I realize cooking for him is like meditating for other people. I smile in a small way, cradling my coffee mug.

Jack's looking at me. "You look like something out of Harry Potter after a bad night fighting Voldemort."

"Great."

And despite this observation he starts going on, in that oblivious way of the young, about his architecture program, as if he had not just accused his mother of looking like Hermione with a hangover. Ernest comes out with the food and the man, and we all sit there, watching the sun climb higher as another New Mexico Saturday finds its glorious form.

It doesn't last long. By noon they have both left me and I stand in the front yard looking down the road at their invisible trails of benign abandonment. I have my hand to my forehead to block the high sun when a guttural hum sidles up behind me. At first, I pay it no mind, because I figure it is a car and will pass. But then I become aware that it will not pass. I turn and find a vintage green low rider with flame detail work idling on the road. I stare. Two vatos with face tattoos mad dog me from the front seat, with Bennie and Mac in the back. Squeezed between his two great uncles is an anemic, expressionless Ángel. He looks like porcelain, bloodless.

I become aware of the insidious silence of Arroyo Seco on a Saturday afternoon. This is why I love it here—the quiet, the privacy. Now, though, I would give anything to be living on a city block with eight hundred people swirling around me. Ernest comes up behind me and for a millisecond I fear they will shoot him if he starts barking or lunging. Instead he does something interesting. He squats next to me, wordless, and mad dogs them back.

"May I help you?" I ask, my throat dry as dust.

Just then Hector rolls up, pulling his wagon and mumbling. He stops when he sees the car, alerted perhaps by Bettina, who growls and snuffles in Ernest's face. He squints and does a buzzard neck maneuver to peer in the back of the car.

"Benito y Maclovio. *Dios mío. Los Muertos revueltan.*" The Dead return.

They too go bloodless and, if I am not mistaken, Ángel appears to get a tiny bit of rosiness back in his cheeks. The two mad doggers could care less.

"*Viejo*, not your business," menaces the driver.

I turn to Hector. "Los Muertos? But they lived . . ." I say, thinking back to Vietnam.

He snorts. "Not their souls." He crosses himself as if fending off the devil. Then he points a craggy finger at them and accuses them with his toothless mouth. "I remember you when you were boys. I remember."

Mac makes a smacking noise as if to bolster himself. "So?" He opens the back door and gets out, his heft outweighing Hector by probably two hundred pounds. His motorcycle leathers creak and his little chains—on his belt, on his boots—clink.

Hector is unimpressed. In fact, he starts to laugh. "What is this getup? You need black leather to make you tough, no?" Now he starts cackling for real, his mouth made even more into a hollow and dentureless cavern.

Mac moves to assault him. I am terrified that Hector's powdery bones will snap, and I stumble to protect him. But Ernest has his own ideas. Danes can move very quickly despite their awkwardness, like moose in the high country, which I hear are the ones you don't want to mess with. Ernest ramrods Mac. He butts his head straight into his thigh and knocks him far off center. We all stare.

I run to Ernest, shielding him. I am so afraid of shot, hurt dogs that I think of nothing else.

Mac lunges at me to get at Ernest, but stops, as if some whiff of wisdom inside suggests that assaulting a probation officer is not a good idea. The other vato, from the passenger seat, is out of the car by now too.

"Señora, we don't wanna make a fuss. Just telling you to back off." His teardrop tattoos crease with his eyes as he squints in the sun.

"Really?" I say. By now it is clear they are amateurs compared to the Octopus, and I rear up. "Or what?" I am mad. "What is all this *for*? So you can continue to deal designer heroin to rich Santa Feans?" My voice has raised, and I am shouting in the middle of a sunbaked street on a quiet Saturday. I realize this is my best defense. "HEROIN?" I yell. "REALLY? You know how many people around here would KILL to get off the opioids?" I am dearly hoping my neighbors come swarming, and sure enough a few people shuffle in the sidelines. "HEROIN?"

Hector is snorting in delight. I hear a small noise of surprise behind me and find Loretta gaping at the car. "It's the same car! That was Chuy's way back when!"

I look at it. Well kept up. "Really?"

Bennie and Mac have not expected so many relatives of Ángel's mother to be milling about, well aware of their history and stories. Ángel cowers in the back, hoping Loretta doesn't see him, but she goes straight there. "Get out of here," she hisses, leaning in the back window. "Get out before your daughter sees you!"

He pales visibly. "Carmelina? You have Carmelina?"

For a second Loretta blanches, and I can read her fear: Now Ángel will come for his daughter in some ghastly, middle-of-the-night raid. But then she sees his frailty and helplessness. He is essentially a captive to the vatos, whose WSL tattoos lie scattered all over their forearms and neck.

She spits. "*Pendejo. Culo.*" Two words for asshole, in descending order of crudity. Tears begin streaming down her face and will not stop. "You kill the only woman who ever loved you. You kill the mother of your child! You KILL!"

By now the vatos look alarmed. I watch them. Women in Spanish culture usually don't swear in public like that.

"Know anything about slitting women's throats?" I ask softly, right at them.

A police car slinks into view.

Mac and the vato are back in the car so fast they peal out in a cloud of dust, Mac's foot hanging out till he can stuff it back in and shut the door. Like some robotic law enforcement officer, I get the license plate number while my nervous system starts to shake.

The sheriff's deputy pulls up. Terri Francisco. Good lady.

"Terri," I say, "I got the plate. You don't have to chase."

She nods, takes the number, calls it in.

By now I am shaking from head to toe. She gets out. "You want to tell me what that was all about?"

I swallow. "Larry Baca knows. Tell him they threatened me. WSL, Ángel in the car. And Bandito great-uncles who lost their souls in Nam."

"Quite a story, I see."

"Yup."

She puts her arm around me. "Okay if I go? Follow up on these boys?"

"Sure. But—can you—can someone do a bit of a drive-by every now and then?" I am still shaking, trying to figure out what might feel like safety.

"Sure thing." She leaves and Loretta, Hector, Ernest, and Bettina and I become a small island in the middle of the street. I turn to any of the neighbors still around. Most of them are easing back to their houses.

"Thank you!" I holler, out to the middle of town. "Whoever called the cops! Thank you!"

A hand waves at me in response, as if to say— Of Course. You Are Our Neighbor.

I tear up. Hector snuffles just like his dog.

"And thank you . . ." I say to Hector. "I didn't know you could talk that much."

He just smiles.

Larry has his Sunday best on. Polished boots, button-down shirt tucked in, bolo tie, Indian jewelry watch on his left wrist and on the right, a stamped silver bracelet with pueblo cloud designs all in a row. His head is in his hands and he's sitting at my dining room table. When he looks up, he seems tired.

"You told them you knew about the heroin?"

I just nod. I know what I've done. I have told them everything I know. Once again, I am a complete ass. I swallow. "I even asked the vato boy if he knew anything about slitting women's throats."

"Christ, Nina."

"Sorry."

We sit in silence for a bit.

"You need to stay somewhere else till this blows over." He seems to be talking to the air, the motes, and silent corners. He won't look at me.

My shoulders slump. "I was afraid you would say that. I'm going to be coming to Seco for my art anyway."

"Yeah, but you won't be sleeping here."

I scowl. "Fine. Taos County can't afford a twenty-four-hour security service, can they?" I am trying to make a joke but it doesn't come out right.

Loretta scoots in through the front door. My screen bangs and she takes a seat. She speaks in a rush. "Ángel isn't going to call that stupid case worker at CYFD is he? And ask to see Carmelina? That lady was all over that idea before he hung himself." She clearly has not lost sight of Ángel in the back seat of the car since they left forty-five minutes ago.

I turn to her. "Really? Even though he's kidnapped her twenty times?" CYFD is the New Mexico way of saying child welfare office. Children, Youth, and Families Department.

She just shakes her head and looks down at her fingers. "'Reunification is our mandate, ma'am.'"

I gape at her. "They can't possibly want her reunifying with *him*."

She sighs. "No. They knew he was a suspect in her mother's death. They know about the kidnappings. But at least be able to see each other." She squints, remembering. "Oh yes. To 'maintain attachment.'"

"Hmmmm," I grunt.

"Take out a restraining order," Larry growls, looking at her. "That way he violates if he gets anywhere near her."

"Knowing CYFD they will get some judge to vacate that." Loretta has been wise to the ways of CYFD since Ángel was a little boy.

I stand up. "Anybody want coffee? Tea? Ángel's re-sentencing is in two days. Let's get him in prison first. Then she can damn well see him."

Larry asks for coffee, but Loretta takes over for me. His cell phone chirps as I get down cups. Loretta measures Ohori's French Roast into my large French press. I look at him over the counter dividing kitchen from living space.

"Got 'em," he says.

"Really?" I brighten.

He chuckles. "Driving around in a vintage bright green low-rider sedan is not a way to get around unobtrusively."

I laugh, hopeful. "Apparently they thought the theater of it was going to have some effect."

"It's all theater," Loretta mumbles. "Why I don't go to mass anymore."

Larry looks at her. "Really? I love all that stuff."

She makes a face. "Allergic to incense," is all she says, not wanting to get into it about faith and lapsed Catholicism. I've seen curandera books lying around, Tarot cards, in her place. The only cross is the obligatory one over the mantel, where photos of her family reside.

"So can they at least stay in jail a day or two for menacing?" I ask. I am angling to stay here.

"They didn't pull a weapon, did they?"

"No," I say. We both frown. This means no felony charge. Just harassment.

"Well, I can question them. They are suspects now in this case and I'll run their rap sheets."

"I am willing to bet small trees will give their lives for them if you print them out," I say. "Prison tats everywhere, WSL like Vegas neon."

Larry sips his coffee, looks at Loretta. "Help her get to Margot's, will you?"

"I haven't even called her yet!" I squawk.

He just rolls his eyes at Loretta, who's grinning. "I have," he says.

"And Carmelina's coming with you," says Loretta.

"What?"

"Ernest and Margot and Carmelina are very excited for this sleepover. Just tonight. And tomorrow night. Bring her in to work tomorrow and I will keep her for the day."

My coffee cup hangs in midair. Somehow they have arranged all this in less than an hour. "You really are afraid he'll come get her, aren't you?"

She draws a hard line with her mouth. "You just do your job and get that boy sentenced for hanging her dog. Then she can come home."

I have to hand it to Loretta, and this case. The shuttle tiles enabling a ship of codependent placation are falling right off. Underneath is one tough mama, reentering the atmosphere at just the right angle.

I sigh and go pack an overnight bag so I can hang with a child, a dog, my best friend, and an Earthship in the Great Hippie Desert west of town.

Chapter 25

IT TAKES THE BETTER part of a week to get through the worst of heroin withdrawals. I've been told they are excruciating, as a body used to an outer supply of endorphins has none of its own at first and so the merest touch can feel like a branding iron. There is a lot of vomiting, sweat, tears, and muscle aches and pains. Probationers repeatedly feel as if opioid withdrawals are going to kill them whereas the DTs will not, though we try profusely to disabuse them of this. America's ICUs are filled with late-stage alcoholics who seized and had to be brought back. A few of my charges, having watched relatives die from alcohol withdrawal, know better. As with the rest of the country, alcohol is endemic around here.

Reza has had the fortune of Gert's testimony upon entering rehab in Santa Fe, as well as their mutual empire of art and antiquities money. She enlists the best autism expert she can find to help the recovery people understand Reza's eccentricities and to make his reentry as easy as possible. This appears in a text Monday morning, and I smile. Maybe the silver lining is that Reza will get legitimate help, and Gert can find support to continue past rehab. Gert says Tom Garcia, Larry's Santa Fe Drug Task Force friend, will talk with him soon to find out what he knows. Meantime, there is a guard.

I heave a sigh and get up out of my chair. Today has the feeling of waiting, of some kind of shift in the atmosphere about to commence but not happening yet. If I were an ancestral Puebloan out on the mesas of the

Jemez, I would be willing to bet my turkeys and dogs would be acting strangely, and the men would be calling an emergency kiva session to deal with the eclipse or comet or wrath of some deity they perceived to be coming. Owls would appear in my dreams. Last night I slept with a four-year-old and a big dog on a mattress on the floor, and though I slept well my mind unraveled, looping paths of dreams about William's family, shiny green cars, Luis's daughters. Margot woke me with a hefty French roast and Carmelina sat on my lap with her hand on Ernest's neck the whole time.

"She seems to know you," is all Margot said, watching from over the rim of her bowl of oatmeal.

"She does," I said back. I hold to the one thing I know to be true: that our souls and bodies and nervous systems are finely tuned to one another's losses, and that out of this—and nothing else—we will save each other from forming too many walls, too many battalions of anger and misdirected avoidance.

"Maybe you should adopt her," Margot said.

Carmelina smiled. "Dopt! Dopt!" She reached around and hugged my neck, letting Ernest free for a minute.

I remember struggling up off the mattress in search of my running clothes. I remember Carmelina looking out the door fearfully as Ernest and I trotted off into the sage.

"Don't worry," Margot said. "They'll be back."

"Better," said Carmelina. She sounded four going on forty.

And so I ran, wondering what I had gotten myself into, my heart balking and bleeding and pounding all over the mesa.

Larry startles me out of my stupor by buzzing my cell phone. Ángel gets sentenced at two and it is barely ten.

"Hey. Come down to the jail."

"Why? You have our vato boys?"

"Yeah. I thought you might want to be a part of the interview."

"You didn't do that yesterday?"

He sighs. "They busted them halfway to Santa Fe. Brought 'em back, found out the two of them have warrants out so we had reason to hold them. I went and tried to enjoy the rest of my Sunday, thank you very much."

I chuckle. "Very well then. Warrants for what?"

"Restraining order violations, of course. Nothing giant."

"Okay. I'll be over."

I waddle on to the fabulous jail. Our whole complex is an elegant new stucco and wood Territorial-style array—courts, jail, offices. The wood is painted white, forming porticos and window frames; the stucco the obligatory adobe pink-brown. Every state building in New Mexico looks like this, a fact I am quite proud of, though when the paint peels and the stucco needs refinishing the underlying poverty of New Mexico's coffers are hard to hide. Sometimes the trim is turquoise, but Taos County has gone for white.

Vato #1 is named Anthony Griegos, a.k.a. Pocket. "Pocket! Why are you Pocket?"

He just looks at me.

Vato #2 is a dude who goes by Weasel, real name Carlos Ruiz y Baca.

"Any relation?" I ask Larry. He scowls at this annoying habit of mine and I ditch the perky school-girl routine.

We start with Pocket because it turns out he has a handy pending charge for pushing a lot of Fentanyl, one of the strongest opioids out there and currently killing residents of northern New Mexico at alarming rates. He bonded out at a fairly steep rate for these parts, a sign that the judge did not think highly of him. Perhaps he might be interested in a plea deal.

We sit across from him in one of the little interview rooms many county jails have. The walls are brick and painted an institutional mint green. It always dismays me how places like this can taint a perfectly good color. Pocket sits back in the insolent slouch patented by young hoods the world over.

Larry starts obliquely. "How long have you known Bennie and Mac?"

He just shrugs. "Around."

"I didn't ask you where you know them. I asked how long."

"Doesn't matter."

I sit forward, remembering Beefy Sleeves' response to the name. "What about Chuy Martinez?"

A faint flutter of an eyelid, the color in his cheeks ever so slightly changing. "Aw, man. Big deal. You know he was WSL. So what?"

"He's dead," I say.

Pocket nods slowly, as if this is the coolest thing on earth to do. He needs a toothpick between his incisors to complete the act.

"People seem afraid of him," I say.

"Not no more. Like you say, man, he's dead."

"Does that make you feel better?" asks Larry.

Pocket's eyes go full hood. "Maybe."

"So he was scaring the wrong people."

"Aw, man. That all you got?"

Larry lets out a sigh. "Okay, square one. What do you know about Liza Martinez?"

"Ángel's bird."

I do my best not to roll my eyes and reveal to him that women are not avian.

"Why'd you threaten me?" I ask. "What'd Ángel tell you?" All I can think is that my information regarding the China White alerted them.

"Ángel's a dumbass. He told us you knew about this drug stash. Blurts it out to us."

Larry blinks. "What, y'all had a meeting of the West Side Locos, Taos chapter?" Larry uses y'all to great sarcastic effect, pulling out an Inner Texan when needed.

Pocket raises both eyebrows and mad dogs Larry. "Yeah, just like you cops do. Usually meet at a donut shop." He lets out a hyena giggle at his own humor.

Larry sighs and stands up. "Okay, that's it. No deal on the Fentanyl."

Pocket sighs back. "Look, man, Ángel's just a stooge for Chuy. We see him at the Taco Bell and ask how's it going, and he says, just says, 'they know.'"

"*They* meaning us?"

He looks at me. "You, meaning you."

"Know what? What do I know?"

Pocket colors a little, debates which hand he will play. "Just about the drugs, that you think Liza was killed cuz of the drugs."

"Was she?" I ask directly. I sit forward and mad dog him back. I get pissed when women go dead at the hands of stupid men.

He blinks again. "Aw, man. Look, we were just trying to protect the drugs. Chuy, uh, pissed some other people off about that. We thought it was just a little barrio deal, a thing between us Westsiders. Chuy and Ángel and us. But he always was too big for himself."

Larry looks supremely satisfied. He more or less has a confession from Pocket right there regarding drug distribution.

But I am not happy. The larger crime remains a mystery. "So, did you kill her?" I ask.

"Fuck, lady, that's not what I said. I said Chuy pissed some people off and when we heard you knew about the China White we—uh—wanted to make sure you shut up about it."

Larry sits back. "So Chuy pisses off someone even scarier than himself. Let's see," he muses, "Chuy made some great friends last time he was in Grants. Mexican Mafia. MS-13. Know anything about that?"

"I ain't no snitch."

"Uh-huh. You're looking at ten years for that Fentanyl. Keep thinking about that."

Pocket is silent. Then he says, "Ángel was—like Chuy's his dad, no? But he was pissed at Chuy about Liza."

"Why?" I ask.

Pocket goes back to silence. We all sit in silence. Sometimes it is better not to talk.

"Ángel's pretty sure Chuy was responsible for killing her." He says it softly. Something shifts in his demeanor, and I see a slight crack in the armor.

"Would you want a dad like that?" I ask.

Pocket, all of twenty-two, kind of tumbles all of his energy down toward the ground. "No, man. I mean, I wish I had a dad. But that dude. Naw."

I think back to Mucci's apocryphal Albuquerque story about witnessing a flaying. "China White's a weird idea, really," I say. "Was that Chuy's idea?"

Pocket nods. "Think so. His dad used to push it. Thought he could start a whole designer market."

"What gave him that idea?"

He shrugs. "Don't know. 'Cept when Ángel had that gallery show—when Kahn Galleries sorta discovered him—Chuy used it to find a market."

I sit up. "Kahn Galleries 'discovered' Ángel?"

"Yeah."

Larry and I exchange glances. That might explain how Chuy met Reza. "So if it's so weird, why would it piss some other people off? Did other people want to horn in?"

Pocket just shrugs. "Turf wars, fuck ... I dunno. But I only seen Chuy look like a ghost once. And that was when this big dude at a party came in. Chuy ran out the back door."

"Really? Who was this guy?"

"Had MS-13 tats."

"At a WSL party?"

"Like I say, he was big. Came in with some others."

"Hmmmm ..." I say.

"They left after Chuy did. Like they were looking for him."

My phone chirps and I fumble in my purse to silence it. I have to take out several items to do so, including the little straw cross Beefy Sleeves gave me that I totally forgot about. It rests in a little baggie, relatively unharmed at the moment despite roaming around the interiors of my bag.

Pocket stares at it.

My hand stops, hovering over it. "What?" I say.

"Where'd you get that?"

"I don't reveal sources," I say, drily.

He sits up. "Well okay."

Larry gets a text. "We should go," he says, looking at it. He glances at Pocket. "Knife in the trunk of that car you used to terrorize her. Dried blood on it." He continues to press into him with his eyes. "Know anything about that?"

Pocket just pales a little. "Naw, man. I swear."

We're done here. I put the cross and my pens and the phone back in my purse. We wait for the jail guard to buzz us out the door and take Pocket back in silence. Pocket seems to know better than to press for a plea deal at the moment. The guard comes and we go out.

"Lady," he says, behind us. I turn. "Cross is a good thing." He nods at my purse. "Good to know."

"Okay . . ." I say. And somehow, I feel I've been given the WSL seal of approval, or at least a token of respect. Maybe next time some vatos threaten me I will hold it up in front of me, the straw winking in the sun. I snort and shake my head, imagining a pamphlet titled *How to Deter New Mexican Vampires*. I will start laughing, bitterly, in spite of myself if I don't watch it, and Larry's in no mood. We get into the sunlight and breathe out a lot of human sorrow and stupidity we want no part of.

"So Chuy killed her or some MS-13 asshole did," Larry spits, glaring out at the vista as if daring it to bug him.

"The MS-13 guy sounds like my Octopus. Who's mad at who here?" I feel very confused. Out loud I say, "The knife might have some info."

"Yeah. I'm willing to bet it's Liza's blood. So that's good. The case goes from cold to hot now. But I am also willing to bet they wore gloves, so no prints."

"Why'd they show up in Chuy's car yesterday?" I shake my head. "This whole thing is weird."

"I dunno, muchacha. Will you talk to Gert about Ángel being 'discovered' while I pay Ángel a visit to get his take on things? Might be interesting to see how the stories differ."

"Okay. He gets sentenced today, you know."

Larry blinks. "Right. I'll talk to him in jail before they ship him to prison."

"Okay. Court's at two. I need to eat lunch."

Bennie Garcia looks wan. On the other side of the court are the prosecutors, assistant DAs who, in Taos County, frequently sport braided ponytails, neatly pulled back, or little earrings, or some other sign of Taos Anglo Cool. Any suits making an appearance are JC Penney specials, with the exception of Bennie, who, like Luis, is physically fit and knows well-cut clothes do him more justice than most. The truth is Bennie's mom designs Taoseño clothing that sells like hotcakes to mavens of the Southwest everywhere, so he grew up with it. Ángel is next to him, with the outfit he had on at Mariposa gallery. He stares straight ahead and offers me nothing.

It doesn't take long, after all that delay. The judge flips through my PSI, questions Ángel about his record, expresses disgust at the dog, Liza's black eyes and bruised ribs. This is a lot, coming from Judge McAfee. He is quite a gentle soul, routinely delaying warrants for twenty-four hours so defendants' lawyers can find them when they don't show up for court, and inquiring after people's rehab progress. But today he is in no mood.

"Now she's dead."

"Yessir," says Ángel.

"Two years," he says, the gavel coming down and taking my maximum suggestion without question. The noise is definitive. I feel relief. I know this will not cure Ángel. It may make him worse. But I have no other tools, and at some point, after your third or fifth or tenth charge, at some point when your wife pays with so much assault and your child with being dunked into your car and peeled away and your family dog with his life—well . . .

Ángel says nothing. Bennie puts a light hand on his shoulder. They shuffle out, Larry shuffles in, and whispers in my ear, "Partial print!"

I jolt, my thoughts on Ángel's receding back.

"What? Whose?"

"Getting that looked at now. More favors, muchacha." He winks and slinks back out to the hallway before the Judge shoots him—and me—daggers for upsetting the courtroom.

Chapter 26

GERT IS A SHADOW of her former self, inasmuch as such a thing is possible. She smokes cigarettes, a habit I have not witnessed in her before, and sits pensively in Reza's office at the back of the gallery. Like her own office, the walls are thick and the vigas low lying, but the windows are a bit clearer and bigger so more natural light gets in. I realize parts of this building, anyway, are very, very old, and consider life in colonial Spain, about 1750, when Comanches and Apaches raided routinely, stuffing burning red chile *ristras* down chimneys to flush out occupants for the killing.

I once had a probationer who lived in Cordova, along the High Road deep in the Sangre foothills, in a narrow adobe that lined the road the way buildings do in small Pyrenees towns and rarely do in America. Half the "windows" there were gun slits, bigger views available only to the side not facing the road. At one time Cordova consisted of just a plaza, where the buildings acted like wagons, circling up against the outside. His family had lived there since that time of ristras down chimneys. As my archeologist friends would say, the place had some rank juju. A whiff of that flits here, in the back half of this gallery. I swallow.

Past Gert, every square inch of surrounding shelving is filled with Reza's fascinations. Blobs of clay with labels citing where they came from. Kitchenware from that same colonial time, crude wrought-iron ladles and cups, darkened with age and fire. They, too, have a provenance. Pottery sherds a-go-go, a small section of Paleo-Indian points archeologists would glare over. Sepia photos of Pueblo governors, old land grant family daughters at betrothals; Arabian horses. I sit back in an overstuffed chair and gaze at Gert.

"You look a little worse for wear, if I can say that," I start. She knows by now I am socially inept, so what the hell?

She smiles, morose. "That's what I like about you, Nina. No pretense."

"No, sadly." I don't tell her that growing up with a lie for a father makes one skittish about even low-grade cover-ups. I ask, "So how is Reza?"

She tamps out the cigarette and wafts her hand about, clearing smoke. "Sorry. An old habit leftover from adolescence." She looks at me. "Well, he's recovering. I think last night he turned a bit of a corner and some of the withdrawal symptoms diminished."

I lean forward. "Are they—is he weaning off with Suboxone?" This is one of the latest ways to get people off opioids. Similar to methadone, it has a milder effect but requires heavy medical monitoring, hopefully in conjunction with therapy, to get off of entirely. Needless to say, there is now a black market for Suboxone.

She shakes her head. "No. I said no to that. He would just get addicted to that. You were right, Nina. After that night in the gallery, with Reza in detox and then transferred to the recovery house, I stayed up reading about autism. I haven't slept much since Friday."

Today is Wednesday. Yesterday I deliberately spent in boring probation land—going in early, catching up on things, attending a staff meeting—and then leaving at three-thirty to spend the afternoon with my art. It was good to have a day to myself, though Carmelina showed up and she and Ernest hummed and slapped clay and made happy dog noises in the corner as I worked. Luis has a show tonight, a special for the Santa Fe Opera crews, who have arrived to begin rehearsals for their season. I thought it would be fun to ogle people who actually sing like that for a living, and to see him. I don't work tomorrow till noon.

"So what course of action are you taking?" I ask.

"Well, I hired a specialist to work with him. He lives in Denver, but I'm flying him down. Right now, I am working with the doctors just to give him whatever comfort he can have while his body readjusts. But the problem isn't normal addiction. It's that hypersensitivity he has lived with all his life. So I hope that between the specialist and, as you say, the right antidepressant or some such, that he can begin a different life."

She gazes off out the window. I just watch her. The silence is not uncomfortable, just a little sad. She wipes her eyes with a tissue. "I wish we had known all this before."

"I know."

"It explains so much."

"Your marriage must have been interesting at times," I risk stating.

She sends me a peaked smile. "Yes. But he is also unabashedly fun. I've learned that, too, about Aspies. They often have this childlike innocence, this utter lack of guile. When you are their special one—well. It is priceless."

This time I do reach out and put my hand on hers. "I think I saw that at my show."

Something in her shifts a bit, the old businesswoman back in the saddle just a hair. "Yes. That was quite a show."

I release my hand and let the glow of that course through me; it feels so good. "Thanks."

She sits up. "Now what did you really come here for?"

I laugh. "Too shrewd, you are. I need to know if you discovered Ángel Martinez . . . and how."

She cocks her head. "The Taoseño whose show you went to?"

"Ye-es," I say, thinking she has no idea why I was really there.

"Reza and I make a point of combing little Hispanic and Indian stores and co-ops where local artists display their wares. Sometimes you hit gold, and above all it is a pleasant way of staying in touch with the real Santa Fe, not the glitz we cater to a lot of the time."

I have to tease her. "You're pretty glitzy yourself, Gert."

She pats her hair and a glimmer of the humor I always thought might be there shows up in the corners of her mouth. "I take that as a compliment."

"Of course." I have to smile.

"At any rate, we get coffee and about every six months make our rounds.

Over the years we have pretty much figured out where the gems are likely to be. This one day, Reza said he wanted to visit an herbalist on Agua Fria. Not for the art, because she was not known to carry any—"

I perk up. "Leila's?"

"Why, yes."

"Let me guess. Reza also likes pot."

Gert colors. "In this state, you need a medical card. I have refrained from telling him that this does not take much, and he doesn't read the news." She shakes her head. "No. He liked Leila's knowledge of plants. Bought some canellas and dried berries. I have no idea how he heard of her, but he has his ears to the ground for things I can only imagine most of the time."

I picture Gert and Reza in their Saturday clothes tinkling Leila's bell. "What'd you think of Leila?"

Gert rolls her eyes a little. "Quite the get-up."

I keep my smile to myself, as well as my thoughts that Leila's style is just Gert's writ working class. "Uh-huh. She's a powerhouse."

"Well, smack on the counter was a retablo. I tell you, Nina, the Virgin Mary looked as if she had porcupine quills coming out of her head. It was harrowing. Next to it was the Christ *Scream* bulto, or one of them."

"Wow," I say.

"I asked her, 'Whose are these? They are brilliant.' She almost beamed at me, as much as a woman like that can be said to beam."

I nod. "Go on."

"Then a man comes out from the back. Scar on his face, something about him making Reza anxious. Reza will pace a bit like a dog when he does not like someone. 'Mijo,' he says to me, 'her grandson,' and he flipped his thumb at Leila. Now," she says, looking directly at me, "I am a businesswoman. I know talent when I see it. So I say to them, 'I'd like to see him get represented.' Reza is almost growling, but I put my hand on his wrist and it calms him a little."

"What happened then?"

"The man and Leila just looked at each other. Something passed between them. Then Leila—I can see she is a businesswoman too—asks, 'represented how?' And I think of my friend Lucy who runs Mariposa and the Young Artist series, and I tell her about it. I told her Ángel should enter into that contest. It would give him a lot of exposure even if he did not win."

"And if he was a success, then what? You undercut Lucy?" Oh dear, I wish I could slap my mouth shut from my brain.

She looks pained. "Heavens, no. Nina, don't be unkind. We specialize in historical artifacts and artists. You are a bit of an exception, but we need a good sculptor in our repertoire. You use clay in a way that picks up on the Indian potters and goes off in a connected but different direction."

I am chagrined. And I had never thought of my art that way. "I do? I'm sorry . . ."

"It's all right. But manners would serve you well."

Shit. I feel twelve and as if I am sitting in front of my mother. I say nothing.

Gert shuffles some papers. "Anyway, the man saw Reza and how uncomfortable he was. Reza was focusing on a shelf of bottles with labels on them. Sumac, serviceberry, piñon. Some in Spanish, some in English. I know he was trying to calm himself. The man came around to him. I think he asked him if he liked that stuff, probably picked up on something, I think."

"Picked up on what?"

"His love of esoterica, I would say. Leila and I were exchanging e-mails for Ángel."

"Why do you say that? That he sniffed out Reza's way of being in the world?"

Gert colors. "Because a week later that man came by the gallery and told Reza he wanted to show him something."

I sit back. I can just see it. A true con man. Could read another's weakness like a book, Reza's anxiety as well as his special interests.

"Did Reza go with him?"

"I think so. I was making a sale." She darkens. "But that was—it was after that—"

"That Reza got weird."

She looks at me. "Yes."

I swallow. "That was Ángel's dad, Chuy. He's dead now," I say softly.

She blanches. "And Ángel? Somehow, I don't think this ends well for him."

"He's in prison for two years as of Monday. Domestic violence."

"Dammit," she says quietly. Her brow creases; hot winds of sorrow seem to whip through her.

I don't tell her it may get worse than that for Ángel. Nor that Chuy might have had some MS-13 honcho in on this, or competing with him, or something. Reza was in way over his head, a conduit for Chuy to find other wealthy patrons. Guileless. Reza wouldn't know how to deal with a con man to save his life, except for that sixth sense, that physical wariness, he had no idea how to connect to his brain power, to warn him off.

I decide, the next morning, that I am tired of waiting for Leila's workshop, and I make a trek to her shop myself. Luis has breakfast with opera stars, so I am out of his beautiful little casita early and make my way slowly down Agua Fria. Cold water. Where is the spring? I wonder. Or is it part of the river? Or some long-ago stream reworked and dried up by now? What did this look like so long ago? I know it was dust, and coyote fences, sloping walls, melons in the sun come August. This is the thing about northern New Mexico—it unfurls me to things so much bigger than myself. I feel like an aspen, connected underground to everything else. Aspens are rhizomes, the world's largest organism, rooted in each other. And I am but one of those tentacles, palpating in the April sun, breathing in remnants of cedar fires from the still-cold dawn hour.

Leila's shop is quiet, unearthly so. Perhaps I am too early. If I ran an herb shop, I wouldn't open till ten, but here I am at eight-twenty. And I think I might find answers. A white girl. Barging in and expecting the world to answer.

Nonetheless my eye catches a whiff of white smoke from behind the shop. I follow it. Around back is a small yard. Old cottonwood leaves pile in the corner of the fence lines. The fence is a mix of coyote-style latillas, slat, even a little chain link. Whatever can be salvaged and put together on the cheap. Probably twenty years in the making. Repaired constantly. The yard is dirt, with a picnic table, and, in the middle, an *horno*, the beehive ovens so familiar at Taos Pueblo but really a Spanish import. Leila is squatting before it, blowing smoke into it to start a fire.

I don't move. On the picnic table are two perfectly round loaves of bread, ready for cooking. Is there nothing this woman cannot do? I breathe out and wait patiently at the side of the yard for her to see me. It is her territory, her yard. I have no real right to be here, and I will make myself known only when she is ready. If I were shooed away with angry shouts I would not be surprised, and I decide I would not take it personally.

She stands up as the fire catches and begins to move toward the back door. I make a small noise in my throat and she startles, swiveling to where I stand. Her body, ready for combat, softens ever so slightly when she sees it is a woman, greying; when she sees it is me, her eyes nonetheless narrow as something clicks in her brain.

"Two years, huh?" she asks. She knows exactly who I am.

"Sorry," I say. "But he had it coming."

She shrugs. "*El mismo. Siempre el mismo.*"

"What's the same?"

"All the men in this family." Leila, Our Lady of the Perpetual Guard, sliding toward admission. It's as if I can hear her heart collapsing.

Her hand remains on the handle of the back door. I wait.

"Want some tea?" she asks. "I don't drink coffee."

"Sure," I say. I feel as if I have won the lottery. Leila! Inviting me to tea!

Inside, in a room behind the main store, I find a small kitchen on one end and a desk full of invoices and paperwork on the other end. The paint is chipped and the Virgin of Guadalupe peers over the stove in the form of a retablo. She puts a kettle on and chooses which tea we will have from one of several jars on a shelf over the sink. She could be poisoning me for all I know, but since she prepares a cup for herself, I decide this is unlikely.

"Licorice, chamomile." She smiles bitterly. "Calming."

"Thank you."

We sit at a rickety little table in the middle of the room. It is a cousin to the one in Ángel's trailer—steel legs, blue laminated top instead of his yellow. The chairs are wooden, matched but each with their own histories.

"Why are you here?" she asks.

I sip the tea. "Chuy and Àngel were here at the store the day Chuy died. That's in a police report."

She goes very still and whitens. "You don't pull any punches, *gringa*," she says, softly, almost a whisper.

I close my eyes, surprised to find my lips trembling. "I am done with that. I am done with being nice, with pretending the world is not full of heartbreak much of the time." My eyes open. "I need to know what their relationship was like. I need to know what they were saying to each other that day."

Leila drinks her tea and looks down into the cup as if reading leaves. "They are my family," she says.

"I know."

She is silent. I let the clock tick. She gets up, goes outside, and I can hear her sliding bread into the oven. The backdoor clicks back open, and she sits in her chair once again. She turns her head away, the nearest thing to humility I think I will ever see in her. "Ángel hated him." Her voice is a scratch, dry.

"Why?"

"*Porque era nunca aquí.* He was never here. Never there for him. Didn't save Lolo from her drugs."

"He has said all that to you?"

"No. But you know your children and grandchildren. I watched him grow up and have his heart broken a thousand times. Dad would swoop in, take him, promise the moon, leave him here with me. All the time." She grimaces. "I would tell Chuy. *Tell* him. 'Don't make promises you can't keep. Better to do nothing, stay away.' He never listened."

"Sooo . . . why were they at the shop together? That day?"

"I needed to have some shelves built. I thought—I thought—with Ángel a success now and Chuy—Chuy hadn't been in trouble in a while—I thought maybe they could reconcile."

Surely she knew how naïve that was, but then the hope of a mother never dies. I finish my tea and say nothing for a minute.

She starts to cry. "And now Chuy's dead! Mijo! Mijo!" Her hands go to her face, and she starts keening.

Fuck, I think. I hate this. *If you are a rhizome, then find her branches and reach out.* I stand up and touch her shoulder. "I'm sorry, Leila. I am so sorry."

She looks up at me, tears black from mascara. Then she bolts out the door. The bread.

When she comes back in some of her composure has returned.

"Do you think," I say softly, "that Chuy's death had something to do with Ángel?"

Her face grows horrified, and she shakes her head violently. "No! I can't think that!"

"But what then?" I feel like a rat bastard to be pushing like this.

"But they were hissing at each other a lot. I heard Liza's name several times. Like they were fighting over her, like Ángel thought Chuy had something to do with her dying. I broke it up by serving posole for lunch. Then Ángel left, all angry."

I consider my next move. "Leila . . . maybe go visit Ángel? He would like that, I think."

She just nods, staring at the far wall now, lost in her own thoughts.

"Thank you for the tea."

I don't know what else to say. I squeeze her shoulder and leave her to her misery, the ghosts of all that failure settling on her shoulders like a rebozo, a shawl of sorrow, black and tightly woven. Out on the street, the sun has decided to glare now that we are past early morning. I wipe my eyes and drive away.

Chapter 27

MY LAST CHORE IN Santa Fe is the same as it was before: pick up a file from the SFSO for Larry. I do so, my mind swimming in thoughts of Leila, crime, hurt. Some vague investigatory question niggles at me, but it is not till Larry texts me with a question that I realize what it is. *Why didn't they ransack the house? If it was a drug killing and they wanted drugs?*

I stare at it. That is my question too. That's what was sitting in the back of my head while Luis stomped and people clapped and I sat through a couple of operatic arias after Luis was done. It is the residue of the interview with Pocket, and Gert's story just confirms the drug angle. If Liza was killed because they knew Ángel was stashing drugs, why not turn the place upside down? Unless it was just a warning. To whom? Ángel?

Larry tells me he is in his office and I drop the file by. He puts his library glasses on and opens it up. Mainly these are blow-ups of Chuy and José Hernandez, the MS-13 thug. I slap Herndandez's picture down abruptly. "That's him."

I look away to the other photo. Chuy's scar is more prominent than I realized, coursing down his face and almost achieving a natural look, like a crease from smiling, by the time it gets past his cheekbones. Must have been a helluva knife fight, is all I can think. He should have died long before he did, given the life he led.

Rap sheets on both men flesh the file out, including prison reports. "Do you want any of this?" Larry asks.

"You'd be sharing discovery." Larry seems to be treating me more as a special agent on the case than a run-of-the-mill probation officer.

"I know." He sits up. "Actually, what I want is Carmelina to look at these photos."

"Why? She didn't say anything about seeing anyone in her forensic interview."

He looks at me as if I am dumb. "People remember stuff all the time they didn't at first."

He's right, of course. I just don't want to expose Carmelina to more terror if she does recognize them.

"Did the partial print come back?" My voice is soft. I think I know the answer.

He nods. "Looks like Chuy."

It drops like a stone in a lake, a clink of keys on a clean sideboard in a silent house. Chuy killed Liza. Chuy killed Liza. His own daughter-in-law. After all this time, these past two months, we have what to me feels like an answer. A thousand lawyers could shred this in court, but I don't care. In my heart, some resolution begins to glimmer, and I let down a burden I didn't quite know I had.

The rest of the day goes by in a desultory sort of way. I find myself stepping outside a lot, restless, unable to tolerate the usual tales of woe and stupidity out of my probationers. I look at them as lizards look at flies on a hot day, with hooded eyes, a kind of numb apprehension. Would they kill their own for drugs? Have they? Everyone is Chuy today.

After work at home, I take Ernest out for a slow walk up Salto Road before coming back to the studio to sit with little mountain goat hooves, milkweed pods carved out of clay. I am incapable of big things today and it is dusk anyway. Working with indoor light has never been my forte, so I just touch up the hooves and turn a curled horn into a nautilus, ridged and out of context. I briefly wonder what it would be like to go through life as adult rams do, with giant nautili on their heads. In fall, I will get mule deer bucks with huge racks lounging in the little space between my back fence and the Rio. We will regard each other casually, but the burden of those racks must weigh on them too. The sound of my tools being put away seems tinny, remote, lonely. The air is very still.

Night in early May falls a little more gradually than a month ago, but this being a high steppe off the Rockies, the air cools rapidly. Sometimes in summer it is nice to visit Albuquerque just to stay out late with no need for a sweater and the feathery dark grazing your skin with a breeze now and then. Then the hot days, the interminable afternoons, start to get to me, and I come home. I feel lucky to perform these modest bouts of transhumance. In my house, I rummage in the veggie bin and find greens, some tomatoes; I have a little smoked salmon left from my last shopping trip, enough to concoct a salad. An hour later, having read this week's edition of *High Country News* and picked up midway through a novel (Italian, Neapolitan, wildly different than here), I hear a knock at the door. Loretta is waiting for me on the other side, with Carmelina in her arms. It is nearly nine.

"What's the matter?" I am alarmed at Loretta's face, the fact of Carmelina, limp and tear-stained, wrapped in a blanket.

"She would like to see Ernest."

I take her from Loretta and lower her onto my couch. Ernest already knows; I tap the couch cushion next to her and he hops up, pressing his Great Dane muzzle into her side. She opens her eyes slightly, smiles, and falls into him, arm on his shoulders. She collapses into sleep almost immediately.

"Thank God." Loretta lets out a big sigh. "That damn Larry had her back in for a forensic interview again this afternoon. I thought we were through with this."

I have to repress a smile. *Damn* is not a word the old Loretta would have used much. "And what did *damn* Larry find out?"

"Mira, he showed her pictures. Two men. One of them Chuy. Her eyes went really big, no?" Loretta makes herself look like Marty Feldman and opens her hands like flowers on either side of her face.

"She recognized them?"

Loretta's mouth goes grim. "Yes."

"From the night her mom was—was—?" I look over at her sleeping form and move us off to the kitchen, where we can keep an eye from the counter dividing the space but not be heard as easily.

Loretta nods to answer my question and goes straight for my pantry.

"What are you looking for?"

She looks at me as if I am an idiot. Great. My second time today, since Larry seemed to think my bulb had grown dim too. "Wine. I need wine, and chocolate."

"Well, gee." I go to the fridge. "I keep the chocolate in here." I toss her a partial bar of Trader Joe's dark stuff. "I'm not sure I have wine."

"What?"

I move her out of the way and look down at the floor of my pantry. "But for emergencies, I have vodka."

I lift out a half-used bottle of Tito's, and she closes her eyes in relief. "If I smoked marijuana, I would do it now," she says.

"Well, that *is* good to know. So I take it Carmelina was a wreck after that? All afternoon?"

She pours herself a finger and finds some tonic water, an ancient lime. "Sí, yes. More restless, unable to sit still. And she wouldn't go to sleep. Helena got mad at her at dinner, so then I had to deal with her. Hector even offered Bettina to pet but something about Bettina bothers her. I don't blame her. Bettina looks like a Chihuahua with hair plugs."

I snort, laughing. "And that little pink dog coat!" I take the vodka and make the same drink.

Pretty soon we are both snorting and giggling and I wish Jade were here. We array ourselves at the dining room table. In ten minutes our hilarity dies off, like fireworks having lit and fallen to Earth, ungrounded. It is a release, and our drinks have served their purpose. They sit there, half-drunk, mostly untouched now. The chocolate is more or less gone. I swallow. "So she saw those two? In the house? The night Liza died?"

"Yes."

"Was Liza—was she already—"

"Dead? Yes."

"So Carmelina hears a noise, comes out, sees them?"

"Yes."

"Why didn't she say so before?"

Anger flashes through Loretta's face like a hawk wing glinting off sunlight, swooping and low. "Madre de Dios. She is four. All she remembers is lying down on her Mamma. At first, anyway. That's all I remember too, that image."

We don't say anything. The silence cloaks around us, small sleep noises emanating from Carmelina and a giant dog sigh from Ernest. Loretta picks up our glasses and puts them in the sink.

"Chuy killed her. Or they both did," I say quietly. "We got a partial print on the knife found in the trunk of the green low rider. And now we have Carmelina's testimony."

Loretta's shoulders slouch and her hands go still in the sink. "His own kin," she mutters. She shuts her jaw tight, as if she might start wailing. She glances back at the couch. "Can she stay tonight?"

I nod. "I will bring her by in the morning."

Loretta wipes the back of her hand against her temple. She leans in and kisses my cheek quickly. "Thank you."

It is an enormous gesture of gratitude coming from Loretta. I realize then how closely she holds her own heart in. I see her out the front door and lock up for the night.

"Well, Larry," I whisper to the air, "now we know why they did not ransack the house."

Grown murderers, thwarted by one little girl. I go to the spare bedroom and find, in the closet, my camping pad and sleeping bag. I move the coffee table and lie down by the couch. I don't want Carmelina falling off in the middle of the night with no one to catch her.

Ángel Martinez looks at his daughter with gutted eyes. He will go to prison in a week or so but for now he is here. The Taos County Jail has a room for families. It is still green, and windowless, but there are some squishy toys in the corner and some carpet and a few plastic chairs of the sort they make you sit on in kindergarten. Carmelina doesn't know what to make of him. Offers up a stuffed dog, which really seems to gall him. A guard lurks in a corner. Loretta and the CYFD worker and myself make up the rest of the crew. I am here at Loretta's request, and because I was his PO—he's off my caseload now that prison is in the cards. The CYFD worker agreed I could come.

It is a terrible meeting. Carmelina starts wailing for her mother and wants Ángel to answer her on that and he just stares at her. Swallows a lot. Shakes his head, scratches out, "I don't know," then says nothing. He appears frozen, and as his emotional inability becomes clear to her, she shrinks back against Loretta.

"She needs to go home," Loretta says to the social worker, in a steely voice. The CYFD woman, all of twenty-four or something, puts up no fight. She can write up her report and say the visit happened and be done for now. It lasts ten minutes.

At work, I sit through afternoon court and try not to fall asleep. I am only there for one probationer. Carmelina went back to Loretta in the morning, but Loretta looked at me in despair. "I need a babysitter. I have a catering gig tonight."

I chewed my lip and thought, *what the hell.* Texted Jade. *Can your daughter babysit? A nine and a four-year-old? Will pay.*

Jade actually got back to me. *I am in LA, but here is Yuki's. Try land line first for real people.*

I smiled at that. I forwarded that to Loretta, without telling her whose daughter it was, and went on with the day.

At five, I close up and walk out to the car.

"Muchacha," I hear, softly.

I turn, find Larry waiting for me, leaning against a cop car parked next to mine.

"What are you, stalking me?"

But he looks like a ghost. I stare at him. "What's wrong?"

He says nothing, as if choking, and holds out his hand.

Two small bultos greet me. One bigger than the other. One has a scar down his face that I would know anywhere. The other looks like him, but younger, smaller, weak. Both have the hungry-dog look each has carried on them all their lives; both take on elements of their religious roots, with long robes, and Ángel's *Scream*, making for a paired agony of spirt that nearly collapses me. I have no idea how he managed to get that carved into wood, but he did.

I look up, alarmed. "What the—"

But something in me knows. "He's dead, isn't he?"

Larry nods. "Hung himself in the jail after seeing you guys."

"And these?"

"We found them in his cell. I have no idea how he got them in there."

I swallow. "Maybe Refugio gave them to him. Sometimes the guards let . . ."

But I die off. Larry knows that. The jail is run by the sheriff's department. I have no idea what to say. My hands start shaking, and in a moment of supreme shame, I get in the car and drive off. I have never felt so vulnerable in front of someone in my life.

It is only later, much later, after I have furiously thrown old bits of useless clay on my back fence, shout-singing the Sex Pistols' "No Future . . ." lyrics over and over, that Larry finds me, hunched over the Ángel-T-Rex, painting its booted toes in the circle of light created by a shop lamp I have clamped to my workbench outside.

"It's getting cold, Nina," he says.

"What are you doing here?"

"Went to Mass at the Pueblo. Not far from here, you know. Clara said I should check on you."

"She did, did she?" But I stop painting and my chin wobbles. I look at him, good and kind and almost disappearing in the dusk outside my lamp. I turn it off and adjust my eyes. "That was a family," I say, my voice a corn husk, and I am thinking all the way back to Lolo, and Loretta's grief at her sister; back to the doomed coupling of Lolo and Chuy Jr.; back to Chuy Sr. and his three brothers, all shattered by a war we should never have been involved with in the first place. I think about Liza and her family; I think about her birth parents and how shattered they, too, must have been.

"I know." Larry takes a deep breath and exhales slowly.

"So, did he kill his own father? Is that the final insult? The thing he couldn't live with?"

"Looks that way. I grilled Pocket some more. There is still a slim chance it is our MS-13 hulk, Señor Hernandez, but he seems to have disappeared off the face of the earth and we have found only traces of China White activity among his buddies in Santa Fe."

"But there were traces?"

Larry nods. "Yeah. Santa Fe is looking into it. Pocket says Ángel found out it was his dad who killed Liza. Said Ángel said he 'would pay.'"

"So . . . we'll never really know."

"No. Maybe not. Unless we find the gun, ballistics, you know."

By now we've reached my front door. I put my hand on his wrist. "Larry. Why don't you go to Mass at this church?" I gesture back toward the hulk of Holy Trinity behind me.

He just smiles. "You know we all have our own sanctuaries."

My home looks dark, lumpy, starkly alone. Is this my sanctuary?

"Thanks for coming by Larry."

"You going to be all right?"

"Yes, but I think I'll call Jack."

He hugs me and leaves. Ernest licks my hand as I enter. We sit on the couch. Jack is out. I leave a message. Talking to Luis does not feel right tonight, so I start talking to William. I tell him the whole story of Ángel and Liza, of the Garcia Sisters of Arroyo Seco; of four brothers named Benito, Maclovio, Jesús, and Tranquiliano; how they went to war in 1967 and in a way never came home. I tell him about my art selling for outrageous sums, and Gert and Reza. I go on about Jade and Leila; and finally, I talk about Luis.

A rich life, Nina.

Yes, maybe, love. But I am still so hollow losing you. And though I have no windows open I feel a small breeze play at my temples, moving my hair. I know it's him, touching it. When I wake up in the morning, I have a blanket over me and a pillow under my head on the couch. I am sure I did not get them myself.